TIGER STRIPES

TOM O'CONNOR

TIGER STRIPES

Positive Waves Publishing
Copyright © 2025 by Tom O'Connor

ISBN 979-8-9859386-0-9 (Paperback)
ISBN 979-8-9859386-1-6 (Ebook)

Published by Positive Waves Publishing

Book Cover & Interior Design: Joshua Frederick
Book Cover Art: © Michiru.K/Adobe Stock

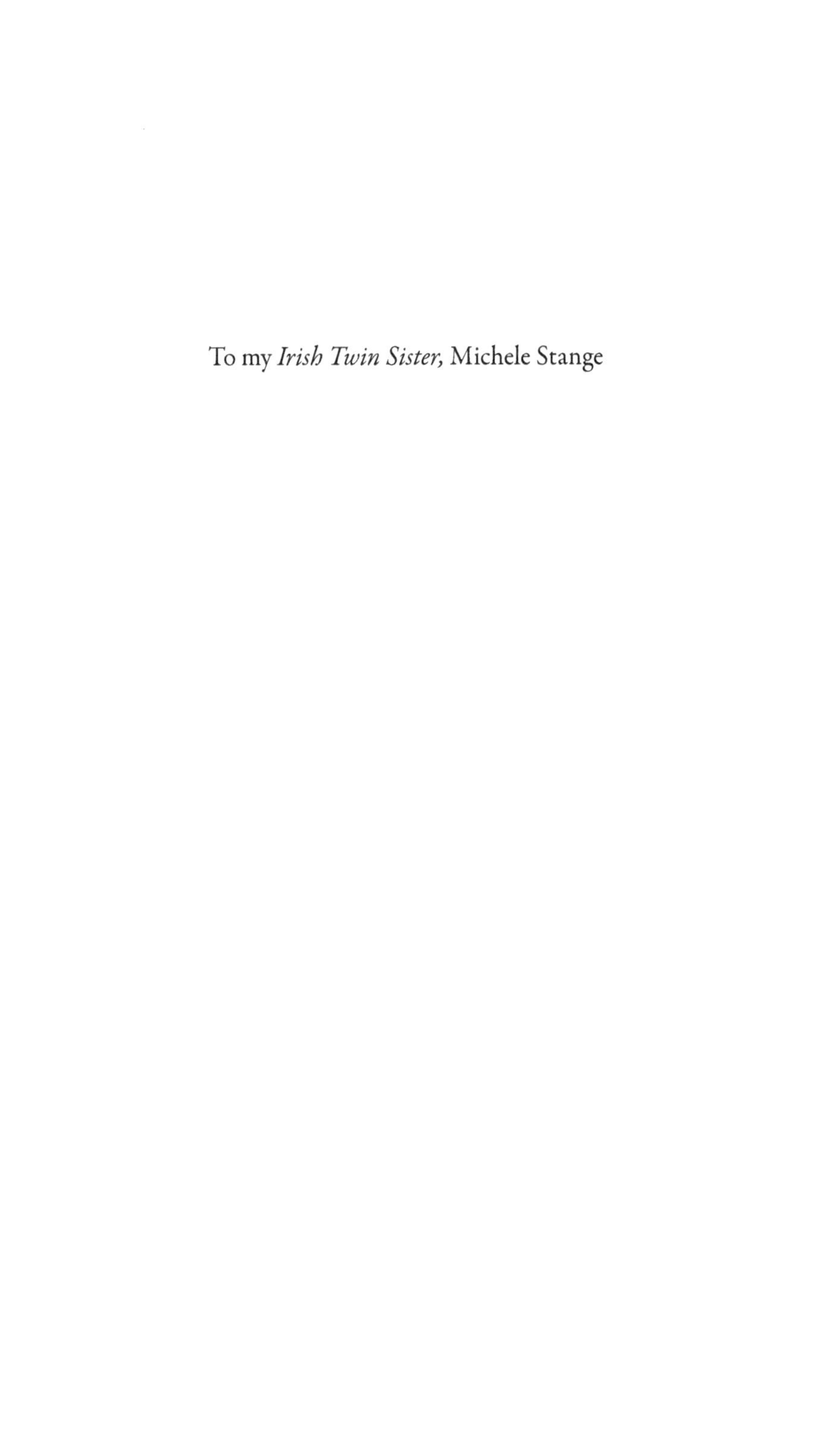

To my *Irish Twin Sister,* Michele Stange

S ECRETS ARE MENTAL and make a path in the forest until the trees disappear. The author makes no apology for not bringing up what's hidden beneath the story, and it's done on purpose, for words have put a spell on him. The real truth is buried in a breadcrumb trail. All the reader has to do is see the pages with a naked eye.

The clues are watching, so hitch your wagon with the horse in front. A tethered person is cursed and often parades around in a shroud of ruin, normalcy, or fortune. Meanwhile, other victims wear masks, numb themselves, and talk behind peoples' backs. They survive by wallowing in blaming others as whispers spread out of their reach instead of counting their blessings. Yet, the brain re-wires itself regardless and for its own accord, with no regard for the person's benevolence. How would one know? Because the thoughtless memories scattered in the mind play on repeat. A mumbling effect takes over in solitude and can often lead to pressing the self-destruct button. Only, it's fool's gold, shining in the moonlight, or shrouded in a darkness like fireflies. A strawberry is not a berry and a banana is. It's uncomfortable to live in our falseness, yet we learn to participate, procrastinate, and pretend.

In this yarn, awareness isn't necessary to enjoy the ride. Like all our answers, they stand behind the questions. One may say: How do we eat a whale? A bite at a time. This book is a writer's first bite.

CHAPTER 1

THE ROAR OF an unmarked C-17 medical transport heading to Beirut kicked over at Baghdad Airport. It was 1997, and the camouflaged plane had a tail number of R96 painted in yellow. Military personnel moved at an accelerated clip, not frantic but alive. Their clothes were baked to the skin from loading under the driving sun, and the temperature was hitting harder than a hammer and nail on a two-by-four. Moisture was deft and dumb to the heat. In order for soldiers to survive, they had to make the sand their friend, and if they didn't a bitterness took hold. The crew chief stood in position like a crow on its perch with a stopwatch ticking in his hand. He was responsible and accountable for all military personnel boarding the aircraft. Nothing could stop the logistic train in motion as he wiped another layer of sandy grime away from the corners of his eyes. It was hard work setting up and dismantling a UN processing center to inspect weapons of mass destruction. It had been sixteen-hour shifts, seven days a week with nothing but greasy oil and jet fuel. He wished for a shower, but deep down, he knew it wouldn't make a difference. The filth would stick in his pores, and it would take years for it to wash off.

Doctors and nurses were present due to the humanitarian security resolution needed for the US Military invasion. The medical staff shared very light moving duties, and they were treating injuries from a recent civil uprising for those opposed to Saddam Hussein. Soldiers pushed off their knees to stand up as they walked with slumped shoulders while carrying rucksacks to the ramp. A whistle blew in a desperate fashion to keep things moving along, as motivation for some and pointless for others since it reminded them of a barking dog. Some complained, but it never helped. They didn't know it yet, but the sickness of sleepless nights wouldn't kick in for a few more weeks. Nothing was over, even if the military said so as they handed out the walking papers. The real healing wouldn't take place until decades later, and for those in combat, it wouldn't occur until they decided that it was time to be free of carrying the burden.

Many turned their heads away from the sun towards two unexpected visitors. The chief followed the pack and saw the expecting Marine arrive with his escort, another hot-shot Sleepy Operator. The Marine got out of a beat-up 1979 Toyota Corolla. What the hell happened to the Jeep? He dismissed the question after seeing the soldier was banged up and helping a woman out of the vehicle that looked to be seriously injured. His orders were clear, they would hitch a ride without any interference, no bullshit. He knew the preferential treatment was deserved, and it was something he admired in them. He readied his attention as they approached. She was dragging her feet and wearing the head garb. He hated not seeing her facial features, but he buried his personal resentment with everything else he disliked about the military. The head nod of acknowledgment let them through a security barrier. Again, he wanted to know the woman behind the mask. He was interested to find out and didn't want to know at the same time. Secure the transit was his job, and he kept it moving. Flight staff personnel stopped briefly while they watched the two go up the ramp, then went back to work securing equipment with ratcheted straps. Everyone knew who she was and went back to it as the sound of torque wrenches clicked into position. Everything was secured.

Marine Sargent Hawkins carried Kayla North. Her reputation was known as a loner. She was the brunette with blue eyes, sitting in the back of all the meetings, rarely asking any questions, and fond of living in the power of silence. Some said that she was the house cat that had a distaste for people and would only let the owners touch it in order to get food. A chip grew on her shoulder after passing through ranger school and living through her second tour of duty. Others said that she was a diversity candidate, but to everyone on her team, she was a first-rate medic. Failure was never an option she considered, and it led to her earning the trust of everyone. The grunts who hit on her received ice baths, and those with rank ate a cold shower. With most of her peers gone, the nickname of Fats had disappeared. They gave it to her because she was difficult to beat in pool. Afterwards, most of them said she won by intimidation. Her midriff wasn't standard issue. The tongue on her could cut through a ten-dollar steak.

Kayla could barely walk, but her hold on Hawkins' arm said she still had a lot of fight left. She'd had a simple mission of picking up intel from a tribal leader in the city and bringing it back to transport. She had no idea of the contents or purpose, and she didn't care. It was a volunteer job and a way to stay motivated. It didn't matter to her, as she hated being cooped up inside the wire. Her knees buckled going up the ramp. Hawkins called out, "Need some help over here." A nurse came by to look under her hand. She pulled out a cloth to reveal that a piece of shrapnel was still lodged in her side. Hawkins said, "We took an RPG and got lucky."

The nurse called for a doctor and Kayla grabbed her arm. "We'll find one when we land. It's a quick flight." They found a seat as Kayla looked up at the ceiling to stare at the rivets in the fuselage. She took a deep breath and closed her eyes.

Hawkins grabbed her satchel as Kayla snapped awake to retrieve the equipment from his hands. She started shaking as he watched her. Kayla said, "I'm fighting from going into shock. It'll wear off soon. Just go get me some water." She blinked and saw his Cammie's stained with patches of blood. "You okay?"

He said, "A small scratch. A lot better than you," and he was gone. She closed her eyes again, happy to see that Hawkins was still around. With the laptop resting nearby, she thought about how things didn't always turn out the way you expected in places where chaos ruled. They had orders, *"You can't engage until they shoot first."* It was good to know Hawkins got off a few rounds. The visions were stacking up with all the other screwups wishing for her to quit, give up, or die. She opened her eyes to gaze at the ceiling again, and all she saw was red, a flashback of her last Marine escort, Sanchez. He got shot in the chest at the rally point. She'd had to find the cricothyrotomy kit in the Jeep while the soldier was choking on his blood. Only the vehicle was empty, and every second counted as she cursed the failure. In hindsight, she blamed herself as she cracked her knuckles while fiending for a cigarette.

Mistakes were forgivable, but when it was a daily occurrence, it took a toll and added up. Kayla looked at what was missing, and the thrill of classified assignments had worn off. Maneuvering behind the scenes was getting uglier by the second. She looked at her Breitling time with the Volcano dial ticking away and thought of an early retirement. A bitter taste hung in the air and was getting heavier with a burden that couldn't be lifted. It was hard for her to pinpoint as she dove into the past as a medic, then to Rangers, upped a level to Special Ops, and for what? What was she trying to prove?

Hawkins returned with plastic water bottles and left them near her arm with some baby wipes. At least they were cold, and the condensation pooled in her hand as she drained the contents without stopping. The BPM's were slowing down, but she was still dehydrated. Hawkins got up to debrief the crew chief as she drained the second bottle of water. She was safe for the time being and closed her eyes again.

Why was she having to prove others wrong? Kayla rested her mind until she saw her younger self getting pushed down at the bus stop in third grade. She was alone. Jake, her older brother, wasn't around and took his bike to school that day. Her elbow hurt with the fresh raspberry scratch from the sidewalk. The kid who did the damage was Jimmy Oliver. He stood over her, laughing. She slowly got up as he turned his back to impress his friends. It was just like Jake, teasing her all the time, only Jimmy was smaller. She wasn't about to take any grief from this fat head and clenched a fist. He turned his head at the perfect time to receive a swing and a hit. The shiner on his face lasted for two weeks. Jake broke Jimmy's arm a month later on the playground, but the real damage was already done. She learned early on that it's best to be the one to do the hitting first.

The chief barked an order. It wasn't delivered over the engine noise. He waved in silence to someone on duty and pointed two fingers down. The vacation ride home was underway as the hatch started to close.

Kayla's bloodbath happened less than an hour ago, and the chunk of metal still inside her was a fresh reminder. It happened in a blink of an eye and, luckily, Hawkins was watching the road because she wasn't. Why was she so easily distracted by the children playing soccer in the alley? Kids, it was an idea for the next life. She sucked in a gasp of air and rubbed the back of her shoulder. Her leg twitched as the image of an RPG exploding in her mind echoed back and took out the Jeep. The memory replayed in detail with the young girl lying still only a few feet away. She didn't have much time as Kayla wanted to run to her aid and provide what little comfort was left in her short, sweet life. Hawkins went on the offensive and fired his weapon as civilians rushed for cover. She was telling her body to move, but it wasn't responding. Hawkins removed a driver from the Corolla and yelled at her to get in. Crawling her way inside, she did the best she could to bounce back, but the explosion had put her in the spin cycle. She pushed on and only took a second to glance back at the motionless child covered in debris. Hawkins blasted off before she could close the door. A few moments later, she woke up, and the engine was screaming. She told him to slow down and avoid the potholes or her guts were going to spill out all over the floor if he hit another one. At least she'd have a chance, unlike the girl. Her eyes burned with fire as she tugged the case on the floor between her legs.

Back in the aircraft, Kayla forced herself to stay awake as she poured water over her face. Her stomach felt as if it was getting chewed up like a meat grinder as the pasty dirt from the road left a trail of grit on the side of her neck. Her mind fluttered in shock as she wiped her eyes with the bottom of the Hijab to remove the jam in the corners. The nagging department opened up in her head as she broke down the mission to retrieve a laptop from a tribal leader. The intel for Fallujah was inaccurate. She barely spoke conversational Iraqi, and now, a child was dead from an RPG. The thought made her sit up as she tucked the laptop between her feet. Then, she threw a blanket over her legs and waited for the contact to find her. She slowly removed the head wrap. The nurse came back to dress her wound, but she waved her off. Finally, Kayla gave in and closed her eyes to try drifting off. It would take more than a couple bottles of Chinaco to get this memory buried.

An unmarked, black, military Humvee drove up beeping its horn. The rear compartment of the plane stopped closing, and then, the hull re-opened. Five soldiers dressed in desert gear waited patiently with their weapons at a neutral position. Everyone moaned inside for the delay. The unmarked soldiers found a row of empty seats near Kayla. She was awake and watched them approach with a masked gaze. Hawkins came back from talking with the crew chief and saw the new arrivals. Guns, tactical gear, and rucksacks were removed. She saw the alarm bells go off inside his head; his orders were to let her make contact, be ready with transport, and support her until the jumper flight landed. She grabbed his arm for him to take the seat next to her. He handed her a couple of Advil. She kept hydrating, and under the blanket, she clicked the safety back on her field weapon. Kayla saw Hawkins put his hand in ready position and she said, "That won't be necessary. I got this." The latch door locks screwed down with squeaky tension and climaxed to a knot. The first hump was under way as she eased her expression while saying to Hawkins, "Just relax. It'll get funny soon enough." She knew the code words and liked that management had a sense of humor.

The bearded meathead nodded to one of his teammates. Kayla smiled with the Glock between her legs. It felt good knowing that it was resting in the saddle. Hell, the only thing missing was a good buzz and some lounge music. The plane raced down the runway.

The paramilitary group had all the trimmings of being experienced, tight-fitted, and part of some elite pipe hitting smoke squad. Her transfer orders were specific about the location for the laptop but ambiguous at best as to when the drop-off would take place. Like she wasn't supposed to come back, but they would find her. It was to be done by a coded Q&A. Real Ian Fleming stuff. It started with her being offered a cigarette. Then she had to ask for a light. Of course the lighter wouldn't work and this key moment would authenticate the correct contact. Geez Louise. Who comes up with this stuff?

One of the soldiers asked, "You look horrible. Can I get you anything?"

Kayla heard the heavy Russian accent and tried to locate its origin. He wasn't from Georgia, probably St. Petersburg. She said in Russian, "U tebya yest' vodka?" He smiled while handing her a flask. She took some.

He asked, "Want a cigarette?" and reached inside his jacket to get out a pack of Kent's.

She took one and put it to her lips.

"Where are you from? Your Russian is horrible."

Kayla said, "Ohio."

The crew chief making rounds intervened when he saw the Russian pull out a lighter. "Tell me you're fucking around."

The mercenary had a blank stare and kept on attempting to ignite the flame. The crew chief had seen these types before and kept a wide berth, but this time was different. He looked around and motioned for support. He thought he was hallucinating and ordered, "Put the lighter down!"

The crew chief was disobeyed. The flame didn't ignite. He kept yelling, "We have open fuselage, yah crapper!" Kayla started laughing, grimaced in pain, knowing that the lighter wasn't going to work. The chief looked at her and then to the Russian. "Are you two nutzo?"

Kayla took the lighter from his hand and offered it to the crew chief. She said, "It doesn't work. Can you give it a try?" He went to reach for it, and she took it back. It looked too nice and fancy. She spun it around in her fingers, and said, "It's a bad joke, sir. Our apologies." The manufacturer was engraved S.T. Dupont with the city name Paris underneath it.

The mercenaries were amused, but not the crew chief. He left in a flurry. Kayla said, "You know what would really work is if you had a Zippo. Those never fail," and gave it back to the man who had taken it out. They heard the crew chief barking orders in every direction. Personnel circled around them all. She took the gun out and put it on her lap. Then, she told Sargent Hawkins, "These were the ones who can't be bothered." She handed over the duffle bag with the laptop.

The Russian said, "Thank you. Nice meeting you, no?" She liked the accent with the beard. He had a smile in his eyes. Or was it a game to him? She didn't second-guess her first instinct and knew that they all had a kill switch. The name patch on his vest was Tretiak. He was broad in the shoulders and long in the arms, and that made wielding a knife in close proximities difficult. She wanted to keep laughing, but it hurt too much.

Kayla said, "I'll save it for later," and tucked the cigarette behind her ear.

He introduced himself as Dmitri and tossed her the pack. Then, he put the S.T. Dupont in her hand while saying, "Needs fluid. Keep it for good luck." She opened and closed the lid in approval. She put it in her pocket while saying thanks.

Dmitri started to engage the crew chief in a stare down and, eventually, the hateful look left his face. He apologized and said it wasn't his fault. "On Russian Airlines, everyone smokes. This is why we have so many problems in our country." Kayla chuckled and held her side as the crew chief called out bullshit and walked away, letting the incident fly under the radar.

Dmitri turned to Kayla as he waited for her to say something, but she didn't, and so he casually turned away to snap his fingers. He turned back to her saying, "Christmas present."

Dmitri smiled and gave Kayla a package from his bag. She said, "You already gave me a present."

He didn't let go of the envelope and said, "This is from someone else. We were told it was for your eyes only. Your friends have friends, who have friends in high places. They say to never take this job too seriously, right? Remember, the first pancake is always lumpy." She didn't know what he meant until she opened up the contents.

Kayla was speechless. Dmitri watched her face in silence as she read the contents. He said, "Take care of yourself," and he left her alone. She saw the photographs and copies of the details of her next assignment all paperclipped together over a Russian Consulate letterhead. The target was a picture of a family friend who was like an older brother to her.

CHAPTER 2

DEEP IN THE jungles of an El Salvadorian Mountain ridge was a lone man by the name of Ken "Duke" Williams. He was six feet four inches with no neck; a Sasquatch in terms of hair. He kept a long beard to cover up a cleft lip. He soothed his deformity by nurturing a penchant for Baby Ruth candy bars. He'd been licking his fingers and relishing in the sweetness as he watched a farm from an advantage point. He had been in the jungle for a few days now, and the sugary snacks were mush within the wrappers. It was heaven to him, a happy place, and he'd endure anything to set up his own cocaine channels into the US. In his mind this place was the mecca for growing a business. They'd been chewing on it for centuries. He wiped his fingers on his shirt, reached into his jacket and pulled out the latest edition of Mad magazine. The slang scrabble page was earmarked. He took his time studying it and circled the word "dweeb." Three years ago, while going AWOL from a field exercise of advanced recon unit, he stumbled onto this farm. The US Army didn't accept his excuse of being lost for two months and properly gave him a dishonorable discharge. He could care less, because now he had found a backer for this great adventure, and his time had now come.

Duke was watching the farm as two rebels stopped a few yards away to have a smoke. They chatted away like a couple of contractors avoiding the day's work and argued about how deep a hole should be for a dry well. He found the conversation fascinating as he watched the bubblegum soldiers with arm bands go back and forth. It was better than a movie theater and the only thing missing was some buttery popcorn. He'd been tracking these two for a couple days. They slept more than they talked, and ate more than needed. These were some pitiful out of shape men that were built for peeling potatoes. He watched as they sucked down water out of a bottle as he licked his lips and decided it was time to go visit the saloon in the village.

A few hours later, Duke watched a green bus snake its way through the mountain pass. In less than ten minutes it was rounding the corner where he was standing in the middle of the road. He boarded the transport and gave the driver some money. Twenty minutes later they entered town, and he found the local tavern dump. It was run by the dentist named Borracho. The clay building had no signs or windows, just a wooden door and holes in the ceiling. His tall frame stood out from the crowd, and the owner came up to him while pointing at the hair on his arm. Borracho gave him a bottle of Cusha and said, "El hombre lobo." Duke accepted the local hooch and found a quiet table to drink alone. He watched the others keep to themselves and talk quietly. A while later he bought a couple more bottles of the horse piss Cusha and walked out back to disappear into the jungle. Then backtracked to a cave he'd found not too far from the coca farm. The accommodations had an underground spring and it connected to the river about a quarter mile away. In his mind, it was the perfect spot for a basecamp, minus the bats, spiders, and occasional scorpion.

The farmers would be up before dawn and even earlier during harvest season. Duke passed the time by giving into his laziness while living off the fat of the land. The place reminded him of his hometown Beaumont in Appalachia, on the edge of Tennessee. He crept around like a ghost, taking food from any place, just like he did as a kid. He had learned to hide from people who ridiculed him. They didn't do it for long because he was shaving by the time he was twelve, and had barely gotten through high school when he enlisted. His strength and speed made up for his lack of education.

The good news for him was the locals had a marijuana field. He picked to his hearts content and smoked himself to sleep in the cave. It was the dark places in his mind that gave him the time to think. He liked the nickname "Wolfman" that Borracho gave him. He howled loudly at the shadows on the wall. The ridicule, his grotesque nature, and lack of civilized behavior was his character and it started to grow on him. It was something he decided to embrace, and a cold calculating demeanor started to develop as he tossed another log onto the fire. It would have been too easy for him to go down and snatch fifteen bundles of square groupers, but then what would he do? He had to come back next year. And who then would he have to battle for the cocaine? Who would do all the packing and prep work? Contact had to be made with a name and a face.

Soon he secured a position where two rebels were hanging out. Duke bit into his fist to wake himself up and stretch his sore muscles. He'd smoked too much in the cave last night. They were far enough away to not hear him flinch as an eight-legged beetle landed in his beard. He had taken the bug off his face and was staring at it on his finger. He started whispering to the creature. "The plan is simple; make friends, purchase the product, and deliver it back to the US by boat. Just like they did it in the 80's, but I'll do it with a different twist, and better than those other yahoos."

Both of the soldiers turned as another man approached. He had on gold necklaces, a cowboy hat, and finger rings. Like a snake in the grass Duke coiled as they moved closer. The man doing all the talking out of his pie-hole was called Tonka. He put a cigarette to his mouth and one of the soldiers struck a match. The rebels said, "Too much grain this year. Not enough coca."

Tonka nodded and said, "Yet we'll have fatter cattle for the winter." Duke curled his lip as the man expressed interest in fortifying the food supply. He disagreed with this rationale and thought they should be focused on cocaine production. The desire for feeding men and not profits was a sign of weakness. He decided to straighten him out tomorrow. Tonka said, "We'll plant more coca next year." The men agreed as they laughed, and Duke sensed pushover.

The next day Tonka was sitting alone on the river bank and fishing. Duke noticed the man was comfortable because he never looked around to see if there were any threats. Duke wanted to scare him and slowly stepped out of the bush with a knife in his hand. Tonka never turned around but said, "Hello."

Duke said, "I've come to steal your fish," and kicked over the basket.

The man didn't bother to look and said, "Take whatever you want, there's plenty in this river."

Duke smiled and kept his gaze on Tonka. His pearly whites gleamed in contrast to the painted green face. He said, "I was moseying in the neighborhood and wanted to talk to you about a business proposition. Would it be okay for me to stop by sometime tomorrow and have a meeting?"

Tonka said, "Sure. Why the knife?" His English was flawless.

Duke replied, "You can never be too careful in the wild," then walked past him and slowly stepped into the river till floating away with the current. Tonka watched him drift downstream and then cast his line in a new spot.

A few days passed and Duke never showed his face as he watched to see if any changes took place with Tonka. He was doing the same casual things of eating, fishing, and walking around the area without a care in the world. The man had a pair, and Duke's intimidation wasn't working. He gave up on waiting any longer and approached the camp the next morning while waving a white flag. Tonka was having coffee and said, "You are the demon in the cave. We knew you were eventually going to show up." Duke looked around as the other men encircled the intruder. Tonka said, "You like the jungle?"

Duke smiled, "Very much."

Tonka said, "It is beautiful. You're welcome to whatever it is you came for. Right now, we have a lot of product and very few buyers." Tonka laughed loudly and then the others joined.

Tonka said, "Do you wonder why...we not kill you?"

Duke answered, "With all respect. Killing me is probably the smartest choice but wouldn't be the best. I was sent here to negotiate for a much larger team. Removing me will only bring long-term negative results for your way of life. What they'd do is just send someone smarter, and with less mercy." The sheer size of Duke among the other men was intimidating and had everyone's attention. Tonka decided not to take any chances. He looked around into the mountain landscape to see if a sniper had his target.

Finally, Tonka said, "How much do you want?"

Duke threw a duffle bag of money at his feet and said, "As much as that will get us." He imagined Tonka wondering about the "us" part. He never let go of the fishing rod and used his foot to peek at the contents.

They started working on his order right away. Tonka invited Duke to stay and he accepted. It was a better place than the cave, and they had an endless supply of drugs. He tried as best as he could to assimilate and the rebels made it easy by accepting him with open arms, no judgement, and it was something he'd never had in his life. So, he played along, but knew deep down the generosity could turn fatal. He smiled when they grinned, talked in broken conversation, and peacocked around camp. His plan grew with confidence as time wore on. It helped that they let him sample the finished product and Duke got higher than a kite while sipping Cusha. He'd fallen in love with the local brew and for some reason it kept the skeeters away. He offered to chop wood for the kettle, and they let him have at it. The energy within him was coursing violently and needed an outlet. At night he slept outside in a hammock till the brown square groupers of cocaine were wrapped up tighter than a Christmas present. His presence made them work harder than necessary and after a few days they had everything ready.

Duke slipped out just before dawn to sneak back to the cave and get the rest of his gear. When he returned, Tonka was enjoying a smoke and drinking tea. He didn't bother to get up, just told him good luck. Duke leaned down and said, "This business is a science and you're a genius. I'll be able to build rockets with your help and will be looking forward to seeing you next month, upon my return." Tonka nodded his head as Duke left with the packhorses loaded.

Two other men accompanied Duke over the mountains. A light rain pelted his shoulders as the path became squishy. He walked along, keeping the men in sight just in case one of them stepped out of line and he had to put a bullet into the back of their head. They waded through the valley and eventually came to a river. He pulled out his side arm and pointed saying, "Vamos." They unloaded the packhorses. Duke said, "Nos vemos luego." Slowly they backed up and walked away. He waited by the shore for a few minutes then backtracked to make sure they were up the trail. He returned a few moments later to pull out a submerged wooden canoe from the water. After loading it up, Duke coasted downstream for the ultimate payoff.

Once he arrived at the port, he looked for the freighter called Little Horn and it's captain. He found the man asleep with a lit cigar in his hand on a deck chair. Duke smiled like a kid in a candy store. He waited for Dolan to wake up and said, "You busy?"

Dolan said, "Ya. Give me about fifteen more minutes." He then proceeded to get up and fire up the stogie to a blaze.

Duke said, "You got one for me?"

"Sure, only it's bad luck for you," replied Captain Dolan.

"Is that a boat thing?"

Captain said, "No. Just messing with you," he then reached into his shirt pocket and gave him one.

Duke took it and said, "What could go wrong?"

Captain replied, "I don't know, maybe hitting a beach at fifty miles an hour or getting arrested by border patrol?" Duke smoked the Cubano as his eyes searched a radius for any unexpected movements. Something bothered him but he didn't know what it was till he saw Dolan's shirt. It had pineapples on it. He hated the fruit, the smell of it and everything about it, including the taste. He wanted to smash him in the face, but he needed this man.

They walked below deck to see the two remote controlled torpedoes that would hold the square groupers. Duke peeked his head inside and thought they'd fit perfectly. Captain would soon have them welded to the side of a forty-six-foot Rough Rider Cigarette boat. He also did some extra fiberglass work and asked Duke, "Where did you get all this electronic equipment?"

Duke pulled out the laptop, "The internet. You should get yourself a Hotmail account."

Dolan laughed and said, "Regular mail doesn't work anymore?"

Duke said, "I keep telling everyone and no one believes me." Duke could see he didn't think much of the technology and knew deep down a lot of people in the world were clueless. To have a conversation go any further would be exhausting, and he needed some sleep. He said, "We're going to do a lot of business together after this."

Dolan replied, "One step at a time."

"You're right," and tossed him an envelope of cash; Dolan opened it up and started counting while saying, "My apologies, you are correct, we are going to do a lot of business together."

Duke said, "The plan is, once I'm close enough to shore, boom, the pods are discharged, and Bing, the remote-controlled devices take over." He held up a handheld console with a joystick. "All our buyers have to do is hit this button and the coordinates are automatically generated. The torpedoes go to the defined area, get picked up, and hot chicken time. I get paid." When he finished explaining, he flicked one of the propellers and it started to spin.

Dolan scratched his head and said, "Seems like a good waste of a boat and a lot of equipment." Duke didn't hear what he said because he was busy smiling at his dream and his reflection on the fiberglass. In less than three days he'd be in Vegas throwing the bones around and hanging out with an Asian showgirl named Nikki. She does a mean Pat Benatar impersonation while taking down Karaoke trophy's. He'd slip one of the groupers into his backpack for the after party and insurance purposes.

The following morning, they hoisted the anchor and set sail.

Three days later Captain Dolan dropped the Rough Rider over the side about fifty miles out. Duke started it up and let the engine idle as he drifted away from the Little Horn into total darkness. It took him a few minutes to get adjusted after checking the instrument panels. Then he took out a pocketknife to get a pinch of grouper, inhaled deeply, knowing things could get out of hand. It would be an added bonus for the trip if everything got out of hand and turned into a haywire express. His hand eased the throttle forward while glancing down at the side storage compartment with two fully loaded mini-Uzi. He was ready for a gun fight and began to day dream.

CHAPTER 3

THE DEBRIEF MEETING was in Beirut, right after Kayla got out of surgery with local anesthesia. She was glad to get the heads up for the next mission, and it gave her time to work on her surprised face for NCO Richard J. Cornick. Two other field analysts silently took some notes in the tent near the airstrip. Kayla was signing paperwork for clearance to documents she had already seen from the Russian hit squad. She'd never met the man before, and it felt awkward to receive orders from someone in uniform, given her position as an agent. It must have been some kind of test that they performed from time to time.

Cornick didn't hold back from saying that she was inappropriately dressed. She responded in Arabic, *"Nothing about me almost getting killed, but you're bothered by the clothes I'm wearing."*

Cornick snapped back, "In English." He wasn't used to getting any pushback. She'd grown accustomed to the head garb and liked how it felt. It was like learning Farsi. It came easy to her, unlike the last mission, which had left its mark. He asked, "What are you looking at?"

Kayla said, "I don't see a combat patch on you, sir. How's life behind the wire?" But her new boss was determined to have no sense of reality and went back to reading the file. She asked, "You know they have a Taco Bell here?" Needling him was giving her strength. Wearing something that he thought was inappropriate was the perfect distraction from what they were going to ask her to do next.

He asked, "You don't look so good. We can do this another time if you're not up to it?" She finished signing the documents and took the file.

She replied, "I'll be fine, sir," and opened the contents. After a few minutes, she asked, "Did you guys find this in a pumpkin?" No one responded. She continued, "So, let me get this straight, my mission is to find a safe and plant a transmitter on a computer?"

He replied, "Correct."

She asked, "Do you want me to have sex with him?"

The analyst responded, "Absolutely not." She was going to be the pawn for bushwhacking a family friend, destroying his life, and selling him out. All so they could run a smear campaign, for no valid reason as far as she could see. Cornick reminded her multiple times to just do the job.

She asked, "Thorpe has been wanting to jump my bones for a long time. It would be a very easy thing to do."

The analyst said, "Negative."

She responded, "Yes, sir."

With Saddam Hussein still in power, they decided pull her out and to tear down Thorpe. He'd definitely stepped on the wrong toes. Suddenly, she saw all the friendlies in the room as the enemy. They had no right to ask her to breach the trust of a personal friendship. The Thorpes had donated to numerous charities, their name was above the door of the medical facility where her father worked. She'd known Christopher Thorpe most of her life, they were close, and her father was Christopher's personal physician ever since he was a child. Why did she say she'd have sex with him? Her mind was getting twisted. When his parents died in a mysterious plane crash, her father took him in like a son. She didn't believe for a second that he was selling secrets to foreign nationals. It had to be some personal vendetta someone had against him, and she was caught in the middle as an expendable asset.

Kayla stood up to leave, but the commanders motioned for her to stop, and she waited. They started to say something, but Cornick pointed to the chair. She looked down at the file again. The analyst that she didn't recognize spoke up, "Your options are to do the job or guard a lighthouse in Nova Scotia for the next five years."

She started to chuckle but held it in with a thought popping into her head. She said, "You're not going to send me to Leavenworth?"

"A dishonorable discharge will suffice."

Kayla sat back and lit a cigarette while saying, "I hope you're not expecting an answer right now? This man is a very good friend of mine."

Cornick said, "Against all enemies, foreign, and domestic."

She stared at him and said, "I'm going to need some personal time to wrap my head around this request. You're asking me to betray a lifelong friend, more like a family member. It's unethical, but I'll do it. I just need more time to come to terms with it first." They looked around the room, took a quick vote, and conceded. She walked out of the tent and into the desert furnace, knowing that their position was desperate. Otherwise, she'd never leave Iraq. Christopher had taught her the trick of giving them an answer they didn't expect or want to hear. It delayed the moment and pivoted each party's positioning, which was a helpful tool in a negotiation. She wondered how many times they had already tried to infiltrate Christopher's estate and failed before reaching out to her. In the morning, they gave her a seven-day pass back home to Florida, to be near Christopher.

A man showed up a week after Kayla's return. He casually followed her around from time to time. She saw him at the clubs, restaurants, and racetrack. He kept his distance. She couldn't care less with all of the sleepless nights and migraines she was having. Drinking at five-star-studded events provided by Christopher was her only cure. Mentally, she had been pushed passed her limit. A seven-day pass turned into a three-week blur. Then, one Wednesday morning, after a heavy night of being out on the town, the agent came up to her at a café to say that her vacation visa was being stamped. He told her to report to Homestead Air Force base on Monday at 0600 and to buy some warm leggings over the weekend for Northern Greenland.

Kayla watched him walk away and get into a car. She couldn't figure out why they hadn't arrested her on the spot. But she had learned early in life that it was best to count your blessings, and she enjoyed her last weekend of freedom. They all learned eventually, like Jimmy Oliver did in the fifth grade when he pushed her to the ground. This situation was no different, and she wasn't going to change. The brass must want Christopher pretty badly to give her the weekend off. She was determined to go live her life by her own set of values. Since getting back into town, it'd been a relentless blowout, despite the lack of sleep and headaches. The ability to say no to any soiree was proving to be lost in her vocabulary.

She woke up the next morning and came to the conclusion that she was in over her head, physically speaking. She couldn't see daylight. There was so much she didn't understand, and it would be easier to tell Christopher everything so she could focus on chilling out from all the stress. He was so young when his parents died. How did he deal with it? He'd had to grow up so fast and live with a chip on his shoulder, as if he had something to prove. That was where they were so much alike. Well, he proved them all wrong, and she contemplated asking him for help this weekend, somewhere away from his fake political friends. Christopher was the whale among the sharks. She scratched her arm like a worm on a hook, itching for a drink, only it was nine o'clock in the morning.

On Friday, Kayla gazed at the first light coming up through the dark tree line in South Florida. She watched with rapt attention as the light peeked through the morning clouds. A nearby street lamp reminded her of the time when most of Florida was swamp land, everglades, and overgrown vegetation, until developers came in with the concrete. She turned her watch into the light to see the time. Christopher Thorpe was standing about twenty feet away. A bottle rocket zipped over her head as she turned to him and said, "Your aim is getting worse with age." They had already been to dinner, casino, a nightclub, and this was the after party. Everyone else had left, and they were hanging out in a field about a mile from his estate. She lit the fuse and held on to the wooden stick of a bottle rocket for just a second longer than necessary before letting the projectile fly towards the intended direction of his face. Christopher feebly resisted the attack by hiding behind his arms. The incoming rocket exploded about ten feet above his head. "Batter swing and a miss! You're getting close, but no cigar."

Kayla said, "Not even." The two of them had been playing this game for years. It all started one Fourth of July when they were kids, but it wasn't supposed to carry over into adulthood. They were acting like children again as she stood across at him, knowing this man couldn't be a traitor. And the millions he donated to the hospital wasn't going to be an influence on her. Or was it? The wine was too good tonight, and it helped her aim. She didn't blink an eyelash for the next shot and cursed the stupid files, and all the "facts" that turned into lies, because everyone stretched the truth to fit a purpose. What is a lie anyway? But a truth turned inside out. Who was hiding behind the assault on his character? Was he the fake cover for something bigger? She didn't see any reason to be the one who removed him from his throne. Instead, she pleaded with herself to tell him what they were asking her to do, but she remained silent.

For the past few years, Christopher would joke with his friends that she was his fiancée. Kayla corrected him in front of everyone tonight when she was introduced, and he laughed nervously afterwards. She would be lying to herself if she said she never considered the amount of shut-up money she'd have if they got hitched, but she always determined that it would ruin their friendship. She remembered telling him to stop introducing her in such a way and he'd replied with, "You can't blame a man for trying." She admired his appetite for power. Most people pretended to want it, but not Christopher. He controlled everything and built a very secure wall around his life. Sure, he made a lot of mistakes along the way, but so would she with that kind of inheritance.

Christopher lit his bottle rocket, and it exploded about a foot in front of Kayla. She jumped back and let out a little scream. The last pop set off a ringing in her ears, and it made her take a knee. She slowed down as the IED came with a hammering flashback. Blood was on her hands, and a pain seared through her body, then it was gone. She looked at her hands again, and nothing was on them, but it made her want to stop playing. Christopher asked, "Is everything all right?" Luckily, the shadowy darkness hid her face. She stood up but was aggravated by the pull that the memory had over her mind. She needed another drink to kill the ringing in her ears.

She replied, "I'll be fine. Give me a second." Everything was getting stressful; she was tired of the daylight sounds, traffic, and noisy machinery. She found it best to hide from people and to avoid strangers. She was grateful to have a friend like Christopher to make these moments in life more manageable.

Kayla pulled out her S.T. Dupont and lit another bottle rocket. This time, she held on until the sparks started to spray off the back of her hand. She wanted it to explode in her fingers to numb the pain and, at the last second, released it in a straight line towards Christopher's chest. It ricocheted off his body and exploded. He yelled, "Ahhhhhh!" After he hit the ground, they both started laughing. He said, "You trying to kill me?" He got back up and took his turn. It went up and into the trees, not even close to hitting her. She put her hand on her hip and watched it explode.

Using the same technique as last time, Kayla channeled her accuracy, holding on for one breath longer than last time. Christopher was oblivious as he checked a message on his phone. A second later, a popping explosion happened two inches from his ear. He dropped to a knee as an oversized rock was inopportunely located under his shoe. He buckled to cover up his ear, then started rolling around in pain with a twisted ankle to say the least. She covered her mouth in surprise. There was nothing for her to do, except to slowly walk over and keep the laughter to a minimum. While standing over him, she asked, "Are you okay?" He remained silent as he held onto his calf with one hand and his ear with the other. She watched him try to talk, then he closed his mouth.

Finally, after a few moments, he said, "We should go back to the car." She helped him up, and they started to wobble away.

Kayla leaned him up against a tree stump as she went back to grab the bottle of tequila. Christopher didn't wait for her and hobbled forward. She knew that he could say nothing against her because this was what bottle rocket wars was all about. The last time they played, he put one in her jacket and ruined the top pocket of a five-hundred-dollar coat. The burn mark almost left a mark on her chest. She didn't feel bad for one second as she watched him struggle ahead. He was a good sport about losing, but these shenanigans made her more on edge. She wished for an easier life and questioned why they both had to prove everyone wrong. Her brain told her to find a man and settle down, to take the easy road for once. Her brow furrowed at the possibility, and then, the resentment of having to spy on Christopher kicked up.

Kayla looked down at the bottle she was carrying over. She became aware of her success at functioning under the influence. Is this what she was going to do with her free time up in Nova Scotia? She took a drink and tossed it away into the field. She had to meet with her dad in a few hours and wouldn't be able to hide her condition from him if she took another sip. He liked to talk while he worked and would require her to start toning things down. His fatherly intuition would probably sniff out her over consumption, and she valued his high opinion of her, even though it did take a few years to comprehend. Why had they not talked since she'd been back? He was always there, holding her accountable and responsible, like a guard in a prison. He'd made her work during the summers, while all her friends went to the beach to perfect their tans. They had money, but not for her. When she wanted a dinghy for sailing, they didn't help. Made her cut lawns, babysit, and work at Jimmy's Pizzeria on weekends to paid for it all. In the pit of her stomach, she knew that it made her stronger. It just hadn't always been easy to understand in the moment. She took a deep breath while strolling out of the darkness and into the light of a new day.

Christopher was at the table full of food that had been set up in the open field near the Rolls, and an old leather-bound suitcase was open. He cut a pink pill in half for her. It was an amphetamine. He said, "This will help you get through the morning." Kayla surmised that he had already taken something for himself. She appreciated the thoughtfulness. He asked, "Where's the tequila?" She replied that she couldn't find it.

Kayla picked up a unique looking bottle and asked, "What's this?"

"My latest endeavor. Water."

Kayla admired the bluish glow emanating from the metal and glass flask. Christopher popped the vacuum-sealed top, and it released a mist into the air. She said, "Is it safe to drink?"

He took a long sip and finished with an, "Ahhhh." She took a step back and, once again, fought back the urge to share with him her stupid assignment. There had to be a better way.

He asked, "What is it?"

She said, "Nothing...what makes it so special?"

Christopher said, "The distance it has to travel." He asked Kayla to give it a try. She took a small sip and then finished half the contents.

After wiping her mouth on her sleeve, she said, "That was delicious. Didn't realize how thirsty I was." He didn't say anything and just stared at her, then started laughing while shaking his head. She looked over to the suitcase of happiness he always carried around and tried to figure out what drugs he'd just consumed. For sure it wasn't laughing gas because she didn't see any containers.

Kayla said, "What's so funny?"

Christopher replied, "It comes from a place near the Bering Sea, an undisclosed location. They bore into the ice about a thousand feet down. It has the highest density of nutrition a human body can handle for the most efficient absorption. Some call it the fountain of youth elixir, others the nectar of the gods. Besides being invigorating, refreshing, and labor intensive, it has a fantastic price point."

Kayla looked at the label on the bottle and said, "Who's Chinook?"

"It's the hometown of the guy who makes it. You like the name?"

"Sure, as long as it helps with the migraines?"

Christopher said, "Take one with you and find out."

"I didn't just drink Molly, did I?"

Christopher said, "And I thought that I had problems."

Kayla replied, "Don't blame me. You're the one who says, *Crack Is Whack.*"

Christopher tapped on the case and replied, "Very true, good memory, but I didn't make it up, Keith Haring did...It's a smart thing to remember, but you'll never be in their category. These pizzy's are for winning votes among the weak-minded. I don't let friends have them." She didn't want to know the extent of how far he could travel down the rabbit hole with the Washington elite. She looked at the car, table set up in an open field, lit candles, fine goldware, and admired his ability to manage this type of existence. She didn't sugarcoat her role as a passenger. He looked at her with soft eyes and said, "Why do you dislike the political vermin so much?"

Kayla waved off the question and said, "What's there to like?" Christopher agreed, and she gulped down the rest of the Chinook. It felt as if it was washing away the dirt and pain from the thorn hanging around in her side from the frag wound. She kept drinking till the bottle was empty. Her eyes opened, and Christopher said, "Thirsty?"

"Apparently. More than I thought." Kayla examined the bottle and said, "This is pretty good. Where can I get some?"

"I'll make sure one falls off the truck during the next shipment."

She pleaded in a respectful tone, "Can I buy a couple cases?"

He said, "Sure. They're fourteen thousand a case."

Kayla asked in surprise, "Twelve hundred a bottle?"

"Roughly speaking."

Kayla laughed and said, "You're kidding?" Christopher didn't say anything, and she deflated, "You're not kidding. I should have known better than to think that a man who flies private could drink anything normal."

"Normal? Nothing normal about me, Kayla. You should know that by now."

She said, "No doubt. You have a way of keeping the party going. What the hell is in this?" and tossed him the empty bottle.

Christopher said, "Dinosaur piss, probably."

They both erupted in laughter as she held back from coming clean to him, and she made a promise to do so in two-weeks. Better to call him from Nova Scotia and break the news in solitude. All would be forgotten by then or at least be out in the open. There were no limits to his ability to sink into the abyss of the good life, and her ability to keep up frightened her. It seemed like he did it unconsciously as if Hunter Thompson, Keith Richards, and Bukowski were all tangled up in his DNA. She had no idea how he still functioned in business. Some people were just made differently, and she was ready for a break.

The weekend had arrived. It was officially Friday, but to her, it could have been a Tuesday or Thursday. Having to see her father in a few hours forced her to sober up. She took a seat next to Christopher at the table by the Rolls.

Kayla recalled a Fourth of July party as a kid when his parents were still alive. They were playing hide and go seek as she crawled through the bushes by the barn. She spotted Christopher hanging out with his friends, the older, and cooler kids. She watched them hitting each other in the arm, smoking cigarettes, and firing bottle rockets at each other. Christopher ran off and came back with his mother's favorite cat, Barry, under his arm.

Then, walking up to the fire, he threw the feline into the flames. His friends laughed, but he was serious, and Kayla ran away.

With the sunrise accenting the curves of her face, Kayla said, "Why did you throw your mother's cat into the fire? You know it messed me up for the longest time about you."

Christopher laughed louder than usual and then saw that she wasn't smiling. "Everyone hated that cat except Mother." She didn't think his smile was sinister. He said, "Holy shit Kay, that was over twenty years ago? I'd forgotten about Barry. What made you think of it?"

"Not sure. Maybe it was the last belt of tequila."

"Well, don't do any more. Just kidding." He paused again and said, "Kids do stupid things. It was my moronic moment. We all get a few of them and can never take them back." He was right. She couldn't blame him, and his honesty was enough for her. She didn't feel uncomfortable for asking. He looked straight at her and said, "I'm glad you asked."

"Why?"

"I loved my mother, and she would have gotten a kick out of you. As best I could remember, it's not what she did, but what she didn't do. It took some time for me to figure it all out with some professional help, and now, who really cares? It's long gone, luckily for me, and best for everyone else. I've found ways to let go of the painful memories, even if it was my fault. Kids do stupid things, and maturity is supposed to change us for the better."

She said, "When did you get all stoic?"

"Since you blew a bottle rocket next to my ear. It won't stop ringing."

She let out a huff and said, "Unfortunately, the ringing never stops. It could be ruptured. Might want to have Dad look at it this morning. I'm going to see him right after this." She started feeling bad for having such excellent aim and suppressed a smile, then said, "It was a pretty lucky shot. I was aiming at your feet."

"You should have aimed at my head, and you would have hit my feet. Couldn't do that shot again in a million years."

Kayla smirked. "Oh, you think so? Don't tempt me, I might try it."

At that moment, Han Lee and Jimmy Young arrived with the horse trailer. Kayla had met them before, but Han was new. They both got out of the truck. She didn't know the other four men in black Chinese tunics hanging out by the road. Christopher waved them all over and told them to get something to eat. The six casually approached to check out the table full of meat cuts, cheese, beers, and different styles of tapas in Tupperware. She could see that they enjoyed his generosity. Two of them started play fighting with each other.

Kayla remarked, "You're always kind to the staff."

"Thank you. That is a high compliment. I found it's always best to work around happy people rather than the angry ones. So, why not keep them happy?"

She watched as the two men sparred in strict traditional format. They got in a horse stance, then touched the back of their lead hands before beginning. She slipped in a nonchalant question, "Why the extra men?"

He said, "For the weekend."

She said, "Is anything wrong?"

Christopher laughed again. "We've had two break-ins at the house in the last six months, and being proactive has its advantages. I'm pretty sure that my resources will soon discover the culprits. We just installed new camera equipment all over the place. What are they teaching you in the military these days? Maybe you can help."

Kayla said, "They have me pushing paperwork mostly, sharpening pencils, that sort of thing."

Christopher said, "Such a waste. They should know your value." He pointed to one of the men eating. "Take Han, for instance. He's not funny, a bit boring, but he's smart as all hell and looks intimidating. It's the stern face I like, which makes for a good poker player. How would one know if he had negative intentions? Only if he told you. But if someone is happy, they're great to have around, and it's noticeable when they get out of line."

"What happens when someone is fake happy? How can you tell?"

"Fake happy people are easy to spot, because they're lazy, and really hate to work. Which, makes them as easy target, like fish in a barrel."

Jimmy went over to remove the horses from the trailer. Kayla watched him remove Biscuit and Ziem. He tied them up near a bale of hay as she went over to say hi to the love of her life, Biscuit. It gave her a chance to take a look at Han, who was observing the sparring. He was Christopher's new attaché. The background file she had read on him was limited, and he didn't fit the profile of a personal assistant. He looked more like a roughneck than an executive secretary. She could see Christopher's inner circle becoming slightly paranoid. She returned to Christopher and said, "Han looks Korean."

"He is. He speaks Cantonese, among several other languages. Might be the most organized person we've ever hired. He's uncanny with remembering names, dates, numbers, places. He's a good egg." The guards stripped the black Chinese tunics off as they continued sparring.

Kayla lit up a cigarette and admired the classical design with the name Paris embedded beneath S.T. Dupont. She thought of the Russian merc who gave it to her when Christopher said, "When did you start smoking, Kay?"

It was an innocent question, but for some reason, it annoyed her. She wanted to think of a good answer, but nothing came to mind as she tossed her hair back while looking away. Then, she said, "A few weeks ago."

She actually never stopped since enlisting, and it picked up since Afghanistan to help mask the smell of scorched earth from all the burning garbage pits and diesel generators. The stench seeped into people's skin like a lotion. No civilian understood; therefore, they could never understand. Smoking was a nasty habit, but it gave her the fix she needed, and she promised herself to eventually quit. Her thoughts sounded stupid echoing in her head, yet she couldn't have a conversation with him about it. Her brain wouldn't let her process a response other than to leave it be. Pretend something else was more important. What bothered her about the question? Who the hell was he? He was just asking. Christopher was just trying to be nice as she remembered the dying soldier. She was getting triggered again and took a deep inhale. Trying not to look vulnerable, she stared right at Christopher and said, "Why do you ask? You don't like cigarettes?"

"No, they're great. You know I used to smoke, I was just looking out for your health."

"Says the man who carries vials of cocaine in a leather briefcase."

Christopher smiled and said, "It's for medicinal purposes. You have no idea how much stress there is in the outside world." He looked into her eyes and said, "Well, you might have an idea. No offense."

Talking always helped her work through a crisis, but Kayla remained silent this time. Christopher had touched a nerve. She knew when to shut things down and sensed a change in him. Or was it in her? He'd stopped bothering about his ear as he chugged away at the Chinook. When finished, he took a napkin from the table and wiped his mouth. They both started changing their socks, putting on their riding boots, and enjoying the rising sun. They'd hit the good times hard in the last twenty-four hours. It was the reason why Christopher would never get married. The man burned the candle at both ends and had a wandering eye. A calm sense of security came over her once she realized how nice it was to be around him. She began to surrender to the desire to think about what to do next after her military service.

Christopher poured another shot of tequila into a bucket glass. Kayla said, "No more for me."

Christopher replied, "We need to hydrate. Take another swig of water first."

"Okay, I'll do one more, and then, we have to leave." The salt and lime were all she needed. They clicked glasses, and he threw it down the hatch. Hers went to the ground. When she looked away, she saw Han had observed the exchange.

Staring back up into the sky, Kayla saw the sun coloring the clouds a bloody hue. She flashed back to trying to find a cricothyrotomy kit for a soldier choking on his own blood. The Jeep was worthless as every second counted. A life was on the line, and her hands slightly trembled as she inhaled the last of the American Spirit.

Kayla arranged the sock in one of her boots. She licked her lips in approval at the leftover taste of salt and lime. She needed something to stop the migraines, which hadn't left her since the desert. The army was concerned with her sodium intake, but she wasn't. It was the only thing that made her feel better. She looked at Christopher and saw a dashing older man with a good head of hair.

Christopher made a face. "Why are you looking at me like that?"

Kayla smiled. "Amazing."

"What is?"

"Sunrises. Not everyone gets to see them. Thanks for everything these past few weeks. I've had a ball."

"It's not over yet. Wait until you see what I have planned for next week." He gave her a friendly salute and said, "It's all in the company we keep." His smile was full of warmth and childlike happiness as he said, "Thanks for joining me." He paused and rubbed a spot on his boot. She could tell that he wanted to say something else, but he let whatever it was fade away. Kayla knew that it wasn't like him to not say what was on his mind.

She reached over and squeezed his arm. "Are you okay?"

Christopher put his hand over hers and said, "Do you have someone in your heart, Kay?" She looked at him and pulled back, saying no. He joked about marrying her with people around, but now, they were alone. She replayed the previous night and caught her breath. She didn't know what to say and didn't want him to ask the question.

Christopher said, "Well, you're in my heart." He got down on one knee and said, "Would you do me the honor of marrying me? Everything in my possession isn't worth having if it can't be shared with you." Then, he pulled out a small velvet box in his hand to reveal a diamond ring as big as her toe. She was speechless and saw that he was waiting for an answer. For a split second, she was going to say yes. Who wouldn't? But no, how could she, knowing that he was her next target? The temptation to tell him everything struck again. If she said yes, she wouldn't have to worry about another thing for the rest of her life. The clock ticked inside her, and the pressure mounted as she put her hand over her mouth to stop herself from saying anything she'd regret. It was a crazy scenario to be in. If she became his wife, she'd have to tell her husband everything. Since most spur of the moment plans like this one failed, it was best to stall and think things over.

Christopher removed her hand from her face and said, "Getting married isn't such a bad idea, you know. Life would be pretty comfortable for us both."

Kayla didn't doubt it for a second and put her hand back over her mouth. She needed more time. As obsessive as he could be, Christopher was controllable. "I know, I know. This is a bit weird, and it's a bit more complicated than you think. Give me a second." On paper, Christopher was the jackpot for most women, and no one else had ever asked her before. She stood on the threshold of not knowing what to do and having to think on her feet for another possible solution. If they had sex, then it would have to be reported, and it would take her off the assignment.

Christopher took her hand and said, "You're going to need to get this sized." He slipped the seven-and-a-half-carat, Asscher-cut with baguettes on her finger. "Got it from a fence named Bull Tuckett. He had a slight tax problem and needed the cash to avoid prison. His only weakness was Pai gow."

Kayla said, "How romantic."

"I'm kidding. Hey, help a guy out, will yah? My knee is killing me."

Kayla grabbed his arm as he got on both feet, and she said, "Enough already. I thought it was the ankle?"

"Everything is going to hurt if you don't say yes." Kayla pulled away and he said, "No, seriously. This is a legit proposal, a real Kodak moment." He pointed at her ring. "I won't be able to sleep tonight—"

She interrupted him and said, "Stop. I get it. Don't rush me. We've been friends a long time, and you're more like a brother than a husband."

Kayla imagined needing a sling to hold up her arm to support the new attachment to her hand. It was stunning, and she'd have to take it off to put on the riding gloves. She said,

"It's ridiculous," and laughed. Christopher smiled and gestured to her to say something.

Kayla said, "It's beautiful, but too big."

"Well, it's a start. What else?"

"How am I going to explain it to my parents?"

"Your mom and dad love me. I already asked them."

Kayla took a step back. "You asked? Dad said yes?" Christopher nodded. She realized then why her father wanted to see her this morning. "Can't mess up the tennis partnership."

Christopher said, "Holy shit, Kayla. Your dad didn't give me his blessing because we play tennis together."

Kayla sighed. "Oh, Christopher, I don't know."

"Listen, this is all really sudden. You need to sit down?"

"Do you think we'd last? Or am I going to poison you at some point for not mowing the lawn?"

"Don't be silly. We have the hired help."

She smiled. "What if I force you to do something you don't want to do?"

"I don't understand?"

She said hesitantly, "There's some things you don't know about me, and it's important for you to understand the truth."

Christopher replied, "What are you talking about? I can get over whatever it is." She knew that he didn't scare so easily, and the shy act he was pulling with kicking at the rocks on the ground were winning her over. For a second, she gave way to an idea that would result in all of her problems working out.

Then, a voice popped inside Kayla's head telling her that it would be for the wrong reasons. She questioned the future of having children together and knew it would be best for her to have a kid sooner rather than later. Could she be a covert agent and a mom? She was looking for a way out, and here was the opportunity. She could always tell him the truth in a few weeks. It could save him and solve her biological clock issue.

If it didn't work out, at least she'd have an interesting story to tell over cocktails.

Kayla didn't dance around her words and said, "You know, if we get married, you'll disappoint all your other girlfriends." He reeled back a notch with a surprised look on his face.

"They mean nothing to me. They're just meaningless relationships to fill a work-life necessity. None of them measure up to you, and I'm not asking them. My purpose is to keep the family business going and leave a legacy with someone I truly love. Everyone around me is after something but you." He looked up at her to see if she was listening and said, "It's pretty cool to keep looking over your shoulder and see the only person in the world you can really trust. It's why I'm committing everything to you."

Kayla hated herself and genuinely cared for Christopher. She softly said, "I need some time to think about it." She saw him hanging by a thread and continued, "Can we talk about this on our way back to the stables?"

He agreed, and they walked over to the horses. "But what is there to think over?"

She turned her head and said, "I'm not blowing you off, Christopher. Dad asked me to see him this morning." He didn't respond and looked down at the ground again.

He tightened his belt and said, "Well, at least you're thinking about it, and that's better than a no. Take all the time you need."

It was a sobering conversation, and Kayla spun the ring around her index finger. Any kind of guilt was falling off of her shoulders as she started to see a way out of finding a hidden safe or installing a transmitter. Of course, they could get someone else to plant a smear campaign, and if they could do this to him, then she was definitely expendable. The marriage idea might be her best chance. "I'll hang onto this," as she tucked the ring into her jeans and slide on the riding gloves. They fit like pieces of a puzzle as she sandwiched her fingers to the knuckle webbing.

The leather made a smacking noise as she punched the palm of each hand. Biscuit's ears popped up.

Kayla said, "One thing we'd have to do is sign a pre-nup."

"What?!!" Christopher laughed so loud that it riled the horses. He said, "For what reason?"

"Shut up. You probably already have one drafted up."

"Of course we did, at our lawyer's request. But we left one part blank." She asked what it was and he said, "The type of work you do for the government."

"You're joking?"

"No, and I wanted to know for shits and giggles."

Kayla smiled at him and said, "You can put me down as a research assistant." She could see his mind contemplating her answer.

He said, "Sounds secretive. So, you're a spy."

She couldn't believe that he'd uttered those words and said, "It's a boring desk job, since you want to know so badly."

"Nothing wrong with boring."

"I'll be out soon enough, and if you ever want to know how to fix a paper jam on a copy machine, I'm your girl."

"How much longer do you have?"

"Less than I realized." She played it off with such aplomb that it caused Christopher to drop the subject.

He said, "You've changed. You seem wiser or smarter, or is it cynical?"

"Just tired of being ordered around."

"Well, if you say yes, then your days of taking orders are over. To be honest, I'm not sure I'll get to tell you what to do when we tie the knot. But let's not go down that road just yet."

"Are you sure? We're down it already." She hoped the response would shut him up for a spell.

Kayla checked her knockoff Rolex. It was a gift from Sargent Copeland for saving his leg as a medic in her first tour. Said he picked it up from a street vendor in Ramadi. She thought it would have stopped ticking a while ago. After grabbing the reins, she hopped up in the saddle. Yesterday was over, and the new day had officially arrived.

Christopher adjusted his saddle and climbed up using the stirrup belonging to Ziem. Kayla could see him beginning to focus, and then, he turned his head with a warm smile, saying, "Why would you want to sign a pre-nup? I thought the subject would get some push back from you." She couldn't tell him that it was window dressing for having an excuse to get an honorable discharge from her commitment to serve. The truth would come out eventually on their wedding night. She'd have to come clean and then get incredibly drunk afterward. Her silence made him say, "I don't get it." Then, he kept talking to himself as if she wasn't there. All she heard was *blah, blah, blah*. The sun was in his eyes as he looked over at her on Biscuit. She was rubbing the neck of the buckskin while Christopher stared at the two of them. Kayla had watched over her since she had finished college. Christopher didn't like Biscuit after the horse kicked him in the thigh.

"What a twist in the martini you are. A fucking fortune is at your feet, and all you want to do is rub the neck of your horse." Kayla pretended not to listen. She took what he was saying as a compliment. He continued, "You don't have any money bumps running up and down your arm?"

Kayla smiled at his exasperation and kept her attention on Biscuit. She had become a horse person thanks to Christopher, and it wasn't her fault that he didn't get along with the horse she liked the most. He said, "Okay. I'll drop the conversation since I'm in it by myself." She needed more time, and tending to Biscuit helped her deal with the stress. Horses kept things simple, and rubbing the side of Biscuit's neck was helping to calm her brain.

Biscuit's soft ears perked up.

Kayla said, "If I wanted your money, Christopher, I'd have it already. Do you think I'm that incompetent? How long have you been planning this?"

"Just came to me the other day." She called him out on his BS, and he said, "Since you went into the military."

"When we flew to Vegas and stayed at the Hard Rock?"

"It was the Four Seasons, but yes."

"Well, this is a big surprise, and you're catching me off-guard. I need a moment. Is that too much to ask?" She looked at her watch again and said, "We have to be getting back."

"Just forget it all. It was a stupid idea. As long as you don't hold it against me, I think I'll be fine."

"No way. I'm flattered."

"It was a long shot. Can't blame a man for trying."

"The humble Christopher. I'm not saying no, and this is a side of you I've never seen before."

"Fair enough. Why don't you come by tonight? We'll discuss it then."

Kayla would need to show up and do some surveillance in case she changed her mind. It would be good to walk the grounds and get some intel. Maybe she could play both sides by telling Christopher one thing and her boss another while planting the transmitter. Thinking about having to follow through with the mission made her feel dirty. The marriage was turning into as good a plan as any. She looked at him with pity, because he didn't deserve what was coming. In no way did she believe he was a traitor giving secrets to the highest bidder, he was too much of a patriot, and she was caught in the middle. She'd tell him everything before she would sell him out.

Christopher wasn't a stupid man and needed to be thrown off the trail a bit. A victory would work for him, but not a planned one like when he just let her win the last bottle rocket battle. As he mounted the steed, Ziem, she saw a meticulously tailored horseman, exuding luxury. If he could win in a race, then it would serve as a necessary diversion.

Christopher worked the reins and said, "When you say yes…after you finish thinking about it…we'll spare no expense on the wedding and honeymoon. It'll be the best decision either one of us has ever made, and nothing will be able to stand between us."

Kayla said, "I haven't said yes yet." Christopher smiled confidently. She circled Biscuit away from his position as one of the horse's hind legs kicked in the air. Both horses were jumpy. She didn't know why, but she suddenly started to get agitated and didn't know where it was coming from. Nothing was ever good enough for her, and now, a proposal was on the table for all the wrong reasons. Something had been ruined. She realized how powerless she was in life, and the anger inside her boiled up.

Everything percolated into a driving headache. She pressed her thumbs to her temples and closed her eyes. Christopher said, "Are you okay?"

"I feel a migraine coming on."

"Want to race back to the stables? It would be a good distraction for you."

Kayla looked at Christopher as if they were on the battlefield. Did he just take the words out of her mouth? The man was a mind reader. She grabbed the reins and backed Biscuit up a few paces. She was going to play this game they gave her, and her only hope was that he'd appreciate her loyalty one day.

"A race? Are you sure you're up to it?" asked Kayla.

"If I remember correctly, wasn't it you who fell out of the raft in Jackson Hole on a level two?"

Kayla remembered and said, "Some people say I fell out, and other people might say that I was pushed by a fifty-year old juvenile delinquent."

"Lucky you knew how to swim." He was trying to goad her, but in her rulebook, payback was a bitch.

Kayla said, "Let's warm up, shall we?" She took Biscuit for a trot. Christopher did the same with the Arabian. They came back together a few minutes later near the Phantom automobile.

Christopher said, "Your ability to ride that horse is commendable."

Biscuit's ears pricked up and turned from side to side. Kayla patted her sinewy neck again. The sun breached the morning clouds. She had her plan, knew her exit point, and Christopher's face was full of innocence. She temporarily gave up on coming clean with him and took a deep breath. The excitement dispersed the throbbing pain in her pre-frontal cortex. This news wasn't going to be easy for him, and his life would be changing regardless. She simmered a bit to digest the strategy and said, "Maybe you're right for once, Christopher."

Christopher said, "Pardon me?" Kayla saw Christopher's confusion; he wasn't ready for what was about to happen. She moved nonchalantly with Biscuit, and as Christopher lifted his chin, his shoulders straightened with the gusto of a hot air balloon.

Christopher continued, "We're going to create some kind of life together, right?" He looked gallant and she said, "Obviously." Biscuit circled again. Kayla smiled at Christopher for always being the gentleman, even in the face of such high stakes.

To the man who swam in a pool with a four-foot alligator, she asked, "Are you going to give me a head start?"

"Of course. How much time do you want? One Mississippi?"

Kayla smiled and said, "You're too generous. Let me ask you something. Were the extra tequila shots part of the plan?"

"Come on? What am I, an amateur? Tequilla is good medicine."

She said, "I suppose," and Biscuit fell into position perfectly with no effort from Kayla. Her mind was cleared of any guilt. She tilted her head forward as her hair fell to the side and waited.

What was about to happen next was for the benefit of her boss in DC and Christopher himself. Kayla looked at the leftover caviar, lobster shells, meats, and cheese on fine white linen. She memorized the scene in detail so she could spin the yarn at a later date. It was part of the peripheral training she had undergone. They'd have to believe her back in the office while sipping coffee and listening to her recorded statement. The investigators would gossip to one another like a bunch of envious Nancys waiting for happy hour to start. The air had a whiff of adventure. She inhaled a relaxing breath and gave herself about a five percent chance of not being given a dishonorable discharge, or they might just leave her out in the cold. She would have to practice her surprised look with a ring the size of an ice cube held to her lips.

"I'll tell you what," proposed Kayla. "Let's leave it to fate."

"How are we going to do that?"

She could see that he didn't like the new contingency. "If you beat me back to the stables, I'll marry you. No questions asked." Of course, she would lose. He needed a convincing story, too. Biscuit let out a neigh and shook her mane.

"What are you talking about?" said Christopher.

Kayla suddenly grew tired of the game and was at the end of her rope. Christopher would eventually understand. She was about to pivot her role in this situation. What could be better than marrying one of the richest men in the world? Her rebellious nature took over as she settled back into the saddle. The headache was going to hurt regardless, and it was coming in waves of anguish. She settled her resolve into a race for marriage.

"How long have you known me?"

"A long time," Christopher said.

"Then, you know I'm not easily swayed."

"That's why we're getting married."

A horsefly landed on Biscuit, and she brushed it away with her tail. Kayla said, "How are we going to start this matchup?" Biscuit sensed a fast departure as Kayla's legs tightened to her belly. She was ready to run and launched onto her hind legs.

Christopher called over to Han. The man looked up, and Christopher waved him over. When he arrived, Christopher said, "Can you do us a favor? Please, take one of the napkins and raise it above your head. Count down from three and let it go. Oh, and stand about fifteen feet over there."

Kayla interrupted him and said, "No head start?"

Christopher let out a huff and said, "You get a One Mississippi. Then, I'll go. We start as soon as Han drops the napkin."

"Two Mississippi. Fair is fair," she said. He conceded.

Kayla gently started whispering to Biscuit. "Easy, baby, easy. Everything is going to be all right, don't worry. Easy does it. I know you wouldn't let me lose."

As she whispered into Biscuit's ear, Christopher strained to hear what she was saying. Both were ready, and the moment had arrived.

Christopher said, "What do you think about Fiji for our honeymoon?" Kayla didn't pay him any attention.

Kayla said, "Hear that, Biscuit?. Fiji." She knew her target. They both were ready. Biscuit pressed Ziem closer to the Phantom.

"Careful of the car."

"Do you have a bad knee or ankle?"

Christopher rubbed his arm. "Nothing hurts right now."

Christopher nudged his horse closer to her. Han let go of the napkin. They both looked at each other. She never hesitated.

Kayla took her foot out of the stirrup and side-kicked Christopher in the ribs. The force of the blow sent him flying into the air and onto the hood of the car. He rolled off and fell to the ground.

"Chop chop." And in a blink of an eye, Biscuit took off like a bullet in the chamber.

Han came over to help him up, and Jimmy grabbed Ziem. Christopher put his hands over the dent on the hood. "What the fuck? I love it. Crazy nutjob. She's something else, isn't she?" And Christopher smacked Han on the back. The two of them remained silent. Christopher struggled onto the saddle as Ziem pulled him away.

Kayla's brain was calm, cool, and collected. Her blood mixed with Biscuit's to reach the speed of pure satisfaction. She cracked a smile when she remembered Christopher landing on the ground. She hoped that he was okay, but she needed a hook to complete her story. Biscuit didn't miss a beat. The saddle, stirrups, and bridle became one with her. Kayla slammed her heels for one swift blow to the side of Biscuit's belly. The horse's eyes widened, and she kicked up dust like never before. Kayla had never used the short Cossack whip before, but today would be different. She let the heavily braided end flex as Biscuit went from a three-beat gait to a near instant gallop. She reached back high and let another one rip off the hindquarter. The sound was nothing for them both, and Biscuit was steaming for speed. Then, Kayla took the wrong turn on purpose.

Christopher wasn't too far behind and saw Kayla's mistake. He knew that she would have to backtrack. She watched the Arabian cut a corner as they met up along the trail. She timed it perfectly and eased up on Biscuit to let him inch ahead. He turned to look and said, "Gotcha." She humbly accepted defeat. She drew the whip and was about to take a swing when Christopher yelled, "Careful!" He blocked the crossing of the bridge and forced her through the creek.

The stables were getting close. Blood dripped from Christopher's elbow. The race was over, and her head felt better, but not by much. She eased up on the reins, when a swarm of gnats engulfed them both just before they reached the yard.

A rage of excitement filled Christopher as he swung wildly at the insects. Kayla wasn't bothered and trotted in behind him. He yelled, "You cheated!" She didn't respond as he looked at her in awe. He wondered how he had even considered marrying her, let alone just being friends. He threw his helmet to the ground as the swarm moved on with the breeze. She hadn't expected him to get this angry, and it played well into her story.

Kayla said, "No crying allowed, remember?"

"Crying? You fucked up my ride! Look at my arm!"

"You'll live." She stared at him. He got off of Ziem and grabbed his knee. She offered him her bandana for the blood dripping down his arm.

Christopher took it and said, "You think this is funny?"

"No."

"Did the thought of beating me fair and square ever cross your mind?" She shook her head to say no. He said, "I'm going to make you pay for my Phantom."

She smiled at the acknowledgement. He said, "I don't know how you're ever going to afford it."

He pointed to his horse and said, "Ziem is the wind. What were you thinking? They have to cheat in order to beat you." She said nothing and rested on Biscuit. He turned back to her and said, "Did you try to hit me?"

"The thought crossed my mind more than once." She tapped his head and let out a demure laugh that men usually liked. It allowed them to relax and stop being angry. She took off her riding gloves and scrutinized his behavior to see how upset he really was. She said, "You gave me no choice. I didn't want you to win. But you proved me wrong, yet again." Then, she lifted up the ring to examine its features.

He saw the glowing engagement ring and said, "Don't worry about it. I'm not going to hold you to anything, just let me know when you're ready." He took a moment and continued, "I don't like the direction this is going. We should call it off."

"It's up to you. I'm still trying to figure out why you needed to get me so drunk to ask?"

"It's not that...it's...it was more for me than you. Didn't know how you'd take it. Now, I know."

"I'm going to plead the fifth until I'm sober."

"Let's go inside."

Kayla did as she was told. It didn't hurt her to think that she took it too far. She had a plan, and if it was going to work, she was going to have to sell the message.

"Wait up," she said. But Christopher didn't. He went inside the stables. She followed him and saw the slaphappy look on his face.

He asked, "So, you really think we have a chance?"

Kayla took a deep breath and said, "If we elope, then I give us a twenty percent chance."

"That's less than a coin flip."

"Pretty much."

Christopher took a moment but didn't seem to register what she had said.

"And the ring has to get sized."

It looked like his knees buckled, but she couldn't be sure. A wave of relief came over his face after she talked.

Christopher said, "Whatever you want. Just name it, and it's yours. We're going to live one happy fucking life together."

"I prefer an intimate setting, and let's not tell anyone."

Christopher locked it in. "Is Monday too soon?" Before Kayla could respond, Christopher remembered the financial tally needing to be delivered, and it required his signature to transfer of funds, which couldn't wait. "Sorry, I'm booked on Monday. How about Wednesday?" She nodded in agreement. She said Vegas, but he wanted it to take place in wine country instead. She knew he loved his vino, and then, he said, "Cali's not so bad with the helicopter. It would give my team the chance to shake down some of those broad-minded constituents." She agreed and chuckled at his ability to kill two birds with one wedding stone.

Every crooked political deal seemed sold for pennies on the dollar in California. It was election year, and Kayla knew what to expect. Christopher said, "We've built up a Super PAC the size of a caribou in the Golden 'Ticket' State. They'll treat us like royalty when we show up." She'd heard all the bragging before and would avoid most of his contacts in the West Coast.

He said, "These next two weeks are going to be insane."

"Can't wait. For sure," is all Kayla could force out. They stood looking at each other.

Christopher said, "You want to grab a shirt or something from the office?" She looked at him as if she'd forgotten something or reality had taken hold.

"What?"

"If you want a shirt or clothes, use the changing room."

Kayla took a look at the mirror and saw the mud from the creek splattered all over her.

Christopher grabbed her hand and gave her a kiss on the cheek, "It's all going to work out perfectly. See you tonight." Kayla went to freshen up and walked back to the main house.

Kayla passed on the large coffee Christopher offered that would have kicked the amphetamine she took into another gear. Instead, settled on decaf. She would be seeing her dad soon enough and didn't want to be too jittery as they discussed a marriage proposal. Why did he agree? As she sobered up, the migraine went from a car horn to a donkey kick. She looked at herself in the mirror and vowed to stop drinking like a fish for the next twenty-four hours. She didn't want to admit it, but the time had come for some professional help, and that was Pops' department.

CHAPTER 4

TWO FEMALE COPS scanned the beach while driving Segways. They were told to keep an eye out for things coming out of the water. They both thought it was a joke. Spring break ended months ago, and the only activity out in the water was parked cargo ships. Their shift was almost over when they spotted a white man on the basketball court doing some kind of strange workout. It was David Wolfe, all six foot two inches of him, and his two-pack of a stomach was on full display. He had the inheritance most bald men envied: a good head of hair. His arms were longer than normal, which made him always choose the aisle seats when flying. He looked up to see them turn around in his direction as he continued counting off a hundred burpee set. The beat cops came to a halt. One of them walked away to take a phone call. The other, Marci, said with a slight Jamaican accent, "What ah you doing over here?"

"Struggling. How about you?" They hugged.

Marci replied, "Looking for idiots doing stupid stuff. Man, this has to be the biggest white boy move ever."

David laughed and said, "How so?"

"You're on a basketball court without a ball."

"I got one in the truck. Does that count?"

"Hardly. A bit windy dis morning for shooting hoops."

"It's what I was thinking. How's Baby Glenn?"

David remembered when they had first met each other at Dandy's Donut Shop on Fifth Avenue. She walked in off duty and had on a pair of white Adidas. He complimented her shoes, and she gave him a signature, sweetheart island grin. He told the lady behind the counter, "Whatever she wants, it's on me." This proven method of breaking the ice was full of good intentions but overly presumptuous.

Marci said, "Don't worry about it. I got money. Thank you." She opened up her purse and pulled out her wallet. David saw the badge and insisted that he pay. She accepted and started talking about her fiancé, Baby Glenn. As he backpedaled in the conversation, she said to him, "We live in the same building."

David immediately recognized her and was glad he hadn't said anything too forward. A pleasant friendship started, and months went by with the two of them seeing each other from time to time at the pool or mailbox. David would wave, partake in some small talk, and then leave. It was strange at first seeing her around, but he got over it quickly when she invited him to a Sunday BBQ at the community grill.

His friendship with Marci lasted because her fiancé allowed it to. For some reason, Baby Glenn approved of him, and David was grateful to get occasional Heat tickets from him. The first few times he went to the game with Baby Glenn and Marci were a lot of fun. It put him at ease, and David made sure to always listen to Baby Glenn's workout tips. It felt good to try some new things at the gym. David gave them one of his paintings as a gift, and Baby Glenn respected the gesture. Still, he said, "My job is to put mother fuckers away and not trust anybody. So, don't think this puts us on any common ground."

David didn't know if he was serious or joking. Today was the first time he'd seen Marci since moving out over a year ago. Marci blurted out, "I'm expecting."

He congratulated her and gave her another quick hug. Then, he said, "You must be going nuts."

"I'm fine. Glenn is the one who's losing it."

"How so?"

"The man is overworked and paranoid. Not a good mix."

David could see her concern and knew that she didn't hide anything. He asked, "You guys have been engaged for a while, haven't you?"

Marci said, "Like two years. But dat's nothing. He made two cops come by the other night to make sure everything was all right with me. They showed up unannounced at one in the morning, looked inside the closet, the laundry room, and left. Said they were following orders." Marci continued, "He said he thought he saw someone parked down the street one night when leaving. I was like, people park down the street all the time and we have a parking garage."

David said, "Maybe it's because it's his first baby?"

"It had better be his first."

He switched things up. "Isn't it good to have protection rather than no protection?"

"I guess so. Dat's what got us in this mess in the first place."

David smiled and said, "I wouldn't worry." He opened up his gym bag.

"It is kind of cute. He won't let me lift a grocery bag. I guess I should see how long it lasts."

Marci saw the goggles and asked, "You going for a swim?"

"Yep, not fooling around today. It's been a year since my mom passed. She loved the water. I figured that it's the best way to honor her."

"It has to be hard to lose a parent. I'm sorry. I hope the day never comes for me."

David stopped talking. He just stared at the bag. Marci said, "You know, I used to be a swimmer when I was younger." He looked up like he didn't believe what he was hearing. She said, "Yes. Black people can swim. I loved it." He looked down and saw her dainty cop shoes.

"Your feet are too small. Not good for swimming unless you have webbing in between your toes."

"Bomba blast. I'm not Aqua Woman. Besides, you wouldn't catch me swimming around here."

"Why not?"

"Too many sharks."

"Thanks for letting me know just before I go in. I had them all blocked out of my mind till you just mentioned it. Thanks. So, what do you do if someone falls off of the pier by accident?"

"I follow them on land, and when they get close enough to shore, I arrest them for being stupid. I'm no lifeguard." David stretched his legs and laughed at Marci, who was on a roll.

"Seriously, you think I can swim out to rescue someone? Where am I going to put my gun? My wallet? Then, my hair gets wet. I'll throw them a life preserver, Miami Dade code toss, twenty-five feet."

"Is that the rule, to be able to throw it twenty-five feet?"

She shrugged. "Well, if it doesn't reach them, then they're going to die." He could see her mind ticking away. She continued, "Where I come from, we don't have a problem with you drowning, especially if we don't know you or you've done something wrong. Grandma told me to learn how to swim, and I did."

Marci's voice lightened David up. He'd known that she was the life of the party when he'd met her and could see why Baby Glenn was always on the lookout for competition. David said,

"Prayers and wishes for a healthy delivery." Then, he gave her another hug as they said goodbye.

Seeing Marci put David into an even better mood, as he stopped thinking of the sharks in the water. With the sun in his eyes, he confidently strolled towards the sound of waves easing onto shore. He squinted at a red boat a couple hundred yards out. It wasn't too far, no more than a couple of stone throws. The twelve different species of sharks popped back into his mind, not including the Barracuda, which were native to the Florida coast. Then, he remembered an incident he read about a week ago where a school of baby Spinner sharks chewed up a wind surfer and left behind nothing but the bones for crabs to gnaw upon.

As David walked closer to the shoreline, the waves increased slightly in volume. The breakers landing were the ocean's heart-beat, as the wind picked up. He tossed his duffle bag near a worn-down sandcastle, ran his fingers through his hair, and closed his eyes to have a listen. After a quick prayer to his mother, he made his way into the water. Keeping his back to civilization, he dove into the surf.

David stood up and sunk his toes into the sand, forgetting once again about the sharks. He smiled at her memory and strength. Thoughts of the day drifted and released into the open sea. Dad had passed years before, and now, David felt like it was time to take a few chances of his own, double down, and go to the next level. Only now, his mom would never know if he ever settled or started a family. She would never see if he found someone. He felt like he had disappointed her as a kid and blamed himself for being so selfish. If he had only said yes to all the times that she asked him to go swimming with her, rather than falling in love with skateboarding. He would have saved himself a couple of broken bones. His psychologist recommended exercise, and this swimming business was the best option.

It was good to be in the water. He moved into a slow-moving breaststroke in the direction of the red boat and the distant jetty. It would keep him close to the shore and not too far out. The water started getting choppy, and he liked the splashing around. He thought about how his mom while cutting through the waves and his appreciation of her existence welled up inside of him. He stopped swimming for a second while his toes still touched the sandy bottom to adjust his goggles and prevent the water from getting into his eyes. Then, he pushed off to start up again.

A few moments later, everything got cold, and he instantly sensed something was wrong. He looked to shore to see that the few people on the beach were rapidly starting to get farther and farther away. He tried to swim to the beach, but it was pointless. A panic gripped his muscles as the riptide invaded reality. He let the tension run for a few seconds before he forced himself to relax. The change in temperature wasn't so bad, and he told himself to remain calm. He breathed out a deep exhale and rode the rip out to sea. The boat he was using for a directional marker was now closer than shore. It made more sense to swim in that direction.

David didn't see any lifeguards jumping in for a rescue because they weren't on the job yet. He pushed the idea of dying an aquatic death out of his thoughts. There was no second place in the ocean, so he freestyled his way with a steady flutter kick in a calm rhythm.

A salty film on the crest of the ocean filled his nose, and there was nothing he could do about it. Life could take what it wanted when it wanted. He heard a sound like something snapping or a gun going off as he rolled in the water to float on his back. He suddenly wanted nothing except to make it to the boat. Fear was the kernel that destroyed people. He resolved not to think, just do.

The water was splashing around any way it wanted with no end in sight as David stopped to tread water. He evaluated what was happening, and reaching the boat became the goal while fate hunted its prey. He slowly started again with a steady breast stroke. He'd save the freestyle for the last push. He didn't want anything negative to possess his spirit, so his arms relaxed as his legs followed in unison.

Another swift current passed through David. People on the beach were just dots, but the anchored red boat was close. It was one smooth stroke after the other, just like Mom taught him. He found another slice of peace and felt like he could swim to Miami. He played a mind game with himself, mentally arguing that surely the sharks didn't want him. They wanted some Yellowfin tuna to rip apart. If they went for him, it would be like trying to swallow a toothpick in a ham sandwich.

No way was he going to drown. He'd have to stop swimming and that was never going to happen. Right now, he just needed to make it to the boat. David discovered a way to remove all doubt from his mind, and his thoughts became about nothing. It was about one stroke after the other, maintaining a solid form.

Marci's voice chimed inside his brain, and he started thinking about the sharks again. David let it go and accepted a fast death; at least the funeral cost would be cheap. A few rotations more, and he'd get some rest.

It was time to start living again, and under some new rules. People depended upon him. Reality got lighter as David rested his arms on the boat. The owner popped his head out from under water. He was scuba diving. "You okay, buddy?"

"Never felt better." They both climbed aboard and sat down.

The man said, "You shouldn't be swimming this far out."

"Riptide took me." The man was dumbfounded as he looked to shore and back. David saw another scuba diver breach the water. Surprisingly, he felt good, as his muscles were loose and energized.

The man said, "You're one lucky son of bitch."

"Tell me about it. You guys see any sharks around here?"

"Shit ton today, but they don't bother any of us little buggers. We do have a harpoon just in case." He laid it down in the boat. "Why don't you rest a bit, and we'll take you in." David turned his face into the sun and soaked up the warmth as he closed his eyes.

The man tugged the line to reel in the water buoy. David heard them talk and was happy to be alive. They'd been catching lobsters and had reached their limit. They proudly showed them off to David, but he couldn't care less. Even so, he didn't dare interrupt his rescuer's bragging. David watched the partner handle the lobsters like tomatoes and scratched his head with one of them before fearlessly tossing them in the cooler. "It'll be some good eating later on. I'll give you one to take with you as a memento. You know, you shouldn't go swimming without the lifeguards around." He pointed his finger at David as they all laughed. They both were having fun and cracked a few beers. "You want one?" David declined but took a bottle of water. After a short chat, they headed in.

David watched the water and remembered his clothes. "This is going to sound crazy, but take me as close as you can and I'll swim back." They both disagreed, but he insisted. They said that they'd keep watch just in case. By now, the lifeguard was on duty and blowing the whistle at the boat. He put his goggles back on and dove off. Then, the boat pulled way back to a proper distance. The lifeguard had David in the binoculars and followed his movements to shore as he radioed in the incident.

DUKE WAS IN the Rough Rider about a mile and half out. He was strapped in and not slowing down as the horse-powered diesels pushed for land. He screamed at the top of his lungs like a rabid fan at a football game. Nothing was going to get in his way when landing the vessel. The hard work had paid off as the hull repeatedly slammed into the water at top speed. He could only think of his power, his moment in time, and gripped the wheel tighter. Willpower was going to push him to victory as he released the torpedoes. The remote-controlled devices were activated and ready to deliver two hundred pounds of mountain-grown bam-bam to the buyers. The handheld monitor showed a reading, and now, all he had to do was find a parking spot.

The beach was drawing closer as Duke looked to see if a white SUV extraction vehicle was visible. They would hand him his payday, and life would drastically change in an instant. He tossed the cell phone into the water and caught a glimpse of something just ahead. It looked like a body, but with the light reflecting off the surface, he couldn't quite make it out. A split second later, he passed the lone swimmer and wished he'd run him over. The beach was seconds away as he cut the motor to brace for impact.

The sun worshipers stood up as a lifeguard fresh on duty blew his whistle. The sound drowned out the music playing from portable speakers of one of the sand dwellers. The boat landed with a thud. A yoga instructor stopped the Vinyasa flow as her students turned their heads in unison for the spinal twist. David treaded water as he contemplated death by motorboat, then counted his blessings again. He looked to the sky to see if a plane was going to fall onto his head. Then, he made a freestyle beeline to shore just in case Fate had any more ideas.

The lifeguard was running at full speed to help. Marci and her partner were calling in the sighting as they headed over on the Segways. Duke hopped off the boat and landed in the sand. He pulled out a gun and fired the automatic rounds into the air. The lifeguard did a 180. The yoga practitioners skipped namaste, and the beachcombers hid under their beach towels. David didn't hear a thing. He was going to make it to land if it was the last thing he did. Duke strolled his way to the street. The sand felt good, and he liked how it worked the ankles. He never looked back at the lone swimmer who was crawling to land. After crossing the fire pits and then the sidewalk, Duke saw the white SUV parked past the palm trees. The door opened, and they were gone.

Marci and her partner had pulled over to watch everything from a distance. Once the coast was clear, they drove the Segways to the area and drew their guns. They walked out to the sand near the boat where David was sitting.

"Freeze! Hands where I can see them!" It was Marci barking orders. David stood up, and she lowered her weapon. Her partner approached from the other side. David said, "Hello, Marci. Good to see you again."

"Yes, it is. A morning to remember." She told him to take a few steps back, so they could look around. The sirens were approaching, and David obliged.

Marci and her partner continued searching around with guns drawn. It was a crime scene now. Her partner asked, "Do you have any ID?"

David said, "In my bag."

Marci said, "I know him. He's okay. But you better go get it just in case, David."

David got up to get his bag, and she said, "Looks like you sure picked a fine morning for a swim."

She continued with, "Not every day you almost get run over by a boat." David got his stuff and returned. Her partner had cut off the engine as police officers started arriving. The one in a suit and tie he immediately recognized as Baby Glenn. He looked as big as a refrigerator with legs digging through the sand.

Marci said, "I'm sorry, you're going to have to wait, but it'll be over once we take a statement." David thanked her as she went to greet Baby Glenn, who was sweating profusely. David held up his arm to wave hello but didn't get an acknowledgement other than a stare down.

A police officer came up to take David's statement, and the man seemed skeptical of his story. He asked the officer, "Ever been in a riptide?" The rookie didn't respond. "It's like getting your feet swept up under you, then getting dragged by your heels. I'm lucky to be alive." He saw the emotionless face in front of him, and it didn't slow him down with the sharing. "I could have been stabbed by a Marlin or eaten by an octopus. Look how far out I was...see that buoy?"

The officer looked out to sea and then back to David. He said, "Let's stick with what actually happened this morning, okay sir?"

Baby Glenn walked up to David, and they shook hands. Marci was right behind her fiancé. The six foot three black man wearing a Brooks Brothers suit, had a shaved head, and looked to possess no personality with the detective's badge in his pocket. His clothes didn't fit, and the top button of the collared shirt was undone. The blue tie matched, but his wingtip shoes were taking in a lot of sand. He asked, "What's so funny?"

David said, "Do you have to wear the jacket?" Baby Glenn wiped his face with a hand towel.

"Part of the job, man. So, Marci says you've had a close call." He turned to the officer and asked, "You finished?"

The officer said, "Not yet."

Baby Glenn said, "It'll have to do. We know where he lives." The officer left.

David pointed to the stern of the boat and said, "You want to take a seat and catch your breath?"

Baby Glenn said, "I'm fine," then wrung out the sweat in the hand towel he was carrying. David could tell the man had contempt for something, he just didn't know what it was.

David said, "Just heard the news. Congrats on growing the family."

"Thanks." Glenn took off his jacket and seemed to relax a bit. His shirt was soaked in sweat as some of the other officers came up to get orders. Then, he came back to the conversation with David.

Baby Glenn asked, "Did she tell you about the physical therapist?" David said no. "Apparently, he didn't want to give out a refund. What was his name?"

Marci said, "Hans."

Baby Glenn said, "Ya, him. The dude with the accent who thinks women swoon all over him, even though he had some messed-up teeth."

"They weren't that bad."

"They were so crooked, he needed to be arrested."

David asked, "What happened?"

Baby Glenn said, "He's flying back to Denmark as we speak. Some of the paperwork had expired."

Marci said, "He gave me the money back."

"Funny how that worked out." Baby Glenn glanced at his phone and looked at David. "You okay?" David said he was fine but was running late. Baby Glenn told Marci and David that the Feds were coming down and that they might need a face-to-face. "We'll let you know. Keep your phone on."

David said, "No problem." He'd be going to the job site, then the hospital, and would keep his phone with him.

Baby Glenn said, "You're lucky you didn't get eaten by sharks."

David said, "Tell me about it."

Marci said, "I told you about it." David agreed and Baby Glenn added, "We'll be in touch shark food." They said their goodbyes, and David walked away while shaking his head to get the water out of his ear.

CHAPTER 5

HITTING TRAFFIC WAS the expected outcome. Instead, David made green lights all the way to the Interstate as an acoustic guitar rendition of "Sarsaparilla" jammed over the radio. Upon entering the on ramp over the speed limit, he could see cars backed up for miles going in the opposite direction. A tractor trailer full of adhesive primer had turned over, and five-gallon buckets where strewn over five lanes. He spotted a motorcycle taking advantage of the lack of drivers going in his direction in the review mirror. It passed him at well over a hundred. The urge to bring the Harley out of storage popped up, but he shrugged it off.

The magnet sign on the side of David's truck read, "Pivot Construction – We're your axis to quality workmanship and stunning results." He'd built his business up from scratch, starting in Cleveland. His family specialized in custom-built homes. Working in the trades gave him the common sense he appreciated, but it also gave him the ability to enjoy his free time. Money burned holes in his pockets, and Friday's paycheck was often spent by Saturday. But that was in his roaring twenties, and times changed as he learned to save his money. Instead of going out on the weekends, he started tinkering around with cars, rebuilding engines, and turned into a motorhead. His dad told him that he was all over the place and should concentrate on becoming an electrician instead. The family business needed one. He preferred to avoid the electrical shock lifestyle and started his own construction crew instead. Barely earning enough didn't matter; it was the free time he appreciated, and all it took was one vacation to Florida for David to want to make a change in his permanent living situation.

As much as David loved to renovate homes and geek out in the garage, he was an artist at heart. He loved to create something from nothing, so he dabbled with multiple mediums. Florida was the place where patrons of his work grew and developed. Many became his friends, and the one he'd been hanging out with the most lately was Dr. Sam North. The man was a bit of a father figure to him, and his wife, Julia, had a graceful power in her that was rare among women. Together, they shared an endless passion for one another, which David found unpretentious. Sam had an interesting theory about artists and how it should take at least sixty years for one to be recognized. David hated the thought and said, "Great, only fifteen more years to go."

When David pulled up to the job site, he saw the crew unloading a supply truck. It was the Norths' home, and they had hired him to renovate the place after hours of scrutiny, references, and endless questions. Someone popped out from in between the cars, and he slammed on the breaks. All of his clothes stacked up in the backseat toppled over, along with some equipment. It landed on a forty-eight-pack of plastic water bottles, which sprung a leak. He took a deep breath and let the worker pass. Then, he saw some cars parked on the lawn. The ground was a bit soggy from last night's rain, and the weight from the vehicles was creating a rut in the grass. He beeped the horn and yelled out to get someone's attention. No one responded.

David soon went looking for his best friend and foreman, OP. They'd met in their teens at a public speaking course in Cleveland. The short Russian immigrant had a temper that put everyone on edge, except David. OP had followed him out to Florida. David looked up before going inside to make sure an alien spaceship wasn't about to crash land on his head, but the coast was clear except for a few clouds.

The home was nestled along the ocean, and it gave the crew inspiration. A line of sea grape shrubs separated the backyard from the beach. The Norths were living in another location, so David's crew had the run of the place without someone looking over their shoulders. It also saved them a lot of time not having to explain every step of the process. David dropped off a box of nails, blue tape, and pair of snips on the kitchen counter. He saw OP out back by the pool and walked outside.

OP was over 190 pounds and had fists the size of canned hams. They looked strange, and he had a penchant for learning things the hard way whenever something triggered his temper. His new girlfriend, Juanita, showed him how to calm down and encouraged him to cook more. She'd been the best thing to ever come into his life. He loved working with spices and new recipes, but he still drank like a fish unless she was around.

David walked up to OP doing his usual meal prep for lunch. He had a portable stove with a makeshift table supporting his dried herb collection in a tackle box, utensils, and lemon zester. A twinge of jealousy reached the pit of David's stomach. The bubbly concoction brewing looked like braised stew, his favorite as a kid, with a Bisquick batter mix nearby for the dumplings. As cheap as OP was, and could rub the hair off Lincoln's head, he always loved to share the food.

OP said, "It's a recipe from the new girl, Cecilia." David had heard good things about her. She was replacing Hector, who'd had an amazing ability to cause more damage than work.

Cecilia was given the stamp of approval from OP after he watched her cut some tiles. She knocked it out with such precision that it reminded OP of the time he floored the Vatican. On top of it all, she spoke good English and had a driver's license. What really blew his doors off was her showing up to work early. OP started calling her the Unicorn.

David watched OP shave some garlic with a Buck knife as the lid on the pot rattled from being filled too much. He took off the top and used a wooden spoon to slowly turn the pork, chicken, and potatoes. Wedged in between beans, carrots, and corn were some sprinkles of parsley and cilantro. A sliced avocado was sitting to the side in a Tupperware container.

David said, "You working today or hardly working?"

"Glad you could finally show up," OP said.

David laughed. "So am I."

"We gave the new hire a raise to $28 an hour. I told her I'd clear it with you first. You'll probably want to pay her more."

"That shit looks pretty good." OP stirred the pot and tasted the cuisine. David reached down and took out a chunk of corn.

Cecilia passed by with a loaded wheelbarrow and smiled. He said hello and was impressed by the agility she showed while rolling over rocks and uneven surfaces. Her movements didn't struggle with the shifting weight, which he'd never seen in a woman before. She had a glow that no one could resist. David was glad to have the positive energy around the place.

Without dropping the wheelbarrow, Cecelia stopped and said, "It's called Sancocho de Gallina." David and OP had no idea what she was talking about. She said, "Hen's stew."

OP replied, "Sancoccodo de Gayyaina?"

"No. No. No. Sancocho de Gallina." She looked at David and said, "Gringos love maize," and left.

David asked, "What's maize?"

OP pointed to him and said, "Corn."

They both laughed, and David said, "That's messed up, homes."

"See, she's worth the extra money."

OP continued, "Oh, and her husband starts tomorrow. That was the good news I was saving for you." David was happy with getting the new replacements. It was getting harder and harder to find skilled tradesmen.

David said, "Now for some more good news. You have to get the floor laid by the end of the day." OP stood up.

"No way! The plumbing isn't even installed yet." He pointed to the house. David explained that they had the Viking stove arriving next week, and it needed time to cure properly.

OP said, "These people don't even cook."

David laughed out loud at the statement and said, "How do you know?" OP didn't say anything and just stirred the pot. David said, "Now the bad news. The electrician isn't showing up, either."

"What's wrong with you?"

"His wife is having a baby, and he needs the time off."

"How come he didn't tell anyone? It's a load of crap." David told him he saw the baby bump.

OP called, "Bullshit." He looked up to see if David was razzing him or telling the truth.

David said, "You ever talk to the people you work with? And you told me you could do it."

"I can do plumbing, sinks, faucets, drains, but this is a heated floor with flex tubing! I've never hooked up the electrical like this before!"

David hated electrical and gave OP a look of encouragement. "I got all the faith in your ability, buddy."

"No way, boss. I told you before that you had to hire someone else for the job."

David dropped the hammer and said, "Well, then, figure it out, Bobby Flay. We need this to get done today."

"Fine with me," OP replied. "I attach whatever I want, and it'll never work. Suit yourself." David knew that OP was right, and he would have to talk to the Norths about the hiccup. But he wasn't going to let OP know it. That was how they communicated. He would call OP later when he was on the road and let him know that he was off the hook. Julia North was not going to be happy, and the bottom line was that he needed to hire another electrician.

OP yelled at David as he was leaving and said, "You know an electrician eventually has to show up on this job." David's predicament was sinking in as he turned back to watch OP grind more pink Himalayan salt into the stew like he was wringing the neck of a chicken.

Then, he said, "We'll be lucky to finish this place in two years the way you're going." David looked at his watch and knew that he was running late. OP yelled, "Where are you off to, the country club? Nice banker hours." It fell on deaf ears.

David worked his way through the house and grabbed a handful of mini carrots. He was hungry and picked up the pace. Between the swim and the hen stew, his appetite was kicked up a notch as he got in his truck to drive to the hospital. It wasn't too far away, and the arrival was faster than expected.

The place was now called a health center, but it used to be St. Anthony's. One-hundred-foot legacy palms guarded the west entrance and had been there before the building was erected. The walkway into the building felt more like a park then a place for the sick to get care. The trees made it easier for him to relax, but deep down, the building made his skin itch.

David saw a woman sitting alone on a bench. She looked as if she was dealing with something heavy. He cursed all these institutions for no reason. They were the depositories for squeezing the life out of people. A sheet of paper flew by his face, and he turned to see a stack of papers blowing away. He tracked a few of them down and started to walk them over to the woman on the bench.

Kayla was standing up as he approached and stepped on another one as it was going to get away. The closer he got, the more he was struck by her presence. She had a hat pulled over her eyes, and it made him focus on her T-shirt that said "Eat Shit" in bold letters. He moved back up to her face and saw her nose. It was like seeing a ghost from a Modigliani painting.

He wasn't ready for the encounter and mumbled, "Sorry, I messed this one up," as he thrust one crinkled-up paper into her hand.

She took it from him and said, "Thanks. Don't worry about it." He pressed the corners of the last one to try and straighten it out before handing it over.

The giant palm trees swayed in the wind as the palm fronds shushed. David saw the cigarette in her hand and a tall coffee placed onto the table next to the bench, where a bag of peanuts was also laying. He joked to himself as if she was from the nut house down the street. He remembered that they let the patients free every once in a while, to see some daylight. He said, "Is your T-shirt an ice breaker?" She didn't know what to say and looked confused. He asked, "You must be from HR."

She grabbed the front of her shirt to see what it said. He confirmed that she must be from the looney bin if she didn't know what shirt she had put on. There was no apology. Instead, she looked comfortable and said, "It gets the point across, doesn't it?"

David looked at the peanuts on the table and said, "Who the hell buys shelled peanuts anymore?"

Kayla said, "It's for the squirrels. Why? You want one?" She looked him up and down as another wind gust blew. More papers flew in his direction, and he snatched one out of the air. Kayla said, "Nice catch."

He liked how seriously she looked at him and said, "Thanks." He was hypnotized by her long hair and nose. Then, Kayla smiled, displaying a nice set of teeth. A silence ensued in a way that indicated he should run along now. He mumbled something about feeling a cold front in the South Florida summer. Then, a squirrel came down from the tree. Her eyes brightened up as the squirrel tiptoed to one of the peanuts on the ground. David watched her dote over the critter. It made him upset that they weren't going to have a home for much longer.

"You know, it's a shame," he said. The words caught her attention, even though she seemed annoyed by his presence. He continued, "These homies aren't going to be around much longer."

Kayla barked, "What?"

He said, "All the trees will be gone in a couple weeks."

"The hell they will!" The squirrel froze in its tracks, and David took a step back.

He said, "Hey, take it easy, lady. They're cutting them down next week. I'm not the one doing it." She didn't believe him, so he went over to a notice stapled to a wooden sign and tore it off. He gave it to her. As she was reading it, he could tell that she wasn't the type of woman to put up with a lot of crap. He felt bad being the messenger and was preparing to go. It looked like she was getting more upset by the second, until she inhaled deeply and folded the paper evenly to slide into her rear pocket. David said, "Well. Glad to run into someone who cares about this place as much as me." She sat down on the bench, and he gazed at her, waiting for her to say something. She didn't.

It was as if the ice princess was sucking the air from David's lungs. He didn't want to leave with his tail between his legs, so he said, "The hospital needs back-up generators, and this is the only place on property with room for it." He could have been mumbling the words in Polish, she wasn't listening. He continued,

"From what I found out, they voted on it last year. The generators will be here, and the rest of it is going to be a parking lot."

Kayla asked, "Do you work for the hospital?"

"No."

Kayla watched another squirrel come down from the tree and pounce on the grass. It took a couple steps forward, then to the side and back. Its head was on a swivel, surveying the environment. They both watched as it tiptoed in search of anything edible. She threw a peanut near the furry creature.

David watched her demeanor change. Kayla said, "Well, lookie here. It's Bonny Cotton Tail."

Joining in to feed the squirrels, David said, "I thought it was Peter the Rabbit, wasn't it?" David felt good about being somewhat versed in remembering his children's illustrated book characters. "You can change the name. It doesn't cost anything." He thought that he was telling a joke, but Kayla remained silent with an annoying stare.

David dissected the conversation and realized it was over. He said, "Well, have fun with Bonny Cotton Tail."

Kayla said, "Thanks."

David took a couple steps back and then walked away. He was glad to be gone. The conversation was like getting his teeth pulled by a longshoreman. The funny farm must be wide open today. She couldn't be married, as he didn't see a ring on her finger. If she was, then some poor guy had his hands full.

CHAPTER 6

FRIDAY
1100 HRS

THE LINOLEUM IN the hospital had a pressed shine of misery pasted onto the floor that was left over from years of waxing. The place made David cynical, but what was he going to do about it? It was where his psychologist worked. He tried not to let the smell of the harsh chemicals and disinfectants impede his inhalations. The sanitation engineers did their job as his shoes squeaked with every step. He thought of the place as a laboratory for human rats being used for the greater scientific good. The beds had to be filled with the sick just like prisons needed lawbreakers. Anyone within a ten-mile radius would fall into the Venus flytrap. The employees of the hospital didn't mind because they got to pay off their student debt, keep golf memberships, and cover their monthly Lexus payments. He didn't know why the place put him in such a mood. Maybe it was because it was a place like this one where his mother had died.

David regretted accepting the invitation to view Dr. North's operation this morning. He had problems with the sight of blood, and the thought of cutting through someone's skin put his nerves on edge. He planned to distract himself when the scalpel began carving by attempting to tie his shoelaces or scratch his eyes. It would have to look casual. By the time he reached the elevator, there was no turning back, but this morning's activities gave him a boost of confidence.

David remembered going up the same elevator a year ago after dislocating his pinky finger while playing basketball. It looked worse than it felt, and after four hours of waiting, the doctor came in, and three seconds later he popped it back into place. Then, the fifteen-hundred-dollar x-ray bill arrived in the mail, and it made him want to go back to school to learn radiology. He thought he could read black and white digital pictures with the best of them. A person could day drink while keeping this job.

On the way out after getting the finger straightened, he spotted a research library. Curiosity won him over as he entered. Inside was a man trying to figure out how to navigate the computer. He looked frustrated with the device and was dressed as an aging orderly. His request for help from David was more of an order than a plea. The man handed him a slip of paper with an email address.

It read, "SamNorth@hotmail.com – password – Sam123."

David showed him how to log in, attach a file, and then send it. The white-jacket-wearing fellow treated him like he was a genius. "It's pretty easy once you get through it a couple of times."

David said, "Now, when you give this address to anyone, there's no postage necessary. The password, Sam123, should be changed to something a bit longer when you get the chance." They soon were chatting it up like a couple of fraternity pals. He thanked him for making him more socially acceptable, and when the pager beeped, he was gone.

Sam was the absent-minded professor who had a face like a Labrador. Over the last year, they'd bumped into each other from time to time, and a friendship had grown through their shared passion for art. He recommended for David to come watch an operation and get a taste of the classic Da Vinci method of artistry. He went on to explain how the great artist mastered his craft by drawing the internal organs of cadavers. Sam said, "Maybe you should do the same."

David said, "I might not be as serious as Da Vinci."

Sam pressed him and said, "The color is a lot different when the subject is alive."

David didn't share the same appreciation of internal organs as Sam. He convincingly said, "Who cares? It's worth seeing regardless." David finally relented, and now, the day had arrived.

With each step getting him closer to his destination, a nervous excitement grew. He wasn't familiar with this part of the building as he rounded the corner, and Sam glanced up from a chart.

"There he is. Hello, David."

"Hey, Doc."

"How is the house coming along?"

David said, "I should be there right now. Is this going to take long?"

"Don't be a hack, and try to enjoy yourself." Sam held the door open for David to enter. "Are you sure you're up for this?"

David said, "Piece of cake," as his stomach flipped over like a pancake. He didn't tell Sam about the last time a nurse took his blood and how he got a little woozy. She'd had thick glasses on and couldn't see very well. Ended up sticking him multiple times with the needle and blaming it on his veins. Normally, the sight of blood wasn't a problem, but today was his official entry into the next level.

David asked, "How's your day going?" Sam said fine, but his response was distracted and something didn't seem right. David asked, "What's wrong?"

Sam said, "My daughter, she should have been here already." He shook it off like a baseball pitcher for a different pitch and said, "Not to worry," and smacked David on the shoulder.

Then, Sam said in a calming voice, "How many psychiatrists does it take to screw in a light bulb?" David said he didn't know. Sam replied, "One. But the light bulb has to really want to change." David didn't laugh, and Sam's piercing blue eyes waited for a response. Sam said, "You'll get the joke later."

"No, I got it. It's a good one."

"You've heard it before. Do you know why the Irish invented chairs?"

"No."

"Because no one could stand to drink with them."

"Hilarious."

"But you're not laughing."

"I'll laugh later."

Sam looked closer and said, "You look like you'll pass out from nerves."

"How can you tell?"

"It's all over your face."

David said, "Van der Sloot already spilled those two onto me last week. You guys hang out too much."

Sam said, "Van der Slootzin is a good egg, and he'll tell anyone a joke who will listen." The look out of the corner of Sam's eye told David all he needed to know. The man was keeping him loose, and David admired his ability to read a person. This was Sam's domain, after all.

Sam said, "Surgery is a scary thing, David. If a patient laughs, then the chances of success increase by eighty-five percent or more. If they know they have nothing to fear, they'll laugh with me. If they crack a smile, it's a red flag. Means more prep work. They're in their own head too much. They're the type of patient who will micro-manage a sleeping dog. So, we dive into the details. Make everything easy in their heads. It gives them peace of mind and lets them know that I know what I'm doing."

David said, "What happens if they don't do anything? Freeze up, I mean."

"Never going to happen. I make everyone laugh in a captured audience." After a long pause, Sam said, "What do you call a guy with no arms and no legs and hangs out on a wall?"

"Dead?"

Sam looked at him seriously and grabbed his arm, saying, "Don't ever say that word to a doctor before surgery again. It's taboo." Then, he smiled, and Sam's banter made David feel better. He no longer wanted to throw up. While putting on his scrubs, Sam gave some background information on the patient. "This is an exploratory surgery. She needs a new liver and was forbidden to have any more alcohol. It drove her crazy."

"How do you know if she drank or not?"

He smiled. "Blood test last night, and we kept her in the hospital. She's had worse news than the surgery. Her husband just filed for a divorce this morning."

"How is she holding up?" David asked.

"Not good. She can barely stand."

"Touché."

Dr. North pressed forward. "No way. This is serious business. Have you ever had too much to drink?"

"Quite often, but not lately."

Sam got quiet and stood in the doorway. He said after a few moments, "Speaking of cocktails, we'll be seeing you at the party tonight."

"The invitation is on the refrigerator."

"One more thing. No talking when inside unless I ask you something. It's how I operate."

David said, "Yes, sir," and took a swallow of dry air.

Sam said, "And don't forget to put on the booties," as he watched David slip them over his feet. The smell of iodine reeked in the next room and slapped David in his face. He looked up at Sam and knew that he was in another situation that was beyond his control.

Sam said, "You know my daughter viewed her first procedure in this room when she was ten?"

"Is that legal?"

"It was for me. She did pretty good, and we all got a kick out of her using a step ladder to watch."

"So, this should be a walk in the park for me." Sam glanced at David as they walked inside the operation room.

David asked, "How long has she been back?"

"Been home for a few weeks now."

"Slootzin says soldiers have a hard time relating to their families after having served. The adjustment to civilian life is more difficult than one would think."

Sam continued, "I've seen them lined up outside his office. One doesn't sleep, the other has bad dreams, and they all have a forgotten look on their faces."

David had heard the stories and was sorry that he'd broached the subject.

Sam said, "The research on trauma is pretty extensive, especially with PTSD, and the pharma companies don't like to broadcast any of the dangerous side effects." David listened as he watched the nurses enter the room. Sam continued, "Can you imagine how they still don't even discuss the issue amongst veterans?"

"How come?"

"Because it's viewed as complaining, so they sweep it under the rug. In the medical field we like to prescribe more drugs, and what's interesting with Van der Slootzin work is that he's tapped into similar responses happening with car accidents, natural catastrophes, or even physical abuse. They all seem to be related with one being no worse than the other. Interesting how they all have a common link."

"What is it?"

Sam said, "The brain."

"It has to be hell waking up in the morning."

"Not all of them make it to see another day."

David said, "It's hard enough figuring out civilian life, let alone adding war into the mix."

"Well, Kayla's been lucky. She's got a strong mother. But a good family can't help someone who doesn't want any."

David thought of Sam's wife, Julia. He had hated the weekly meetings she requested with budgeting, forecasting, progress reports, and completion schedules. But, as strange as it sounded, he'd started to look forward to them. She was smart enough to want to be around during the renovation, and the accountability she demanded gave him the chance to learn how to scale the profits in his favor. He never told her how much he was making, but with her number-crunching ability, she probably already knew. He relinquished access to the supplier pricing, receipts, and labor costs. On her own, she figured out insurance and worker's comp. Giving up control actually resulted in him gaining a sense of freedom.

"So, is your daughter as thorough as our project manager?" David asked.

"You got that right, and don't forget it. The best move you ever made with us was to put her in charge. Wake up on the dark side of Julia, and even I couldn't save you with all this equipment in front of me." David didn't need any scare tactics, but it worked.

Sam got close to David and said, "Don't forget about tonight. Julia wants you to show up, and she promised not to bring up work."

"Fine with me. All I was going to do is relax and watch the game." Sam glanced at the door, then turned to the anesthesiologist and gave him the green light. The patient started counting backwards from a hundred. She never made it to ninety-seven. David asked one of the nurses, "Am I in your way?"

Sam said, "Why are you whispering? Stand over there." Then, Sam pointed to the left of the monitor.

Kayla walked in and said, "Hey, Poppa Bear. Sorry I'm late, and…" She saw David and stopped for a moment. She didn't know for sure who he was, but the eyes looked familiar.

"It's okay. How are you doing?" Sam asked.

David felt embarrassed because Sam's daughter had the same shape and size as the lady with the squirrels. After looking closer, she had the same nose, too. He went over his conversation to make sure that he hadn't said anything stupid. Had Sam set this up from the beginning?

Sam said, "Just stand where you always do."

Kayla quipped, "You mean where I'm standing now?"

David liked her ability to dish it out to everyone. Sam didn't waste any time with the first cut; it was clean, and David saw that he forgot to tie his shoelaces. He glanced at Kayla and was now more determined than ever to watch the surgery.

Sam said, "I asked around like you wanted me to."

Kayla asked, "What did they say?"

David gagged slightly while Sam and Kayla talked casually. Sam briefly looked at David and said, "The trauma gets washed out or trapped in the background noise. No way to filter it through a self-diagnosis. It can feel like you're dream walking. The mind replays the trauma, and the only way out is reprogramming or attempting some sort of re-wiring."

Kayla said, "How?"

Sam replied, "Machines, light therapy, computers, dance, whatever it takes. They have a number of different corrective therapies."

She said, "Jazzercise?"

Sam gave her "the dad" look, and she said, "Okay, what else?"

He continued, "The memory is what gets influenced. The harder the recall, the more it affects decision making or response times. It's all connected to the brain, specifically the hippocampus, and survival mode. Quite fascinating."

Kayla said, "What else?"

Sam said, "They say it can be easy to spot the changes. Only, no one really knows for sure the trigger for attacking everything in its path. It goes for the throat, vision, hearing, or any other type of normal behavior. My guess says that it would depend on the patient."

Kayla asked, "Is Van der Slootzin the one with the brain machine?"

Sam replied, "I wouldn't use that terminology, but yes. The results after one session with the electrodes can be extremely positive in some patients."

Kayla said, "Probably reading brain wave frequencies."

Sam never looked up and said, "You're set up for a session right after lunch." After he dropped this piece of information, nothing was said for ten to fifteen minutes. The room went silent except for the beeping monitors.

David thought about breaking the ice, but he refrained from saying anything about little Miss Bonny Cotton Tail.

Sam said, "Van der Slootzin said the most difficult decision is to just start, don't think about it, and begin as is."

Kayla said, "The starting of what?"

"Recovery, of course."

David looked at the liver, intestines, and who knew what else while getting anxious. He zoned out after "the slush of the blood" and was glad that he hadn't eaten anything this morning besides the corn and carrots. Kayla looked back at David and asked, "You going to be all right?"

He was going to respond, but Sam said, "He'll be fine. You hungry, David?"

Kayla said, "I'm starving. How about you, Dad?"

"Oh, yeah. Time to get some lasagna after this."

Kayla said, "I have something important to share, but I think you already know what it's about."

"We'll take care of that soon enough," Sam replied. He then went on to explain how reservations had been made at the family's favorite restaurant. Julia would be waiting. The owner made the lasagna early for them. Normally, you couldn't get it until after five. David was actually wanting to skip a meal, which rarely happened, but no one cared.

Kayla said to David, "I didn't expect to see you again."

"Small world."

Sam said, "You two know each other?" She filled him in on the details and expressed her grief about the trees. He replied, "If you can stop them, then be my guest. David is the contractor doing work on the house."

Kayla dropped the subject like a hot potato and asked, "So, when are you going to be finished with the house?"

David said, "Oh, a couple years from now."

Sam said, "Not funny."

David got self-conscious and folded his arms. Sam said, "Take a picture, Cheryl." The nurse went over to the monitor and pressed a button. It clicked, and David looked at the clock on the wall.

Kayla asked, "So, what are you doing here?"

Before David could answer, Sam asked, "How's my tennis partner?"

Kayla said, "He might need a couple days off from playing. Rolled his ankle, but all in all, he's doing okay."

Kayla asked David, "So, where did you learn to rebuild houses?"

"Family tradition. You in town long?"

"Not sure just yet."

"Then, you should stop by, and I'll give you a tour of what we're doing."

"Mom's keeping me updated. It all sounds really interesting." David picked up the hint of sarcasm.

Sam said, "My guess is it should all be done in the next two months, assuming we pass inspections."

David said, "That would be great news." Sam shot him a glance, and David knew that it would be longer. Then, he remembered that he needed to find another electrician who could do heated floors.

Kayla asked, "How many contractors did Mom interview?"

Sam looked up and said, "Seven." David's chest swelled as he realized all of the competition was crushed. Sam continued, "We went with the cheapest bid."

David coughed and said, "On the contract, I have some tiny print, and it says the price is subject to change according to the contractor's wishes." Sam said he hadn't seen any such print. David said, "You better have another look with a magnifying glass when you get home." Sam kept silent. David was earning enough and knew that Julia got carte blanche on the project after forty-four years of marriage. She had all the taste in the family. What the Norths liked about David was his transparency in explaining the process. He saved them a lot of money in the build-out. They just forgot about it, like all wealthy clients do.

Sam said to Cheryl, "Pinch these two. Clamp. Suction. Take a look, David. Nice, huh!"

David grumbled, "Gorgeous," and coughed again. He stepped around to get a closer look and hit the blower mister. The tube popped out of the machine, and a harmless solution started spraying all over the room. The nurse tried to grab it, and it took a few extra seconds. She wrestled it down and reattached it to the outlet. Everyone stared at David.

Sam said, "Don't worry about it. It's okay." David felt better and asked how often it happened.

Sam said, "Never." David tried to squeeze out an apology, but it landed on deaf ears.

Kayla said, "Is this the guy who made the dresser in the foyer?"

Sam nodded.

David didn't say anything at first but, after a few moments, asked, "You want me to get some paper towels and clean this stuff up?"

Sam said, "Leave it."

Kayla said, "It's beautiful."

David wasn't ready for the acknowledgment and now was embarrassed. He kept silent.

Sam announced, "Good news. We don't have to remove the gall bladder."

"I thought it was a liver?" asked David.

Sam said, "I thought it was supposed to be the left toe? No damage means we're done early."

Kayla asked David, "Do you exhibit?"

"No, but I'll ship anywhere. They take a long time to make. It's more of a hobby." A splash of blood sprayed against David's smock. He said, "That's disgusting."

"Sorry, David, it gets a little dirty in here sometimes." David could tell Sam was smiling under his mask. Once he saw that David was unfazed, he said, "You better go get cleaned up. We're almost finished, see you tonight."

David said, "You don't have to say that twice. Nice meeting you again." He was glad to get out of his Jackson Pollack smock. The place smelled awful.

Sam said, "Tile delivery today, correct?"

David turned and said, "Yes, sir. Bye." Kayla gave a short hand gesture to say "so long." Outside in the changing room, he was glad that the blood hadn't soaked through to the T-shirt.

KAYLA CHUCKLED AND said, "Where did you dig him up?"

Sam said, "We met at the research library in the hospital. He helped me with the computer. You know how great I am with those things."

"You're the only person I know who hasn't bought a Blackberry yet."

"Land lines work perfectly fine, thank you. His mom died about a year ago. It's been hard for him. He's been seeing Van der Slootzin. I'm surprised you haven't stopped by the house and taken a look." She said she meant to, and he nodded. "You have to go." She was happy to see that he was enjoying himself, and it seemed David had more going for him than met the eye. He was someone who could think on his feet. She would have to run a background check on him to make sure he wasn't an agent. It was not easy to win over her father's approval.

Sam asked, "So, lets hear it."

She squeaked. "You know what happened. How long ago did he ask?"

"About three months ago."

"You gave your approval?"

"He's the first one but might not be the last. I was torn, and, in the end, this is your decision. We've known him a long time. It didn't feel right to say no given the circumstances." After a long pause, he said, "This is where you should lean on your mother for answers. My department is moral support." She saw the logic in his response.

Sam said, "You know, for a guy with a hurt leg, I wonder when he'll be able to play tennis again?"

Kayla looked up. "David has a bad leg?"

Sam looked at her thoughtfully and said, "Let's go get some lunch."

CHAPTER 7

RICO'S HAD BEEN around for over twenty years and was located across the street from the hospital. Sam and Kayla avoided the two-minute drive and elected to walk instead. Coming from a desert climate, it was fun to see the cracks in the sidewalk with grass growing in between them. Her dad pressed her about Christopher. She didn't waste any time and confessed her assignment. Sam paused his walking from time to time to reflect. She knew his silence indicated that he was forming a controlled, logical answer. They stopped for a minute under the shade of a tree, and there, she laid out a half-baked plan. She liked his reply of, "You signed up for an adventure, and now, it keeps taking you down the rabbit hole."

Kayla knew that he hated her job, and yet, his reply was always positive. It wasn't much of an answer, but at least she had found a way to get it off her chest. He was a good listener. He told her to give it some time, and she responded with, "Time is the one part of the equation that is running out. I leave first thing Monday morning."

Sam said, "It's hard for me to believe that he's a traitor. The only problems I've seen with him was when Beth was alive. But he was only a child." If he was willing to believe in Christopher, then she was willing to give him a chance as well.

She said, "What was his mother like?"

"Cold, she raised him as best she could. Only child, heartless environment, and considering all he's been through, I thought he turned out pretty good. His mother was something else."

Kayla asked, "What do you mean?"

"She was a woman who had fallen in love with the material world and needed her quiet time. She was superficial in conversation and talked endlessly about the weather or herself. But what I remember the most was how vindictive she was and how she could hold a grudge. I stayed clear of her. Christopher didn't get a lot of attention for being an only child. I'm sure it was hard for him as they struggled like any family." Kayla had never heard many stories about Christopher's parents because she was so young when they died. It all seemed forgotten to her, but she felt bad for him. Sam saw her getting nostalgic and said, "Let's not keep your mother waiting."

Kayla loved her parents and knew that she compromised their safety, but this mission was too close to home, and time was running out. In a way, by telling them, she committed herself. She said, "Maybe I can work it out with Christopher?" She covered up her stress with a fake smile. No sleep, excessive drinking, and overprescribed medications was the current recipe for her disaster. Tiny, black dots randomly floating on her retinas made her self-conscious.

Sam reached out to hold the door open. Kayla trusted her dad, as his mind never wavered in a storm. He said, "Everything will work out regardless. Just be patient." She composed her emotions and reached over to loop her arm around him. He smiled brightly. They had always been close; he was the reason she joined the army, and now, it was time to do what needed to be done.

Mario, the owner, was at the bar drinking a cappuccino with Julia when they entered. He was an old school Italian who owned an excess amount of Paco Rabbane aftershave, something she had bought for her dad as a teenager. They had so many great memories in this place. Sam called out "Buongiorno" when they entered. Mom came in for a hug, and Mario was next. He was always parked next to the cash register. Her dad liked him because he was a street guy from New York who left school in second grade. No one really knew what he did prior to owning the restaurant, and it was a local favorite for the entire hospital staff, who could afford to spend a couple of hours on lunch. His story was simple: the family had made a small fortune from selling a couple buildings right next to each other in Queens. A real estate developer came in and made them an offer they couldn't refuse. The rest was history in sunny Florida. She never believed it, and after doing some digging, she found out the family never owned any property in the state of New York. His life was a mystery, other than his burglary arrest record.

After the warm greeting was given, the three of them were quickly seated at a table by the window. The mother-daughter connection was so strong that they couldn't hide anything from each other, even if they wanted to. Julia said, "What's wrong? You should be happy."

Kayla said, "It's a work thing. I've made an important decision."

"Of course you have! You're getting married!"

Kayla looked at her dad, who turned to Julia, and the look he gave her shifted the mood.

Julia asked, "Can you talk about it?"

Kayla didn't say anything, just shook her head.

Without looking up, Julia told the waitress, "We don't need menus."

Kayla said, "You should get a chardonnay, Mom." The waitress stood near the table waiting patiently for the drink order. Kayla said, "Arnold Palmer with unsweetened tea." Sam ordered the same.

Julia said, "I guess I'll have the chardonnay, please. What's going on?"

Kayla was about to say something when Sam said, "Kayla has a neurofeedback session with Van der Slootzin after lunch."

Julia said, "It's nothing serious, is it?"

Kayla replied, "They're saying I have PTSD, and if I do, this is the new electric shock therapy to stop me from getting hooked on prescription drugs."

Sam said, "Be serious."

Julia took hold of Kayla's hand to squeeze it. She said, "And now, Christopher asks you to marry him. The world must be caving in a bit. How are you holding up?"

Kayla started blabbering away about the proposal, how they've stayed in touch through the years, and the issue with their age gap. Julia saw Kayla gazing out the window for too long. She said, "What's outside?"

Kayla apologized, and Sam said, "It's a lot of pressure, given the circumstances. We just need to give her some space to figure things out."

Julia said, "What's there to figure out? She's getting married to Christopher and has PTSD. This is something we can handle."

Kayla's lack of enthusiasm made Julia ask, "You're not happy?"

Kayla shrugged.

"Let's see the ring."

Kayla pulled it out of her pocket and said, "It's all he could afford." Julia wiped the top of the ring with her napkin. "It had some smudge on it. Can see it much better now?"

Julia continued, "You're going to need a squeegee to keep it clean. I had no idea you felt this way about him."

Kayla said, "I didn't either, a bit of a surprise, really. You know how Christopher is."

Julia asked, "How did it all happen?" Kayla's facial expression contorted uncomfortably. Julia turned to Sam and said, "This is going to be interesting. Do I need to wait for the wine to be delivered?"

Sam said, "It's complicated. She might need some time to go over the particulars this weekend."

The drinks were delivered, and Kayla described the proposal all the way up to the race. She left out the job assignment of planting a bug on his computer and finding a mysterious safe room in the mansion. Julia listened to her story and, in the end, said, "Sounds like a fun night. I didn't know if you'd say yes."

They had lunch, but it didn't feel like much of a celebration while eating in silence. After dessert was served. Kayla polished off the tiramisu by herself. She looked up from the empty plate and said it was horrible. "They should take it off the menu."

In the back of her mind, Kayla thought about Christopher asking her dad for permission and was grateful. It was a small condolence for consenting to disobey direct orders. She looked at her mother and knew that it would only be a matter of time until she was filled in. The world was shifting, and nothing could be done to change it. Kayla left the table to go outside and have a smoke. A dose of fresh air wasn't going to help, but it made her feel better to sit on the bench. She didn't want to play this cat and mouse game anymore. Sam came out a minute later to get Julia's car. Mom sat next to her and said, "Don't worry, we'll get through it."

Kayla said, "I know."

"Sorry I don't know anything about PTSD. But I'll find out." Kayla gave her a hug. They sat together, hugging each other, and Julia said, "It's a hell of a ring, isn't it?" Kayla was glad that her mom had backed down from the tough questions and moved to some easy ones.

In the short car ride over to the hospital, they discussed the EMDR process, which stood for "eye movement desensitization and reprocessing." She was meeting with a certified practitioner, and Dr. Van der Slootzin said the treatments would help with the headaches, insomnia, and problems with focusing.

Julia asked, "How long has it been since you've had trouble sleeping?"

Kayla said since she'd been back, and she would forgive the sleepless nights if the headaches went away. It didn't surprise her that Mom and Dad were already solving her issues without her help. She'll always be removed from these types of discussions. The passion they had for each other was a gift, and her mom's acumen drove the line of questioning. Kayla started to relax when they started finishing one another sentences.

While glancing at the diamond reflecting the light of the sun, she asked herself if she could learn to love Christopher and how long she could remain silent about the purpose of her saying yes.

Everything was happening so fast. She couldn't second-guess herself. Now wasn't the time to be a Monday morning quarterback. The Thorpes had been valuable friends, and marrying Christopher was Kayla's only choice. She hadn't even considered having children yet, but now, it was on her mind, playing on her heartstrings. To be emotional in the spy business was a disaster. They liked you single. All of the sudden, she was engaged, backstabbing a family friend, and her career world was turned upside-down. The chances of it all working out in her favor were slim to none. She rubbed her fingertips on her forehead as the migraine metastasized on her neck and face.

Dad looked in the review mirror and said, "Leave it be, Kayla. We'll figure it out this afternoon." She laid down on the backseat and closed her eyes.

CHAPTER 8

THE MAN CAVE at Thorpe's mansion was exuberance on ste-roids. Very rarely did he allow guests into his personal sanc-tuary. A Neanderthal would blush after viewing it because they would be frozen in awe. It was chock-full of animal heads, fish trophies, and a six-foot replica of a velociraptor from Jurassic Park stood in the corner. They were all comically dressed with hats, sunglasses, and smoking pipes, and one had a bloody shirt in its mouth. A standing bear at one end of the room had a vin-tage Topper Model 48 Model shotgun between its teeth. This room could be found in the nightmares of interior designers.

Tugboat models and tanker ships lined a glass bookcase. A full bar, poker table, and jukebox also fit spaciously in the room, and it wasn't overcrowded. He had demolished his mother's greenhouse and doll room to fit his vision. It happened not too long after his parents' death, and it eased Christopher's mind knowing that the sacred flower sanctuary was gone. His only regret was that she wasn't around to see its destruction. She used to have all of the varieties carefully marked and enjoyed handfeeding the carnivorous plants. The room which gave him the most annoyance was the dolls room. He cringed every time he passed it by. She always put her favorite doll sitting at center stage, staring at all who entered. It was dressed like the movie character, Chucky, but worse, and it had no face. She said it kept out the rodents.

The hidden den was a perfect sanctuary. It had three TVs placed on a wooden entertainment center with one remote control box for them all. Sitting on the couch and chilling out without any disturbances recharged his batteries. One of the walls had a replica Rolex clock from Wimbledon Court. Next to it was a row of seats from the stadium, which he bought at Sir Winston's Annual Charity event.

The temperature-controlled wine coolers were stacked to the ceiling. Next to the gun rack was a series of small photos of past hunting expeditions. Christopher enjoyed the original print of the illustrated duck sunbathing with bullet holes above its head. He had the classic painting of dogs playing poker, and a highly-prized, signed Michele Pfeiffer photo from the movie *Scarface*.

Christopher was a bit on edge as he glared to the right. He hated anyone being in the room, and yet two government employees were sitting on his couch. They were drinking his soda and watching Alonzo Morning lead the Heat past the Bulls. The sound was turned off. Which meant they could hear what he was saying. Both had earpieces and carried Glocks with the spit and polish Florsheim's. These agents were sworn to protect his guest, James Farnsworth, National Security Advisor. These were US government employees, and he wanted to shoot every last one of them. He contemplated having someone visit their homes by tomorrow morning. This had happened before on the boat, but never so close, and why did they insist on meeting in this room? Someone had been talking, and trouble was brewing. He let it all slide away to make sure the eighty-five billion dollars in funding was transferred to a bank depository by tomorrow morning.

Next to the bar was an old billiards table resting on a Persian rug. It had been restored after he purchased it from the previous owner, the inventor of Velcro. The felt top displayed a map of the world. James was lining up a shot. Christopher looked at his pasty face and beady eyes with no sympathy. He would lose the game on purpose to give the man a sense of power and control. James said, "Seven ball corner pocket." It went in. Christopher suppressed his vexation and faked a casual attitude.

"You know that I play better when I'm drunk." Christopher got up and went behind the bar.

"It explains why you've won the last three fucking games. You're amazing." The errand boy was here for a purpose, Christopher knew it, and they knew he knew it because they wanted his microchips. The need to be diplomatic with the backstabbing Washington hotshots was part of the game. He respected the brokered border dispute James managed between India and China. His thirty-year career meant he had plenty of favors in the bag, so he treaded carefully. His ego was rattling his cage because they were uninvited, but luckily, reason prevailed. He prepared for the worst. They could take it all and kill him by accident without any questions asked. Which meant that he was outgunned. He who fought and ran away, lived to fight another day.

"So where do you plan to tie the knot?" asked James.

"We're heading to Vegas, then wine country."

James said, "Why? The French should be the only ones allowed to make wine. I prefer real wine made in Bordeaux, Burgundy, or Loire Valley. Machère déuxime maison. J'aime Paris." Christopher's facial expression remained emotionless.

"Fuck Bordeaux. We're going to California."

James held up his hand and said, "Hey, okay. Wow. Never hear me knock the best political system in the world. They pay off like slot machines. No state in the union sells out their taxpayers faster. Got to love it. It's because of the weather. Lulls them all to sleep." Christopher was amazed at the guy's bravado and felt like he needed to take a shower after being in his presence.

James said, "I'd go to Fiji if it weren't for the fifteen-hour flights."

Christopher didn't bother to inform him of the bedroom and entertainment on the jet and said, "It would be nice to sail there," after taking a deep breath.

James asked, "Where's the bachelor party?"

Christopher replied, "A small one tomorrow. One last hurrah before the plunge." He'd smoked too much weed this past week, and it was catching up to him. He bent down behind the bar to wash his face and freshen up. Then, he blotted off the moisture with a fluffy, white towel. Deep down, he loved this one-up-man-ship, and started to imagine the wine he was going to be drinking in the morning. It was too late in the day to start. Kayla would be on his mind for the rest of his life, but tomorrow was for him. The morning's events were already planned for an escape. It cheered him up to think about what was in store.

James said, "The only annoying part of California is the people. They get on my nerves. We went into a restaurant in San Francisco, and they charged us for butter. Can you believe it?"

Christopher said, "Who cares? It's not like you're paying for the meals."

"It's the principle."

Christopher let it go and remembered the time he didn't get into a nightclub in Beverly Hills. The next day, he bought the building and gave notice to the owners. Afterwards, he gutted it and made it into a commercial office location. He had his own way of destroying adversaries. James looked like the kind of man who would extract revenge in any way possible. Christopher needed to listen and popped a pizzy.

The ability to tell the truth in Washington was an impossibility and if funding was involved, then all the attachments were wrapped up as donations with none of the hooks showing. What else was James fishing for? Christopher knew how everything worked as good as anyone, and he made sure that they all got a slice of cake. He was the pimp of the chocolate chips, and James always had his hand in the cookie jar. In the back room political arena, everyone called Christopher "Uncle Sugar." Playing corrupt politics was a unique craft taught to him by his father, and he guessed his father before him. It was time to keep the foundation growing. Thorpe Inc. needs a legacy. It was connected to everything from health care, Hollywood, Silicon Valley, and eastern Europe. They infiltrated the Asian markets, India, and created ties with a few African dictators. He was at full power and had invested in a considerable amount of security resources. His people needed to pay attention to where the Farnsworths of the world were hiding. They'd crawl out from under a rock and gut him for sure, if given the chance.

The writing was on the wall with the changes coming, and Christopher had to lobby his way to keep men like James from taking control of his company. They were growing stronger, and so would Christopher. Media connections should be his next venture to gain any future advantages. To be successful and wealthy was to be attacked. It came with the territory. Well, it was time to mark out some new positions and fly low for a while. Christopher watched how the man looked at him out of the corner of his eyes like a greedy bastard. Maybe he'd give him a gift to keep the filthy animal happy. Would a Honda NSX satisfy him? How about backstage passes to a U2 concert? He had to figure out a way to give him some more rope before Christopher could find a loophole. Now was not the time to be getting married.

This craze for all things relating to the Internet was changing the game and the talk of the town. Christopher had hired a few hackers and was impressed with the results they were producing. He could manipulate targeted areas with a blink of an eye. The only downside was the risk of getting caught. He didn't need to be told to proceed with caution when the government showed up in your house. After this weekend, he would set in motion a plan to get better intel on James' habits, website visits, and past behavior. Everyone had something they'd like to erase. This unannounced meeting with a goon squad was a message, and it was being received. They smelled like fertilizer a mile away. The anger began to boil inside Christopher again. What were these yahoos up to? He forced himself to let out a cackle at a stupid joke James was telling.

"We're in a pissing contest with you Mega Group people," James said. "Who can go the farthest?" He buried the nine-ball in the corner pocket, and the cue ball continued on off of two bumpers and knocked the two-ball in by accident.

Christopher said, "Nice shot. So, why are you really here?"

James said, "That is the question. We've run dry with firepower in the middle of a negotiation. Not good. They're asking for an American manufacturer to host in their country. We thought of you."

"And what do we get for this generosity?"

James said, "The sale of your business will be in the billions."

Christopher replied, "I already have billions. What if we..."

James said, "Decline?"

"Something like that, or tell you to fuck off?"

James looked offended and said, "We'll settle for ninety-two percent of your manufacturing to move off-shore. You keep eight percent in the States and lose everything else overseas. Then, after posting a win in the negotiations, we'd be in your debt."

Christopher had anticipated a raw deal and said, "Makes sense. We've been told as much already, and now isn't a good time to sell."

James said, "Why not?"

Christopher took a second and said, "You guys used to have the best parties at Pennsylvania Ave. It's been a while since we had a sleepover. But the wedding has me tied up right now."

James took a sip of his drink. "See, boys, my man here knows how to play ball." The two screws looked at them both, then went back to the game.

James said, "Ever been to Camp David? Better yet, have you taken out Marine One for a spin? We can give you one of those to fly wherever you want for a week. Your balls will vibrate on the seat, it's a blast."

"Already have a helicopter and Camp David smells like an old rug," said Christopher.

"Nothing like the White House, huh," James continued. "Forget the West Room, the place is cat piss, thanks to Lady Johnson. Lincoln's bedroom is my favorite."

Christopher said, "A couple days wouldn't hurt. It'll take at least that long to go over all the paperwork." He knew the guy didn't have authority to negotiate and would play the rest of this conversation out as dumb as a stump to delay. Either way, the proposal was out in the open, but the contract wasn't signed. A lot could happen.

James said, "Deal. Come down anytime. We'll roll out the red carpet for you. Dinner, drinks, dancing, you name it. Then, we'll surround you with a bunch of celebrities who think they're important and talk your ear off about kale or the Oscar they won. It'll be beautiful," said James, smiling. "Bring the new wifey. The more the merrier." He then finished his drink.

Christopher said, "I don't know. It's hard to trust the word of a man who drinks single malt with water. A person could look past it all if you didn't use also a straw."

"You're right, you shouldn't trust me because I can be a nightmare. No one even likes me/ I'm vulgar, lazy, and the only reason I drink this stuff is because my doctor says it lowers my cholesterol." James took his glass and sloshed the ice cubes around until he finished it off with a slurping noise. That was Christopher's cue to make him another one. He went behind the bar and pulled out an ice pick, then punched away at the block. At the center of the bar was a taxidermy tiger encased in darkness. The light was off, and the voyeurism glass was preventing anyone from viewing it in the room. With a push of a button, the centerpiece would be noticed. James said, "Can you make it look like a snow cone this time? I used to love those in the summer."

"The machine is broken."

The scotch was a forty-year-old Macallan from Speyside. He poured it generously and applied a topper of water. It hurt watching the barley get diluted.

James said, "Not too much of the clear stuff. It'll throw off the flavor." He inspected the libation and said, "Momma's milk."

Christopher smiled and said, "Nothing but the best for you." James didn't know that Christopher reused the expensive containers for certain individuals. He would pour Dewar's into the premium bottles for people who didn't know the difference and needed to be impressed. He wanted to hear their bullshit retelling of the flavor profile. Since James was in the silk-stocking crowd, he got the liquor store special. Christopher hated being so close to the slug as they clicked for a toast. It was all a ruse and an old game of perceived value. James took a couple of gulps like a dog at a bowl on the floor. The face-to-face meeting started getting old as Christopher looked at his watch.

A framed black and white photograph had caught James' attention. It was an image of a whale slaughter from years ago in Northern Canada. Christopher sipped on tequila and liked how it mixed with the drugs he was taking. James said, "Jesus H., Christopher. Are you friends with Eskimos?"

Christopher said, "Yes, I am. That's me right there in the boat."

James did a double take and responded, "You look like a kid who never missed a meal." Christopher went back to lining up another pool shot and missed. James took his turn and started shooting again.

Christopher said, "Things change."

James said, "Call me on Monday, and I'll get back to you by Wednesday about this manufacturing sale."

While James lined up his shot, Christopher said, "What? This isn't Sri fucking Lanka, James. It's going to take a little bit more time with proper planning. You act as if you're ordering McDonalds at the drive-thr. We'll get to you when we're ready. Now, get the fuck out of here. This meeting is over."

ames got closer to Christopher. "So stupid. Sorry about that. Sometimes, I got to ask, and it can be messy. We can make life very difficult for your business if we so choose. Unfortunately, your computer chips are now on our time schedule. We don't want to put a freeze on things, and we won't as long as you follow orders. We're making a play for the Asian market, and your company buys us a lot of capital gains with interest. Take your time, though. We'll figure out the new system and let you know. See you in a month. Actually, two months, forget the pressure. The most important thing about today is that you're getting married. Congratulations."

Christopher kept silent to the forced agreement. James asked, "If you're interested, we have disaster relief funds waiting to be cleared. It's a construction contract. You skim the down payment, and we provide the red tape. Everyone makes out like a bandit. Except the ones who needed the help the most, of course." Christopher rolled out a smile and said he was done with the meeting.

James gave him a "suit yourself" shrug. Then, he looked back at the pool game. He took aim at a difficult shot, and Christopher heard a wretched tear. He turned to see that the cue had dug into the middle of the felt. Slowly, James pulled back the stick as they gathered around to inspect the hole in the table. Christopher put his hands near his head without touching it and then crossed them on his chest. He silently walked out of the room while saying, "You know your way out. We'll be in touch."

After the door closed, James said, "I think I wiped out the Canary Islands."

CHAPTER 9

T HE SUN WAS fading, and the cirrocumulus had a fire apple glow. Kayla pulled into the driveway of Christopher's inherited mansion and passed by the twelve-foot iron gates with an embossed family crest displayed on both sides. The perfectly manicured grounds sat on six and a half acres of prime real estate and surrounded by tree-lined vegetation. She'd been visiting the Thorpes' home for years, but now, it was different. Today, she saw the possibility of living here, raising a family, and the stables in the back added to her speculation. But then, she let it gently pass because she wasn't in love romantically with Christopher. She wouldn't turn her back on him, but the decision had repercussions. She chose their friendship and accepted Nova Scotia or a dishonorable discharge. The government would need to find someone else.

The meeting with Dr. Van der Slootzin had been mind-altering. The eye movement desensitization and reprocessing therapy was easy. The procedure took an unknown weight off her shoulders. She didn't care how the brain manipulation worked; it put a spring back into her step and made the headache vanish. But how long would it last?

A peaceful feeling filled her heart as the tires rolled across the cobblestones. She was driving Mom's M5 and found solace in the navigational chamber. The four-hundred-horse-powered machine was always hungry for the open road, and she had barely tested its speed on the way over. Kayla smiled, knowing her mother owned such a vehicle and drove it below the limit. The aggravation of fellow commuters wasn't her mom's concern.

The car slowly edged its way forward as fond memories playing on repeat danced in her head. The place was unrecognizable from the front. She always entered the property from the back in order to check up on Biscuit. It was the first time seeing the facelift to the entrance, and it was somewhat unrecognizable. She glanced in the mirror to check her makeup and instead saw a strength to endure the upcoming struggles. It didn't seem strange to think of herself in this new light.

The valet was running around as Kayla pulled up. She got out wearing a blue dress from the consignment store. It was the stitching that drew her attention. She would have bought it regardless of the label, because the Victorian neckline made everything pop. A bow gave it a couture feel. The shoes were knockoffs. All in all, she had put the outfit together without a thought and for less than two hundred dollars. She strutted past the welcome table while saying hello to a few of the familiar faces. The four security guards at the front all acknowledged her entry by smiling and nodding. No one was going to stop the future Mrs. Thorpe, and everyone had been instructed how to behave.

Kayla ran into Mrs. Sandra Kelly, who had a Yorkie stuffed inside her handbag. It had been a while since they'd seen each other. Standing close beside her was Ruth, her personal assistant. Kayla gave Roscoe, the Yorkie, a little rub. The two women exchanged pleasantries and fawned over the seven pounds of adorableness. Sandra exhumed philanthropy and thanked Kayla for her service. Kayla smiled at the compliment and asked Sandra about her sons. She said they'd be arriving in town tomorrow. Sandra asked, "When are you going to find yourself a man?"

Kayla said, "Might be faster than you think. Any advice?"

"Find them before they're rich."

"Why is that?"

"They get a little pushy after becoming accomplished, but I don't think you'll have anything to worry about." The chitchat continued, and Kayla liked Sandra. She had a polish about her, and it commanded respect. She would have been a great field agent with her down-to-earth personality. Both sensed that they could talk for a while and agreed to meet up later. Sandra was directed away and further into the estate.

Kayla glanced at Sandra leaving and saw the poise in her walk. She watched how people with money moved differently through a crowd and dress impeccably. No knockoffs in her closet. It was easy for Kayla to believe that she ran a five-billion-dollar foundation and funded several political candidate's careers.

SANDRA DIDN'T RECOGNIZE any of the guards while passing through the entrance. She felt it was a bit extreme to have so many for a fundraiser. The outfits they were wearing caught her eye, with buttons shaped as flowers. She dismissed the notion of asking for their origin. The task at hand was tiresome enough, and it was best to get it completed so she could enjoy the rest of the weekend.

Walking past the foyer, Sandra saw a woman hanging from the ceiling performing a cirque du soleil act. Playing in the corner was a trio of classical chamber musicians. Sandra rubbed Roscoe's chin. Her personal assistant, Ruth, was two steps behind.

The French country, natural stone flooring in the hallway led away from the crowd. The polished paneling hinted of old money. She liked some of Christopher's taste and appreciated the row of vintage guns saluting Smith and Wesson, Colt Paterson, and Winchester. The displays looked to be precisely measured in distance from one another. The musket encased in glass was conspicuous, and she kept walking, but came to a full stop at the tag on the Henry Rifle. Next to it was a black and white photo of Benjamin Tyler Henry, the inventor of the first reliable, lever-action repeating rifle. The ability to think on her feet was the only measured device she needed.

At the end of the hall, a security guard opened the door for Sandra and Ruth to enter. They walked into a dark space that was noticeably colder than the rest of the house. A woman dressed in a business suit watched them enter. It was Miriam Hayden, Christopher's personal assistant. She took off her glasses and closed her laptop, then walked around an eight-foot folding table to greet them. She had blonde hair, longer than shoulder length, and was stylishly dressed in a white suit with black trim. The only light in the room was a lone lamp on the table, making it look like an interrogation chamber.

Miriam greeted her. "Mrs. Kelly. Thank you so much for coming by. I know it isn't normal procedure. We appreciate you taking the time out of your busy schedule. How are you today?"

"Fantastic. Who are the goons at the door?" replied Sandra. Miriam gave Ruth a quick hug hello. They were friends and talked a lot while managing the bosses.

Miriam waited for the door to close and said, "New private security detail for Count Thorpe. They just showed up an hour ago."

Sandra looked confused and asked, "Count?"

Miriam continued, "He's just been awarded the title in a private ceremony. He's been testing its usefulness."

"Who made him a Count?"

"Belgium or Norway, I'm not sure. I can find out if you like?"

Sandra clapped back and said, "It won't be necessary." She looked around the room as if expecting someone else. "Well, you know what they say about titles, don't you?"

Miriam didn't answer, and Sandra didn't wait for a reply before saying, "Very few people live up to them?"

Sandra smiled at Miriam, liking that she never pretended to know an answer she didn't have. Sandra saw it as a remarkable stroke of luck for Christopher to have found such an employee working as a VIP host at the casino. She knew he was a gambler with a never-ending bankroll to help the winning percentages. He was known to always give action and by definition a true high roller.

Sandra had done some checking up on Miriam and knew that she had paid her own way through law school. Now, she was getting firsthand experience on what it was like to become someone's personal slave. She saw the worn-down heels and stress bags under her eyes and had some empathy for the young woman. Sandra said, "I'll help you find a good position if things don't work out with you and Christopher."

Miriam leaned in to say, "Thank you. That would be great. Once I pass the bar, I'll be sure to reach out." Sandra didn't like the idea of stealing her away from Christopher and shelved the topic for another day.

"How about doing me a favor and turning down the air conditioning? It's freezing in here," said Sandra.

"Wish we could," came a voice from the shadows in the back of the room.

"Who the hell is that? And what are you doing in the dark?"

Slowly, Aaron Chapman walked towards Sandra. Ruth looked over to Miriam.

Sandra said, "Look at what the cat dragged in." Ruth had already prepped Sandra about Aaron being hired by Thorpe. Miriam took a step back to let them hash it out.

"I didn't mean to startle you," said Aaron.

"Thank you, but I don't get startled. I heard you were here, but I didn't think I'd run into you just yet. What a pleasant surprise." Aaron moved to stand behind the folding table near Miriam.

"Well, when you let me go, I was devastated. Made me re-evaluate my priorities after all the work we did together."

Sandra said, "Yes, we did a lot, and I'm grateful for the results. Glad to see you landed on your feet. My brother is enjoying being the Sheriff."

Aaron kept silent. Sandra continued, "I'm sorry, Ruth, why did we release Aaron again?" Ruth looked Aaron straight in the eye.

"It was for multiple reasons. The software he created was encrypted for other priorities outside the scope of our foundation. We're still working out a few of the bugs he installed from the last election results. If they weren't illegal, they are now, and it put us at risk. We still have the opportunity to pin a few illegal rules of conduct on him as our scapegoat. But unfortunately, cyber security laws are changing by the week, and we would have shared the blame with him. Second, he leveraged money from the foundation's account to collect interest off of a personal investment. He used the London Vex Corp account specifically, then exited the position before they defaulted on the loans to our investors. He would have gotten away with it if we didn't back check on the ledger with an Ernst & Young audit. To pour more salt on the wound, camera footage showed Aaron's car crashing into your Bentley. He told security that he had no recollection of the accident." When she finished talking, she handed Sandra an envelope.

Aaron smiled and said, "We won the election, didn't we?"

Sandra said, "Yes, we did."

"And Christopher still hired me. Seems like the age of computers is taking over."

Sandra opened the envelope and handed a cashier's check to him, saying, "I think we still have a while yet before that happens."

Aaron said, "Thank you," and took the check. He continued, "You hired me to do a job. It got done. Sorry about the car. If you are ever in need of a software engineer, mathematician, or an upgrade on your firewall protection, let me know." Aaron pantomimed putting a phone to his ear. Then, he gave her a nicely wrapped gift box. Sandra passed it to Ruth to hold.

She asked, "What is it?"

He said, "It's a vintage music box. I know you collect them. It's an apology gift."

Sandra said, "Apology accepted."

"Like you always said, Mrs. Kelly, longevity is the key to this business, and it's a marathon, not a sprint."

"You have a lot going for you, Aaron. I hope the Count can teach you what we were unable to."

Sandra and Ruth started to walk out. Ruth told Miriam, "Please, tell Christopher that Sandra would like to meet with him about the waterfront expansion. She has a few resolutions he might like." Miriam agreed, and then, they were gone.

———————

AARON WISHED THEM luck as they exited, then called out, "Do you want a receipt?" No one came back into the room. Aaron said, "She's really a nice person, isn't she...once you get past all the hair."

Miriam shook her head in disgust and said, "Get away from me."

He shrugged his shoulders and took a few steps back. "What did I say?"

Everyone knew that Aaron was an over-talented youth in an adult body, but he could write code, and the position was in high demand.

Aaron reached over to the computer to eject a flash drive. He attached the cap of a flash drive that looked like a miniature skateboard. Then, he looked at the cashier's check for two hundred thousand dollars and stuffed it into his breast pocket. He said, "She's got bags of money."

He invaded Miriam's space again, and she said, "Remember the three-foot rule, Aaron. We have two more hours of this, so give me some space."

He said, "You got two more hours, but my job is over. So, I'm going to go and enjoy the party while you finish the spreadsheets, in this cold dark room, with your rules. Burrr."

DAVID TURNED INTO the drive and was stunned by the size of the property. He lowered the music to admire the details. The signs along the drive said to "elect State Representative Allison Baker." He made a mental note to not talk politics or voice an opinion on anything, especially to the homeowner. He hoped the place had the Heat game on.

There was something about meeting Sam's daughter that had him thinking about her, and he found that he couldn't stop. He wouldn't mind if she showed up tonight.

David got in the valet line and went over what needed to be done at the job site. They were at an impasse with the floor until a backup electrician was found. Then, a new window needed to be ordered because a ladder went through it. Finally, he would have to give up on fixing the lawn and just have it resodded. A pinched knot in his shoulder happened when unloading a late lumber delivery. While rubbing at the kink, he felt good enough to not be totally exhausted, as the iced coffee gave him a much needed boost. Tonight was all about making an appearance, eating as much free food as possible, and then pulling a David Copperfield vanishing act for a final goodbye. He curled his lip in angst the closer he got to the mansion.

The place grated his taste. The sidewalks had thickly trimmed frames of grass wedged in between each section. Which meant no baby carriages or grandmothers were hanging out at this residence. If any did exist, they'd have to choose between the cobblestones or grass because the sidewalk gap would be too extreme. The grand entrance made him lean into the windshield of the truck to see the collage of architectural gaudiness. He thought it best to tear down homes of this style with so many different designs.

The normal eye would think it's fantastic, but he had a different opinion. He never understood how Roman columns matched up with modern architecture. He blurred his vision to see if it would make a difference, but it didn't. In between the rows of cars popped out a man walking on stilts. David missed putting him on the hood by inches. The guy told him to watch where he was going. This day wasn't going to end peacefully for him. The valet took the keys to his truck, and David walked through the front door.

To the immediate right, just past the foyer, was a wall of flat screen TVs showing images of nature. To the left was a bare room filled with a pile of bricks. He looked to the ceiling to see if they were doing any work. A woman with nose rings and tattoos took her foot off the wall and said, "Nice jacket." He thanked her and asked about the bricks. She said, "Would you like to get a picture with one of the bricks?" David complied. After the Polaroid was taken, she gave it to him.

"Do you work here?" he asked.

"No. I'm just taking pictures."

"What do they call it?"

She pointed to the sign on the wall that said, "Human Confetti."

David picked one up and got the point. He said, "So the artist is a realist?"

"Not really," she responded. "I think a pessimist." He decided to not understand and tossed the brick back into the pile.

"Very inspirational. Thanks for the pic." She nodded as David strolled away while tucking the picture into a custom-tailored suit with quilt patterns and a montage of homespun cotton yarn. He felt comfortable wearing it and didn't care if it looked out of place. A person didn't have to get close in order to notice the not-so-subtle differences in color. He casually followed the arrangements of historical artifacts as they were displayed. He stopped at a Medieval Heraldry statue from 1508 that looked priceless, or at least was an excellent fake.

David turned to see Sam and Julia approaching.

Dr. North said, "Nice dinner jacket."

David replied, "It must have been hard to eat in such a thing," as he gently knocked on the metal.

Sam said, "Nothing like a suit of armor to swell a man's confidence."

"Hello, Julia, good to see you."

Julia said, "You look dashing."

They hugged, and he could see by the look in her eyes that she had a few questions to ask about the job. No way was she going to let tonight be a social meeting, and he was ready for it with his patent catch phrase. Which was line number 346 on the contract; if you didn't have the time, then don't hire Pivot Construction. But the Norths were becoming good friends, and he would go easy on them.

Julia asked, "Did the floor get set today?"

David said the job was on hold for a bit because the electrician's wife was having a baby.

"It's a hard excuse to be upset over. Was it a boy or a girl?"

David said, "Boy."

"How long will he be away?"

Sam said, "As long as he needs. We can wait." Sam dismissed the further Q&A, and Julia took the hint.

Then, Sam asked, "Do you think we really needed a bathroom permit?" Now, Julia gave Sam the eye.

David said, "It's important to have an inspector double-check our calculations since we're not perfect. I know it seems like a formality, but after it's all set, you won't have to pay someone else to tear it back up again and start from scratch." He could see that he had their attention, and Julia's mouth tightened into a fine line.

She said, "You make a convincing argument. Let's sit on it until Monday." They didn't say anything else, and David breathed a sigh of relief, knowing that he was out of the conversation until then.

———

Kayla was outside in the back and entered the main room. David spotted her looking for her parents. She had an elegant stride, and the dress stuck out like a metallic, flake-blue Ferrari on a dirt road. What the hell was she wearing? The gold pinstriping was a nice touch. He was glad that she couldn't see him staring. He turned away to eat some food. It was a great coping mechanism, and he was proud to have one. While chewing slowly, he watched her weave through the crowd.

Kayla stopped at the front of the room, where a performance painter was going to transform an empty canvas into a work of art. David had scarfed down his second bite of lobster macaroni and cheese by the time the painting started flying around and she had made her way to where they were standing.

Julia looked to see if any paint had splashed onto Kayla's dress, then they both laughed and kissed. David noticed that Kayla wasn't wearing her engagement ring. Her mother held up Kayla's hand without saying a word. She took the ring out of her purse and slipped it onto her hand. Moms had a way of sending a message without saying a word. He gave the engagement a seventy-five percent chance of making it to a church. No chance of it lasting longer than a year, since to him, their love looked like one big lie, even though he had no idea who the groom was. If it was the guy who designed the front entrance, then he felt sorry for her, but that was his ego talking. What a roller coaster ride she must have been on right now. He objectively observed how love showed up when you least expected it, or in a twisted fashion. It looked as if it took Kayla by storm. He was glad to see her, and it made him think of an excuse to stay a bit longer.

"How are you feeling?" asked Sam.

"Terrific. Never better. I'm shocked at the world of change I've gone through without any self-medicating," said Kayla. "No urge to have a drink or a smoke, and I'm at a party. Does the military know about this treatment?"

Julia said, "You should never have a reason to start smoking." Kayla and Sam didn't look at her as he explained how the treatment has been rejected by the military. The adoption and testing had been an uphill battle from the beginning. Kayla couldn't believe it because of how much had physically shifted in her. David listened intently and was amazed at how she described her physical status, tranquility, and the newer version of herself. She stopped talking and turned to him.

He said, with some food in the corner of his mouth, "Sounds like you've been reborn." He felt awkward when she didn't respond. Maybe she didn't hear him, and he let it go without pressing.

Sam was happy to hear it and gave her a bear hug filled with love. He held her in his arms and said, "We have another appointment set up for you on Monday. Just enjoy the weekend, and we'll resume treatment first thing next week." He started to tear up, then Kayla turned to David.

"You seem to be showing up a lot lately."

"Synchronicity," said David while glancing over to Sam and Julia, knowing that one of the two were influencing the connection. Only, why introduce him to Kayla when she was engaged? Nothing made sense, and he was just going to roll with whatever happened.

Kayla smiled as she brushed some crumbs off of his jacket. He sensed something was brewing and looked down at the clothes he was wearing to knock off any more debris. It didn't stop her from smiling and feeling his custom-made sport coat. "Nice material. You make this?"

David brushed off the shoulders and said, "I wish. No. I got it in Miami. Small shop right outside of Wynwood. The designer is Miss Kane." David promised to take her there if interested.

Kayla said, "No. But it looks good on you." A server came by, and David grabbed some sushi in a martini glass.

Kayla asked her mom, "They don't have any plates?" David brushed off his sleeves and straightened out his outfit. Kayla looked at her watch, and it made him look at his for no reason. Kayla asked, "Do you have to be someplace?"

David replied, "Not right now."

Kayla looked at his shoes, and it made him feel self-conscious. He asked, "What's wrong?" She dismissed the question as if it was nothing.

"It's how they're serving it," Julia replied. "They even put bacon in my vodka." David watched Kayla talk to her parents about some boring medical chatter. She talked with her hands, and then, a tray of Kobe sliders passed by for him to lasso. He glanced her way and caught a glimpse of the yellow trim again around the lace of her dress.

David ate his way to feeling more comfortable in the setting as Kayla was hitting on all cylinders. He kept telling himself that she was engaged. His feelings weren't confusing, it was the situation, and all he needed to do was chill. He told himself to toe the line like a trained soldier on guard duty. Thoughts of being a homewrecker told him to back up. The best play was to continue to keep looking cool, fill his belly, and leave. What a crackerjack of a day! Swimming with sharks, feeding squirrels, watching a surgery, and enjoying this tall drink of water in front of him torch his mind. He forced some thoughts about tomorrow morning and visiting the job. The urge to drink whisky came and went, and he found himself listening to Kayla again. Something was definitely different about her. She had changed since this morning. He spotted another server and took a sample.

After getting his fill, Kayla glanced his way again. He figured that she was probably starving herself, so he offered her one, but she declined. Julia said, "Doctors know too much. They would put an x-ray machine in your brain if they could. You're going in for a check-up first thing Monday morning," and pointed at Sam.

Alone in thought, Kayla interrupted by saying, "They have a buffet table set up outside if you want a real meal."

It was music to David's ears. He was hungrier than usual and rubbed his belly at the suggestion. He thought the buffet line was sarcasm, but she was smiling too naturally. He approved of the suggestion.

"This party is so odd," Julia said. "I never understood all this circus stuff he puts together."

"It's all for show, Mom." Kayla said.

"Eccentric is more like it," Sam said. "And he is not to be underestimated. I am surprised how fast he came back from knee surgery. Never give him the passing shot."

"Life isn't all about tennis, Sam," Julia said.

"Of course not, it's a horrible game." He snuggled closer to give her a kiss on the cheek. The artist had left, and a Bossa Nova group started playing. The music echoed in the room and moved some of the guests to the dance floor. Sam asked "Madame?" and held out his hand.

Julia said, "Oh, I don't know. You still got it?" Kayla had watched this routine over and over through the years and turned to David. He watched them rhumba, and it reminded him of a salsa lesson where he learned about his two left feet. He silently begged her to not ask him to dance.

"I need some air," said Kayla as she started walking outside. She was having doubts about her strategy and wanted to do some reconnaissance. It would be good to scout around and have a backup plan. This general contractor was either a tool for someone, or a nobody. Couldn't hurt to see if she could spot any weaknesses in Christopher's defenses.

David followed and was happy that she didn't mind his company. She seemed to have no rules or pretensions, and yet, her tone was like a boss. He watched her figure move, the profile, and then the ring. It looked like it was slowing down the swing of her arm. He knew that she had chosen a man, and he was comfortable with not getting out of line with her. She didn't seem too interested to be at the event, which was fine by him, his only concern was to look out for the groom.

They walked out of two, ten-foot, double French doors to a DJ spinning music and a full piece band setting up. Champagne was being passed around from a fountain while magicians performed card tricks. David recognized the juggler on stilts performing for a small group of kids. Beyond the backyard was a large, open field, which lead to the seventh hole of a golf course. Going down the middle of the fairway was a wild man running for his life. He had a metal plate on his back and a wooden stick in each hand. On the far end of the fairway was a motorcycle getting ready to run him over, and it successfully flattened him out. The victim immediately got up and started running in the opposite direction while laughing hysterically. The motorcycle turned around and chased the man out of sight. David witnessed the perfect image for the day.

"Looks like some people forgot their invitations."

"He has those two at every party." Kayla passed on the Veuve Clicquot fountain and had no urge to celebrate. She turned and asked, "You want any Champagne?"

"No, thank you," said David, "But I'll take a cranberry and soda."

She said, "Sounds exciting, I'll have one of those, too."

David asked, "You don't drink?"

After a slight pause, she answered, "I'm taking a break."

Next to the open bar was a drink special on a handwritten sign; mint watermelon lemonade. They both got one, and David proposed a toast. "To the world of Salvador Dali. Who might have lied when he said he didn't do any drugs. And to your engagement, of course." They took a sip together, and he saw her hesitate before putting the concoction to her lips. They started strolling around and stopped at a mini stage with a contortionist.

"Dali might have been easier to understand than this place," David mused.

Kayla asked, "Have you met Suzy Backscratcher?"

He admitted he hadn't and said, "Is she a regular, too?"

"Nope. But it says it on her card." She took one and handed it to him. It was pink with gold, embossed lettering, and eighteen-point font. It said, "Suzy Backscratcher for live events, parties, and social gatherings. *I Have All the Moves.*" He kept the card just in case he needed a bookmark.

"How is the house coming along?" Kayla asked.

"Pretty good if you're looking at the brighter side of things."

"Well, you made it past Mom. That counts for something." They eased their way through the crowd to a more secluded spot. Kayla said, "I really like the elephant dresser." David was touched by the compliment; and it felt good to receive one from her. She was the type of woman who could make a man feel good about himself.

"A friend of the family used to say, 'If you can't work with your head, then you have to learn to work with your hands.'"

"Then, your hands saved you from a lot of school work."

"I could have become a doctor, but it wasn't very appealing to me. It didn't help when my biology teacher threw me out of class."

She asked, "What for?"

He replied, "My version of dissecting the frog." The scars he left on the croaker should have put him into the Frankenstein Hall of Fame. He looked over her shoulder and saw an object nearby in the shade of the trees.

David walked away from Kayla and toward an outdoor sculpture. He scratched his head.

He said, "It can't be."

"What?"

He replied, "It's a Calder," and he looked around. Stains from leaves, soot, and sun had faded the sculpture. He touched the mobile, and it still moved. He smiled in astonishment.

"Christopher's family has always been into art. This one doesn't look too important."

He responded with, "It's made by Alexander Calder, a national treasure. This doesn't make any sense." He got closer and inspected the installation, then slowly gave it a gentle turn.

Kayla asked, "Would you like to see some more?"

He nodded while saying, "Yes." They moved along the stone path, away from the guests, and approached a side-door with a single guard.

The hallway was dimly lit with wood paneling. Light was coming from behind a large, honey onyx fixture embedded along the wall.

"The idea was to have the feeling of a beehive," she said. He touched the dark wood preserving the hallway and let his mind drift away with the sense of mystery.

"This is some dark timber," he said.

"I always get the feeling of being underwater on a bright day when I'm in here."

"It's probably because of the ship wood."

"Ship wood?"

"You know. Old vessels, Spanish Galileans fallen on a stormy night." He knocked on the side. "Yep. Ship wood. Spanish."

"Spanish Galileans? You mean galleons."

"I think I said galleons."

"You would have been better off saying it was the Portuguese."

"I like them, too. Portuguese galleons are the best." David pretended to be a dead crew member and made scary noises as they walked to the end of the hallway. "AAAAAAAhhhhh-huuuuuggggg!!!!"

She told him he was weird and ordered him to stop. He agreed and was ready for the tour to continue. Unfazed by the banter, he was surprised that they were still hanging out. He didn't care that she was acting way too cool for school, probably some kind of brainiac nerd thing. *Just enjoy the ride*, he told himself, *for as long as it lasts or until the fiancé shows his fat face.*

Kayla jiggled a door handle, but it was locked. She asked David to take a step back. "There's a trick to these original doors in the old house." She put a shoulder into the frame while driving forward. A large cracking of wood exploded through the frame, and they stepped inside.

"Ever play professional hockey?" David commented.

"Seven and half years of military service and an older brother will teach you a thing or two." David wanted to say something flirtatious but drew a blank. So, instead, he thanked her for her service. He wanted to ask about the war, only he was distracted by the new layer of limestone that was intoxicating. Most builders wouldn't give so much attention to such an insignificant space. What for? It was easier to put up some type of linen wallpaper or upholstery fabric. It said something about the owner. He wondered who'd had the idea? Credit to her man with the blank check for budgeting requirements on materials. The creative possibilities were firing away in his mind.

The walnut flooring trim contrasted with the sunken lighting. Then, he saw the main attraction: a beautiful, spiral staircase with a chrome plated anchor in the middle. In any other home, these stairs would be near the entrance. Here, it was a throw away, and it looked to be one piece. He got closer to inspect it, and its beauty was beyond anything he could imagine. Kayla started walking up the sandstone spiral staircase and stopped halfway to glance back at him. David was looking at her reflection in the polished chrome. He didn't see a single smudge print.

Kayla reached the top and waited for David. Her legs were waiting, too, and he didn't fail to notice them. Pinned by her beauty, he stopped before reaching the last step. She said, "The truth is, I'm a little confused by you. What are you doing here?" She was close enough that he could smell her scent. It was an unusual question, and he swallowed a cotton ball before speaking.

He said, "I'm following you."

She pressed on, "Who hired you?"

"Your parents. You're still engaged, right?"

CHAPTER 10

KAYLA LEFT DAVID frozen on the steps. He tried to follow what she was asking, but the woman had too many curves and notches. He told himself to avoid her at all costs, that she was a death trap, but he couldn't help himself. He said, "Let's go back a few. What were you saying?"

She told him to forget it and walked into the room. He scratched his chin and thought of the Marxist quote, "Behind every work of art lies an uncommitted crime." Which was complete lunacy. He wondered if she had committed any felonies. The top of the stairs opened up to vaulted, thirty-five-foot ceiling and a private setting. This room was the chieftain's lair.

"Are we in *Jumanji*?"

"Robin Williams is the best." Kayla replied.

David agreed and watched her walk over to the pool table and start racking up a game. She said, "Not my favorite place, but it's the only room with a pool table." She saw David staring at a bear with a shotgun in its mouth. She said, "You like dead animals?"

"No. I prefer them alive. But I am getting some decorating tips." He came over and slid a few of the balls down from the pockets, and they ran over the world map imprinted on the felt top. She grabbed them and racked up.

"What kind of ideas are you getting?"

"Well, for one thing," he continued, "I've always wanted a couple hundred cans of bear spray stacked up on a wall." He picked up one and began examining the instructions. She cautioned him to be careful, saying if any of that stuff got into his eyes that it could cause permanent blindness. He slowly put the repellant back.

"Anything else?" Kayla asked.

"Sure. I'm thinking about getting into the roadkill industry. It looks to be lucrative." The other thing David noticed was the guy's love for guns. He looked to be someone to make friends with immediately and whose squirrely nutjob fiancée would best be left alone, unless David wanted to end up mounted on a wall. A red flag waving by itself was the elephant in the room telling him to keep the flirtatious behavior to himself. Even so, he hadn't played pool in a while, and one quick game wouldn't hurt. Give her a quick lesson and make an exit. He said, "I haven't played billiards in a really long time. Do you partake?"

Kayla took the eight ball and put it in the middle of the rack and said, "Billiards? Partake? Moi? Juste un petit peu. Est-ce qua tu? Jouez-vous."

The words sounded like a hummingbird landing on the palm of his hand. He said, "Your French sounds horrible."

"Vraiment, est-ce que vous parlez français?"

David said, "You must suffer from imposter syndrome." This statement made her laugh and, surprisingly, it helped him relax. Normally, he'd miss everything, but she was different. Today, he wouldn't give her a chance. Then, he'd be gone unless she wanted to get murdered by another game. He remembered the dogs waiting at home. It would be a fast smash, but not too hard, because word might get back to her mother. He watched her rack the balls and knew that it was going to be a fast slaughter. He looked at the Rolex wall clock and gave her a few minutes until she started crying.

"You look like you know what you're doing. I'll give you that," he said.

Kayla took the rack off the table and threw it on the couch and said, "I'll take it easy on you." He wanted to laugh but instead nodded in approval.

He said, "Listen, as long as you don't get upset, I'll be fine."

Kayla grabbed the white ball, tossed it up in the air, and caught it in her hand. She was looking for a good spot. David saw the determined look, recognized a competitive spirit.

She said, "Why would I be upset?" David found his cue and placed it across the table. He rolled it back and forth to make sure that it was straight.

"Well, someone with your assets...I mean, skills, has a lot of character, and losing can be difficult. It's a stupid, little game, and it requires...how do the French say it? Je ne sais quoi."

Kayla had her cue in hand and leaned on the stick. She paused for a moment and said, "Are you suggesting I have no chance?" She took the cue ball and moved it to the opposite side of the breaking line.

"Maybe after a couple years of practice, but not today." She put her pool cue down so she could walk behind the bar, and once there, she asked if he wanted anything to drink. He said, "Any can of soda will do. No glass." She took out a couple bottles of Perrier and slid one over to him. He rubbed his fingertips over the fossilized, wooden bar top. It had eased edges and one ammonite fossil inset as a centerpiece. He took the cap off and drank. He saw that she was watching him inspect the work. The buildup to the match was getting hyped, and both sides were playing an angle. He didn't think that she was just being nice by offering a drink, but instead a sandbagger. Doubt crept in for a second as he saw her eyes itching to get it on. He watched her go back to the table and line up the break. He took his stick and laid it down in front of the white ball.

"Excuse me," said Kayla. David lifted the cue up and put it back down.

She stood up.

"Your cue is in the way." He agreed and asked what they were playing for. She said, "Well, let's figure it out. You're working for my parents, so they can't be paying you much. And you probably left your glasses at home, so why not just play for bragging rights?" He smiled at the quip.

"I generally don't like to turn down easy money."

Kayla said, "Pardon me. Do I look easy to you?" He saw the vexation pulsing out of her neck. He knew that she would try to punish him, and it was the perfect setup.

"Listen, no offense. I'm just seeing if you're interested in a wager. Won't break the bank. No sense giving yourself a wedgie over it," he said.

"No one's getting a wedgie over anything."

"Okay." He could see the aggravation take effect. "I'm going to leave it alone."

Kayla said, "I generally like trash talkers. They're so predictable and usually underdeliver." The gloves were off. She continued, "I'll give you ten to one of whatever you have in your pocket." Then, she walked over to her purse and dug out a crisp Franklin and put it on the ledge.

David said, "Does it usually work when you squint your eyes like Clint Eastwood?"

"I'm not squinting."

"Of course you're not, my bad." David reached into his pocket and pulled out a C-note from a rubber band stack. He liked to keep his extra money in coffee cans and shoeboxes for gambling purposes. He didn't trust the banks and preferred a cash-ready lifestyle. Things could pop up from time to time, and the greenbacks always took care of business. It was a contractor thing and, in this moment, it served as a reminder of what he had to do. David put the money on top of hers.

"Let's keep it simple. Straight up for a hundred." David then said, "And if you want to press your luck, let's say that whoever wins can either take the money or trade it in for piece work." Kayla looked intrigued by this option.

"What kind of work?"

"Piece work, manual labor," David said, "I could make you dig a few ditches at your parents' place or clean out the inside of my wheel wells. Better yet, I'll have you chop a pile of firewood for winter and haul it two hundred yards up a hill on a tarp." Kayla took a sip of her drink and eyed him like he was crazy.

She said, "We live in Florida. No fireplaces around here."

He thought about what she said. "Okay, then, I'd make you pick up after my dogs for a week...what's so funny?"

"I'm just looking at your jacket. Where did you get it?"

David smiled, "You don't know. This is Miami baby. First class."

She shook her head while lining up the break. "If you say so." He put the stick in the way again. She put her head down and then stood up.

"What's the problem this time?"

"We have to lag to see who goes first?"

"Who said so?"

"It's a rule somewhere, but it's a rule. You're always supposed to lag for break when cash is on the line."

Kayla seductively said, "This a lot of money to you?" She adjusted the collar on his suit. David stood frozen as she continued, "You wouldn't let a little male pride get in the way of a lady going first, would you?" He took a sip of the fizzy stuff, and she went first.

David watched her do her thing as her face switched to one of laser focus. A second later, the cue ball was lined up and connected with lightning speed. The power cascaded, with balls spreading in every direction on the table. The number two solid went into the corner pocket.

David was shocked at the sound of the break because she held the stick like a newbie. No V shape for the hand bridge, but balls were still disappearing rapidly. She was good for a hack. He saw that she only had three shots left to end the game, so he went to go grab the rack. A few seconds later, two of three were off of the table with no effort. The game was all but over; only, she pushed the cue ball too far past for an easy final shot. Then, decided to cut the ball and missed it off the lip. Something in the center of the felt had diverted the path.

"Did you see what happened?! There's a hole in the table!"

"Of course, I saw it. You didn't? It's been there the entire time." David continued, "You didn't see it?" Kayla put her finger on the hole and then stepped away from the table.

He said, "You're squinting again. Does that help at all? Had it in the palm of your hand," as she looked up to the ceiling. His eyes were planning his series of moves.

David didn't pay any attention to the lighting fixtures, fire alarms, or sprinkler heads that were all done in a walnut finish. He didn't want to think of the dogs, the job site, or the cost to upkeep this place. Everything was centered on stick control. It balanced perfectly in his hand, ready for the shooting exhibition which was about to take place.

"You had one more ball left and couldn't put it away. Not going to lie, I was on the ropes." Kayla knew it and wasn't bothered by anything he was saying. She told him to not be so much of a shit talker.

"Can I ask you something?" asked David.

"Go ahead."

"The way you hold the cue. Who taught you that?"

She didn't respond. The fact she even made anything was an astonishment. He'd seen a player like her before out in Colorado, but that is going back fifteen years. He gave her a lot of credit for being able to make long string shots like she did with an open-handed bridge. No brace of the thumb and forefinger was truly a one-of-a-kind playing style. He chalked the stick so loudly that it made an alarming noise.

"Any chance of you getting your money back on the suit?" she asked.

David said, "You can have the money, but you can't teach taste." He was impervious to anything else she had to say. "I'm stripes, right?" She didn't say a word, and the silence was golden. The sequence was mapped out in his head. He saw where he wanted the cue ball to end up after each targeted spot. In a blink of an eye, three balls were buried in the side and corner pockets. He had a long shot to the opposite end and took a pause.

"Every dog has its day."

With a quick alignment, he struck the cue ball with extreme force. The ball went straight into the corner pocket with a penetrating sound. She flinched from the blast. He lined up the next one and said, "This is my favorite jacket, but not my only one."

The twelve ball was sitting on the rail. David applied some left English and just enough before the ball. It went past the side pocket all the way down the rail in slow motion. Then, it fell in the corner pocket on the last rotation.

"We call that getting surgical," he said, "and it looks like I'm going to have to stitch this one up all by myself." Kayla started shaking her head as he went for the closeout.

The nine ball was in the middle of the table and not in an easy position. He looked directly over the spot, then put his hand over the ball to see the shadows. He stepped back to the cue. The cut was perfectly sequenced as it coasted gently into the side pocket. The cue ball bounced off of the side cushion and rolled about fourteen inches from the eight ball. Smack near the corner pocket. He twirled the stick behind his back and rested his tush on the rail. He was about to say eight ball in the corner pocket when Christopher walked in.

CHAPTER 11

DAVID WATCHED THE door open as four men entered. He didn't have to be told which one was Christopher Thorpe, as he led the way. His hair hung past his ears, and he was wearing a white dinner jacket with snazzy, blue loafers and no socks. He looked to have some kind of injury because he was walking with a cane. He watched the man's eyes scan the two of them at the table. Trailing behind were some Asian bodyguards. One looked fairly normal and had a briefcase handcuffed to his wrist. The other had the stride of a man with no neck and only shoulders. He would be hard to beat up with a baseball bat, to say the least. David maneuvered a few steps away from Kayla and kept his back to the wall. Kayla started walking over to Christopher, and they hugged in the politest fashion.

The Flintstone bodyguard looked a bit old for this type of work and certainly wasn't going to win any foot races. Still, David deduced that Thorpe wouldn't hire someone who wasn't capable. The bodyguard had a face like a tomato can and was clearly a fighter, judging from the carved lines around his eyes, which held a tale of misery.

The odd one of the group was a plump fellow in a peacock costume with a thick, gold chain around his neck. David cooled his jets and reminded himself that it was just a friendly game of pool. He didn't need to be so defensive and could certainly work on his politeness.

Christopher was smiling from ear to ear from being next to Kayla.

"Hello, beautiful. How's my fiancée?" He went to give her a kiss as she delicately turned her head so he hit the side of her cheek. Most wouldn't notice, but David did and gave them some space. "Are you two enjoying yourselves?"

Kayla said, "You can have the next game. How's the ankle?"

Christopher said, "Oh, it's nothing, and no more games today. I'm beat up enough. Besides, your parents just agreed to fly out with us on Wednesday. Hello, there, I'm Christopher Thorpe." David shook the other man's outstretched hand and introduced himself.

"He's the contractor Mom and Dad hired for the house."

David felt Christopher's eyes examine him as they both let go of the fireman's grip. He rejected any softness in the man and appreciated his generosity in inviting him to such an event. He remarked, "You have a beautiful home, and the artwork is first class. Nothing short of spectacular."

Christopher said, "Thank you, and your work comes highly recommended, too. You'll have to give us a quote for some roof damage in the guesthouse. It's leaking a bit. You do roofs, don't you?" David told him he did and put the pool cue away against the rack on the wall.

David asked, "Did you do all of the designs for the place?"

"God, no. That would be entirely too much work. My only participation in the development is strictly through financial means. Hunting, working, and making the future Mrs. Thorpe as happy as possible are my only interests. Although, an extra bedroom or two might be needed in due time. How about you help us out when the time comes?"

David said, "No problem."

Christopher then looked directly at Kayla. David wasn't going to ask a follow-up question and got the hint that it was time to leave. "Wow. I didn't realize it was getting so late, and I have an early call tomorrow. If you don't all mind, I'll be running along."

Kayla said, "Are you forfeiting the game?"

Christopher insisted, "Go ahead and finish up, David. We want to get a drink first. What will you have, Kayla?" She declined, and Christopher looked at her in shock.

David pushed the eight ball into the pocket and said to Kayla, "It would take too long to finish two out of three. Another time."

"It was fun while it lasted," she responded. Her voice was soft, and David jumped to the conclusion that she didn't want him to leave. But as much as he wanted to stay, he was the third wheel. The best move was to leave. Christopher rummaged around behind the bar and seemed like he couldn't care less what the two of them were saying. He flicked a switch to turn on the lights for the display of a life-sized tiger in a glass case. David left the money on the ledge of the bar and saw the animal. He said, "How did you get it?"

Grabbing his drink, Christopher walked over to Kayla and grabbed her from behind, saying, "We hunted it. Hey! Where's your ring?"

David wanted to know, too. She had it on earlier.

Kayla said, "It's in my purse."

"Why aren't you wearing it?"

"We talked about this before. It doesn't fit. It's oversized." Then, she casually went over to her handbag to get it out. After slipping it on her finger, she held her hand facing to the ground. The ring slipped off of her finger. Then, she casually put it back into her purse while saying, "It'll be safe here until Monday when we go to the jeweler."

David saw Thorpe accept a temporary defeat. Kayla said, "Now, tell our guest about your tiger."

Christopher said, "My apologies." He saw David had picked up a book titled *Wild Kingdom* and was turning through the pages, pretending to be interested. The room was a bit silent, and Christopher said, "For a second there, I thought she was having buyer's remorse," and then filled the room with his laughter. David reciprocated with a fake chuckle and concluded that his chances of being hired to fix the roof were slim. Then, he put the book down and walked back over to the stuffed tiger.

David said, "It's magnificent."

Christopher looked at Kayla and said, "Of course it is, seven and a half carats. It's why I bought it. Only the best for Kayla."

David said, "Naturally, she deserves it, but I was referring to the tiger." Christopher turned toward David to give him his attention. David continued saying, "Then, you have to tell me about the solid wood panel door at the front entrance. One of a kind."

Christopher said, "Don't know where they bought it, but I know how much it cost." David waited for him to say the price, but it never came up. All he saw was a condescending attitude building up in the man's eyes. It killed any desire David had to keep the conversation going.

"It was killed in the winter. We set up a bunch of traps, but we were surrounded by too many trees. We baited the animal, and one of the hunters in our party got off a shot, but it didn't do any good. The beast turned on me, and the element of surprise was gone."

David scratched his jaw in politeness and said, "Sounds like a nasty piece of business. Were you hurt?" David glanced over at Kayla, who waited for Christopher to answer. David slowly began to realize that the tiger story was probably a fanatical charade that Christopher played out to guests. Either way, David was intrigued to find out who the man was behind the façade. Behind the story of the tiger, David saw Christopher as having had a life full of screw-ups, failures, and hidden disasters just like himself.

Christopher said, "Not even a scratch. It all happened so fast. The poor critter...looked like a pasta strainer when we were finished shooting. After the smoke cleared, the lesson was to never hunt alone." David looked closer and saw all the parts the taxidermist had to rebuild. He watched Christopher scrutinize him. David didn't need to be a fortune teller to figure out he was being a thorn in the guy's side. It was best not to aggravate the multi-billionaire NRA cardholder. Maybe that was the real purpose of the stuffed tiger. To serve as a warning for all inter-lopers. David looked at the men in the room to see that one was on the phone and the other two were watching Jerry Springer.

David couldn't resist and said, "What a horrible way to go."

Christopher scoffed. "One second, you're alive, and the next, dead. That's just life in the Boreal Forest," and snapped his fingers. David nodded in unmarred agreement and decided that he would have to look up this place called the Boreal. It couldn't be too far from his fate this morning.

It seemed people could either be fish food or tiger bait. The old-time security guard, a man who David had overheard Christopher call Han, with a sturdy walk, moved over to the bar. Christopher said, "Gives you an appreciation for being alive, doesn't it?"

Kayla said, "Come on now, Christopher. No need to scare David."

David laughed and said, "Scared?" Neither of them believed him. He continued, "Try getting dragged out to sea a quarter mile out without fins. Then, talk to me about a stuffed animal. If it was alive right now, Kayla would be telling me a different story about you."

Christopher loosened up and said, "You got that right." David saw Kayla was amused but didn't add anything. She was content to be in the peanut gallery.

David asked, "Was the tiger able to put up a fight?"

"It has four-inch curved meat hooks that can cut through steel. The teeth go through bone like they're crackers, and this particular tiger was a monster. It could drag a thousand-pound carcass across the state of Florida if it wanted to. So, yah, it put up a fight."

"Man, you got lucky. I plan on staying away from any tigers for the rest of my life."

"We're hunters, it's what we do, and it was a different time. When my father was still alive, the kill was inevitable." Kayla sat on a barstool. David walked behind the bar to get a closer look. Christopher said, "It was a long time ago. Let's not harp on it any further. Honey, we have to talk about the wedding, make plans."

Kayla said, "What's wrong, Christopher?"

He stared daggers at David and said, "Who is this guy?" David was holding something in his hands.

"This a Yinwyan? It looks like a Zimo Yinwyan right next to a bottle of Bacardi." David looked at the back and the bottom, then felt the weight. It had value and looked authentic. He saw an insignia on the bottom but couldn't make it out. Christopher took the statue from his hands.

"It wasn't next to a bottle of Bacardi—it's Dictator Rum from Columbia."

David said, "What's the difference?"

Christopher put the statue back and moved him gently away from behind the bar. David ran into Han, who was getting closer and looking at him with a blank face.

David said, "I'm amazed at what you've acquired. A Calder in the woods, a stuffed tiger, and now a Yinwyan. I have to hang out with you more often." Christopher chuckled and poured himself some rum. "I shouldn't mix tequila with rum, but just this once. We're friends with the distillery in Cartagena."

"What is it?" Kayla asked.

Christopher said, "The bottle doesn't even look close to Bacardi."

Looking back at the statue, David said, "Not sure about the rum, but the statue could be a famous Chinese artist from the 1930s. Started out with ink drawings, then worked his way to wooden objects while in exile on some remote Japanese island. No one knows what happened to him. A lot of his work is lost, and he was a hell of a painter. I only heard rumors of the sculptures." David couldn't authenticate the object, but he assumed that it had to be a fake if it was on a bar shelf. Kayla didn't look surprised, and David could tell she was probably used to phenomenal works of art. He had a sudden urge to go back behind the bar to give it another look, but the host had closed him off.

"Is it valuable?" she asked.

Christopher said, "Yinwyan? Hard to say for sure, but a collector might put it around a quarter mill."

David said, "You're fortunate to have such a piece."

"Everything isn't what you think it is," Christopher replied. "To be honest, it can't be very authentic because we picked it up at a bazar in Cairo about fifteen years ago for a thousand Egyptian pounds."

Kayla said, "Fifty dollars?"

David believed him and made him an offer to fix the roof for free in exchange for the statue. Christopher graciously declined. He said, "It sleeps next to the booze for sentimental value." David understood the attachment and took a few more seconds to record a mental picture for later. He had enough to replicate the model into something original, even if it was a fake.

Christopher wasn't having it and said, "This is nothing—let me show you something really special. Follow me," and he started walking out of the room. David gave in and let the meatball security guard hold the door as they were herded away. Christopher and Kayla walked out the door. David, Han, and Aaron were in tow. The guard with the briefcase was staying. All three took one last glance back at the statue sandwiched between the rum and Drambuie, but all with different intentions.

Kayla smiled. "Love the orchids," she said before giving Christopher a hug.

CHAPTER 12

FRIDAY
2115 HRS

CHRISTOPHER AND KAYLA walked arm-in-arm. He said loud enough for all to hear, "Playing bridge was Mother's way of socializing, as long as she won. But the greenhouse was her sanctuary. I was outlawed from the place, and as it turned out, she was years ahead of her time."

David asked, "How come?"

"Seems that plants aren't just for looks. Found out when I tried to sell the collection that some of them would be highly effective as natural cleansers. The appraisers recommendations ended up producing a tiny fortune for us."

David was dumbfounded at Christopher's ability to take plants and generate revenue. It made him want to grow a green thumb. David said, "Are you part of the marijuana craze?"

Christopher continued, "Not really our thing. Our current project is a chemical patent for a weed killer. Only problem is it's too toxic for the handlers. They should have it figured out pretty soon."

David said, "Sounds like a good business model." No one laughed.

Kayla said, "And dangerous?"

Christopher explained, "Very, but we're not going to sell any of it until we finish doing the proper test trials and soil samples at a secure facility. They only allow the fragrance division at this location."

David said, "So, were going to find out how Armani gets it done?"

Christopher said, "He's okay, just make sure you give me a good price for repairing my roof. I'm on a budget."

David started to like the guy. He said, "Ever get lost in this place?" Christopher and Kayla pushed on.

David continued, "You know they sell orchids at Home Depot?"

Kayla turned back and said, "So does Lowes."

David said, "You can get them for about fifteen bucks, I think. Super cheap."

Kayla said, "You buy a lot of flowers, David?"

Christopher laughed and said, "They bought about twenty-five thousand from us last month."

David almost didn't believe him for a split second. "Can we drop your name at the counter and get a discount?"

Christopher stood at the doorway and said, "Only in California. They give everything away." David hadn't been to the West Coast but had always wanted to go. Christopher and Kayla walked out the door. David, Han, and Aaron followed.

The hallway was peppered with pottery, and David stopped to admire one of the pieces. Han gazed on with him, and Aaron was busy texting.

Han said, "Ming Dynasty, fourteenth Century. One of the famous Dragon Jars."

David moved a few inches from the jar to get a closer look. He said, "You can see the details of the tree blossoming."

Han smiled and said, "Real artistry."

David said, "Don't play any basketball in this house."

Kayla and Christopher forged ahead arm-in-arm. They went through another door, and the sound of a large cat made David turn his head away from an Inca pot.

The door automatically opened to a balcony overlooking an outdoor courtyard. Aaron was the last to enter while still texting. David looked over the enclosure and then up to an opened dome. Christopher said, "Damn birds." A row of crows on a ledge kept watch as they squawked in a high pitch. David looked down to scan around, and his attention was pulled to a tiger sitting under the tree. It was staring back at them, and it seemed to be hyperventilating. He was stunned to be so close, and it didn't feel safe.

David asked Han in a hushed voice, "What's to stop it from climbing out?"

"An electrified fence and a cage door." Barbed wire scaled the top of the enclosure, and inside was a glass pool.

David asked Christopher, "What's wrong with it? And why has it not taken its eyes off of you?"

"Who knows? Tell her to get in line." He looked at Kayla and said, "Now, listen, Kay. We've been having some problems with getting Tatiana to a sanctuary."

Kayla grabbed at her necklace and said, "It's been a while since I've seen her. She's lost a lot of weight. What's wrong?"

David saw Christopher getting busted for something and watched him stumble around. He said, "It's not too bad. She looks fine. If there's anyone who needs to lose some weight, it's me," as he rubbed his belly.

It was a bluff of an answer, and Kayla said, "Tell me the truth."

"The truth? The truth is it's hard to find someone to adopt an Amur tiger. You need certain conditions to imitate her natural habitat. We're not going to just give her to anyone. She means too much." The crocodile tears must have worked, because Kayla didn't press the issue. It was as if she had forced herself to believe him. David peered down at the animal, and it was clearly in some kind of discomfort. He listened to Christopher go on about the cost of upkeep as if it was a status symbol, and David couldn't help but notice the scent of fresh manure from his speaking.

David appreciated Christopher's charisma and asked, "It doesn't look too friendly. Ever play string-on-a-stick with it?"

Christopher said, "Perhaps you can come back another day and give it a try."

Kayla said, "I wouldn't if I were you. She looks famished and needs something to eat." David didn't want it to suffer and regretted seeing the condition of the beast. What could he do? The rich had expensive tastes.

Christopher said, "Listen to me. We've been trying to find her a home. Two places canceled at the last minute." The more Christopher talked, the more David believed in his efforts. He could see how Kayla loved the man, even if he seemed off his rocker.

Kayla said, "It's not the point. It's the fact that you told me you had a home for her, and now, she's still here."

Christopher said, "Sanctuaries have the right to reject our specimens. I just didn't get a chance to tell you yet."

She said, "This is an abused circus animal that was passed from zoo to zoo. You know tigers have a long memory? And they don't forget."

Christopher said, "So they say. What does that have to do with me?" Kayla was silently staring away from him. Christopher said, "We're going to find her a home as soon as possible. I promise."

She said, "The sooner the better."

Christopher put his hands on her shoulders and said, "I know how much she means to you, after all the time you spent freeing her from captivity with your team. We'll find her a new home, even if we have to push back the wedding."

This promise seemed to take the edge off of Kayla. Aaron chimed in by saying, "We have a place picked out right now in Colorado. We're just waiting for the application to be approved."

Christopher kept his eyes locked onto Kayla. He said, "See. We're trying. It's all we can do."

Kayla said, "Why is she chained up?"

Christopher scoffed. "One of the handlers got stupid." She asked, "What happen?"

Christopher replied, "The trainer was merely scratched, and the mistake he made was turning his back to her in the cage."

Alarm bells started ringing for David when Aaron said, "The guy only took 127 stitches." Kayla moved away from Christopher's touch.

Christopher said, "The kid's exaggerating. It was a few staples, and they didn't even use stitches. Hey, Aaron, don't you have something else to do?" Aaron uttered a "yes, sir" and made a hasty exit.

Kayla again remarked how thin Tatiana looked, as David saw some ribs showing with each breath. Christopher continued, "We're doing some medical tests right now for a liver sample before shipping. So, the feeding schedule has been restricted. She'll start eating again tomorrow. It's supposed to produce more accurate results."

David laughed, and Christopher asked him what was so funny.

"I could work as a crossing guard and figure this one out," David replied.

"What do you mean?"

"It's an old philosophy called 'To feed a tiger is logical. To starve one, risky'."

Christopher said, "Kayla, we've been told these liver tests could save the world from possible extinction and prevent diseases from spreading. It's an entirely new way to develop antibodies." David watched him and didn't see the logic, or even understand what he was saying. Christopher pulled Kayla over to have a private conversation.

David turned to Han and said, "What's it like to be on the forefront of modern medicine?" Han didn't say a word. He continued by saying, "Money sure does buy you a lot of intelligence."

Han said, "Carnivores have to eat. If you don't feed it, then it will find food by any means possible."

David said, "Keep it simple, it's what I've always been told." David peeked over his shoulder as Kayla and Christopher argued in a controlled murmur.

Christopher said, "Can we talk about it later, and I promise to give it my full attention?" Kayla relaxed a bit, and David knew that she would be the one to take action when the time was right. He feared the worst for the helpless animal. Christopher opened his arms for everyone to keep moving along.

Tatiana started roaring louder as they walked away, then fell silent. It sounded more like a cry for help to David then an expression of dominance. The sound tore at his insides. Christopher was leading Kayla away when David took one more look at the enclosure before the door closed. Just above the pen on the opposite side of the courtyard was another balcony. He pictured the approximate location by the last of the sun's rays and took a bearing in order to reach the veranda.

In the elevator, Christopher said, "The greenhouse area was expanded from the original foundation by two thousand square feet to accommodate our mini laboratory." They went three levels below the surface. After the doors opened, a fluorescent, hydroponic light bounced off his face as darkness loomed in the corners. The air was filled with wet soil and wood chips.

Lab technicians were milling about. A ballet of earthy scents danced off the nose. Christopher pressed his thumb into the soil of a potted plant.

David asked, "How far down are we?"

Christopher replied, "About a hundred feet. Why?"

"You must have hit water building this place under ground."

"We did." Christopher didn't want to talk about the building and David noticed he was measuring his words carefully.

Christopher swirled his hands in the air and belted out, "Nessum Dorma, Nessum Dormaaa!" He stopped and closed his eyes to listen. He then said, "It's amazing how well plants react to music. We designed this area to mimic the Palmenhaus Schönbrunn."

David didn't have a clue what that meant when Kayla said, "It's in Vienna."

David said, "Of course it is. Where else would it be?" He noticed an echo and then yelled, "Marco!" The word rang back, and he followed it up by saying, "Polo!"

Christopher frowned at his childish behavior, then pointed to the corner. "Over there is an olive tree. It's over a hundred years old."

They passed a fountain, and Kayla warned David to not to touch anything. He picked up a fallen petal, and she said, "Careful."

David asked, "Is it poisonous?"

Christopher moved David to the side and grabbed the petal from him. "This is a Purple Lady Slipper."

David said, "It looks thirsty to me. Are you testing this plant for resistance purposes?" Christopher told him to not be ridiculous. David put his finger in the soil and said, "It does feel a bit dry." Christopher touched the soil and quickly snapped his fingers.

A technician came over immediately.

"Isn't this supposed to be covered by glass?"

The assistant pulled out a glass cover from below and said, "We were just getting ready to get some samples." Then, he sealed off the orchid. Christopher lifted it back up and gave it a few spritzes with a spray bottle.

When Christopher turned towards everyone staring at him, David said, "Will it live?" Christopher got the joke and laughed heartily. Then, he apologized.

"It's an incurable hobby passed down in my DNA."

David said, "I know how you feel. My dad liked working on cars. So, now, I like to drive fast."

Christopher said, "We don't want to be rude, but it's time to go. We have guests to meet." Kayla's back straightened up a bit.

"Not much of a tour, but I have a show to catch," David said.

"What show?" Kayla asked.

"Mario's on Federal. Killer band if you like some funky beats and spicy wings."

He saw her interest, and Christopher said, "Another time, perhaps? Thanks for stopping by."

David replied, "Congratulations to you both," and left with Han to see him out for a more normal version of reality.

CHAPTER 13

DAVID AND HAN took their time walking back to the party. Both of them slowed down at a painting displayed in a hallway grotto. Silently, they inspected the composition. It fit perfectly in the setting, but David couldn't place the artist. He could picture the face, and the name was on the tip of his tongue. He waited patiently for the words to work their way to his voice. Han was content in his own world.

"May I take a picture?" Han approved. "Who is this? I forgot. I think it's Jasper Johns?"

Han said, "Keith Haring."

David recognized the name but not a connection to this work and said, "It doesn't look like his style."

Han gave him a double take and said, "Johns was famous for the target shapes and flags. This one has too much color."

David said, "Too much color? I think you got the wrong guy. No offense."

Han pointed to a plaque next to the painting with the artist's name engraved on it. David said, "I was close. How many times do you walk by this painting a day?"

"A few thousand."

"I stand corrected. Where did you learn about art?"

"Hong Kong."

David couldn't resist asking more. "I hope you're not insulted, but you look Korean?"

"I am by birth, and I went to the Royal Academy for schooling. My father got transferred to the Beijing finance ministry and became a collector along the way." David felt a heaviness come upon the man as he remembered the past, even though his face seemed naturally expressionless. Regardless, the man seemed shy for having no neck.

David asked, "This guy, Christopher, has a Calder in the woods, a Yinwyan on a bar shelf, and a Haring in a nook. Does any of that seem strange to you?"

Han paused and said, "No. Why should it? Art is to be enjoyed for those who can afford it."

David pressed on to say, "Yeah, but does he appreciate the value?"

"Who cares? His money."

David said, "I guess so, I'd probably do the same thing," and dropped the subject.

Han said, "No one ever stops at this painting. To Christopher, it's a business expense, a tax write-off, or an investment. His specialty is seeing value when no one else does, and he has a good eye for the unusual."

"And a talent for making a lot of money."

"The Thorpes have been around a long time. They can afford to make mistakes."

David listened while getting closer to the brush strokes.

"Most don't want to know how they earned it, just how they'll spend it."

He nodded in agreement and felt comfortable around the man who looked as if he could crack open a coconut with his bare hands.

David said, "I guess you're right." They both checked the time and started to walk away. Inconsequential pieces decorated the stroll back to the event with everyone mulling about to the music. They moved silently closer to the noisy crowd, and David avoided discussing any more subjects. He found Christopher intriguing, the home okay, and based on the magnitude of wealth, it helped explain why the rich man wouldn't feed a tiger.

Han broke the silence by saying, "Something always happens when the whole is more than the sum of its parts." David was amused by the fortune cookie talk.

"Is that Confucius?" David asked.

Han didn't answer and stared silently at the top of the stairs while they overlooked the guests. David asked, "Who said it?"

Han replied, "Aristotle."

David pretended like he understood but said, "I don't get it." Han let the statement stand for itself. After looking out over the crowd, David said, "It's times like these that make me hungry. I think I'll go now and contemplate your words of wisdom on the buffet line. Good talking with you."

They shook hands, and David left Han at the top of the stairs as he glided down the steps. Even though he was critical of the mansion at first glance, it had some charm, and maybe his first impression had been off. He took out a notebook and made a fast sketch of the chandelier. He decided that he liked Christopher and let go of any misgivings he may have had. Keith Haring, he needed to remember the name. Then, the Yinwyan popped into his brain. Something about the wooden statue made him forget the painting. He doodled the shape as best he could from memory and stood patiently in line as guests picked at what they wanted. By the time it was his turn to grab a plate, an image of the Yinwyan was on the page. It was time to get some grubstake and go see OP at the bar.

David's mouth watered at the smorgasbord. He looked downrange and saw the mashed spuds, barbeque ribs, and rotisserie chicken. Layered in between was street corn on a spigot, coleslaw, and a carving station. It was an immediate assult past the salad option, and he dove for the bowl full of super colossal shrimp. The trimmings surrounding the crustacean crypt had a dipping bay of cocktail sauce. He looked around to see if anyone was paying attention and tried a sample. It wasn't polite behavior, but he took the risk and complimented the man in the chef's hat with a chewing nod and got a smile in return. David moved along after stacking the sliced naan. He was at the carving station when his conscious hit him with a rabbit punch. He remembered Tatiana and thought the worst.

The last bite of food was hard to finish. David spit it out in a napkin and rolled it up into a ball. The starving animal gnawed at his mind. He looked around at the decadence as thoughts raced about how to feed the hunter. Youthful choices came without regard for consequences, and he justified his thought process while moving forward. A plan had been formed, and it was raw but required less than a teaspoon of courage. David scanned the room to see a server walk away with an empty tray. He followed her into the kitchen.

Inside was a twenty-foot-long counter top and looked to be over four inches thick. It served as a workstation for the help. Three copper range hoods popped against the marble-clad backsplash as it spread over the entire wall. He soaked up the layout like a kid in a candy store. This guy, Christopher, knew how to spend a dime. Two sub-zero refrigerators with reflective panels stood to the side of a drop-ceiling. No one would ever notice the detail, not even a five-star Michelin chef. He passed on the Kobe sliders being prepared under his nose. Some of the staff were staring at him, wanting to talk, but no one said anything because they were on strict orders not to engage in any conversations with the guests. They were also to keep a six-foot distance from everyone unless asked a question.

David sat back in one of the chairs and watched the staff in action. He looked to the left and saw another kitchen just beyond the main one and got up to investigate. This one was the pastry room with breads cooling, homemade pasta hanging, and cookies ready for service. Towards the back was another large walk-in cooler, and he looked inside the window. There, hanging on hooks, were enough slabs of meat to ride out a winter.

Upon entering the cooler, a wave of fresh herbs and garlic assaulted his nose. Neatly stacked on each shelf were containers of precut steaks, tenderloins, chops, and whole chickens. Hanging off to the side was half a cow cut into sections of chuck, brisket, shank, and sirloin. David took one slab off the hook and went out to the back kitchen. He grabbed a fifty-gallon trash bag and a small carving knife. After wrapping up the meat, he slung it over his shoulder to exit the kitchen and work his way through the crowd. He avoided Han talking with another guard. They were having a private conversation, so it was easy to go undetected. He bumped into a woman, and her wine almost spilled. She gave him the proverbial "excuse me," and David apologized. The two he couldn't avoid were Sam and Julia, smack dab in front of him.

"Are you working?" she asked.

"Yes, ma'am. I have to take this outside. It's what happens when you can't pay the bill." They both looked confused.

Sam said, "Are you all right?"

David nodded. "Wonderful. Couldn't be better," and Julia asked about Kayla as David looked around. "No, I haven't seen her. I think she's with Christopher someplace. Hey, I'm going to be leaving soon. Thanks for the invite, great party, I'll see you two on Monday."

Julia said, "No problem," but he had already left the conversation.

She looked at Sam, and he said, "Glad he could make it."

With each step, David was entering uncharted territory. He didn't think it was foolish to feed a tiger under the given circumstances. He avoided second-guessing himself and pushed any negative thoughts out of his mind. If he didn't feed the thing, then who would? Christopher and Kayla would have to understand. The thought of dumping the bag in the corner and leaving crossed his mind, but yet again, a sense of determination pressed him forward. He wasn't going to back down from the personal challenge, and he disregarded any further mental interruptions. It was on.

The guards were absent from the stairway. David skipped up and down the hall. Sam and Julia watched and were confused as to where he was going. Another song started, but they didn't go back on the dance floor. Instead, Sam gently took Julia's elbow and pulled her to the exit.

With each step down the long, dark hallway, David got more excited. The carpet gave him a cloak of silence. The thought of asking for forgiveness rather than permission made him smile. If he got caught, then there would be some explaining to do, but nothing was going to stop his instincts that were driving him to feed the poor thing. He looked out the window and knew that he was close upon seeing the barbed wire mesh on top of the fence posts. The door in front of him could lead to the tiger's den, and he deducted that the balcony must have been on the other side of this room. He looked down the hall to see if anyone was following. The coast was clear. He tried the handle, but it was locked. Then, he put down the bag of meat.

Inside the room, Aaron was taking pictures of the Yinwyan with his phone when he heard the door handle jiggle. Next came a pounding noise as the bag hit the floor. Aaron didn't know what to think as he froze inside Christopher's office with the door locked. David rapped a few knocks around the frame. Aaron thought someone wanted to enter but couldn't. If he could silently unlock it, then he would say it was always open and blame it on the age of the door. He waited a second longer to see if someone had a key. No one entered. On the other side of the door, David put his ear to the door to have a better listen. Aaron was about to release the latch as David tried the handle again.

A split-second later, David used Kayla's hockey move and snapped down on the handle while pressing his 220-pound body into the center panel with his shoulder leading the charge.

The lock was released, and a solid oak door slammed into Aaron's forehead. He was launched into the air as if it was an uppercut from Mike Tyson. His lights were out before he hit the carpet. David stood in shock as the peacock landed like a sack of potatoes. He only heard music in the distance as Aaron's body lay still. He checked for a pulse. Luckily, the kid was alive, and David cursed the first casualty.

After getting the plastic bag, David closed the door and surveyed the room. He saw the Yinwyan on the floor with a small piece broken off. Aaron must have had it in his hand when he fell over. David didn't want to touch it, but he couldn't resist. The pattern, the grooves, and the shape seared into his memory. The mental snapshot was for later. Then, he pulled out his drawing to make some changes. The broken-off part fit together perfectly, and then, he heard the roar. To the left was an open parlor with double French doors. He picked up Aaron and put him on the couch, then elevated his feet. Lastly, he tucked the Yinwyan on his side between the cushions. As he picked up the slab of meat, he saw a small skateboard figurine sitting on the floor. It was a keychain, and he put it in his pocket. The roar increased as he went into the courtyard. The bottom of the threshold hadn't been cleaned in a while and was filled with leaves.

The balcony was forsaken, to be left alone, like a man's fiancée, but he was already there, and the Atlantic winds were gusting through the palms. It wasn't just another balmy summer night. David combed his hair off to the side with his hand. He was safe, high above the tiger's reach, but doubt still touched his thoughts. The place looked like a vacant ravine with a smell of wounded pride emanating from below. He whistled like he was hailing a cab, then pulled out the carving knife from the kitchen to shave off a piece of raw meat. He tossed it like a hand grenade into the middle of the pen.

Tatiana came out of the shadows, and he saw her disdain for domestication. Each paw moved with precision in a line of bitterness as she sniffed out what had landed. She looked up at him and then licked the snack. A second later, it was gone. He cut out another and tossed it below. The nocturnal hunter instantly snatched it in the air. He'd seen enough and picked up the carcass to swing it over the ledge. It broke some branches, then got stuck in the tree.

Tatiana laid down in a strike position, set her focus, then leaped into flight as if a chef were flipping an omelet. The razor-sharp talons hooked the mass of beef and tossed it to the ground. She descended back in silence and voiced her approval to the stranger. A split second later, her canines dug into the hide and lifted it with ease to drag it back to a more secluded location. It looked to be as light as a tennis ball in her mouth. David heard another roar. He hoped it was one of appreciation as he went back inside. A good deed was done for the day, and he felt that it was payback for surviving the knock-on death's door that morning. Back in the office, Aaron was still unconscious on the couch. David took a moment to watch his chest go up and down, then disappeared. He informed one of the guards on his way out that a man had fainted upstairs and disappeared.

CHAPTER 14

ABOUT TEN MINUTES later, Aaron woke up with two of Thorpe's security guards looking down at him. One was eating an apple.

"What the hell happened to you?"

Aaron couldn't say anything. He had no idea where he was or the time of day. The only thing he did know was that his head was throbbing as he touched a goose egg.

The second guard said, "It's an improvement." Aaron started to get up but fell back down as his hand touched the Yinwyan in the cushions.

The first guard said, "You don't look so good."

Aaron was speechless. The second guard said, "Thorpe is asking for the skateboard. They have a meeting in thirty minutes. Hand it over?"

"It's on the desk. Tell him that I'll be right there."

"It's not on the desk, we looked."

Aaron said, "It's not on the desk?"

"Just bring it down after you clean up." And they were gone.

Aaron pushed himself up from the couch, and in his hand were two pieces of the Yinwyan statue. He grabbed his backpack and stuffed it inside. Then, he went to the mirror and inspected the knot on his forehead. It was the size of a Roma tomato. He reached inside his jacket pocket for the skateboard, but it was empty. He checked all his pockets and found squadouche, except for two chocolate chip cookies wrapped in a napkin. A frantic search around the room produced nothing. A panic attack set in and took control of his vitals. He knew this kind of stress was going to give him a rash.

DAVID PULLED INTO the valet at Mario's Supper Club. He had the skateboard in his hand and was rolling it around on the dashboard. He left it in the console and got out. A crowd was waiting to be let in, and Mitch the bouncer was at the door. Normally, this restaurant was one where anyone could get a table, but not tonight. This evening, they had a guest list for a band called the Snow Bums. They were a funky, electronic group who specialized in a new age music, a local favorite. Mitch had the unfortunate job of holding back the crowd due to the size of the establishment. David got along with him but knew the man had an unpleasant demeanor if necessary. Life was fun and games until the person you mess with plays by a different set of rules. He patiently sat back and waited his turn to get past the ropes.

The guests were in a football huddle surrounding the entrance, which wasn't too far from the street. Some were smoking cigarettes while others stood back like birds on a wire. Mitch was looking at a fake ID of one Candy Hartung. She was as cute as a button, living faster than her age. The name on her driver's license made him smile. He walked away from her and opened the rope for David.

She said, "Excuse me?" She put her hand on her hip as David slipped past, and the two shook hands.

Mitch said, "OP is already inside."

Mitch turned his attention back to Candy and read her name off the driver's license. "Okay, Dolores. What year were you born?"

Candy said, "1967." Candy had found the ID on the floor at the cafeteria. It had been working well until now.

He ignored her answer and gave her the ID back.

"You just let him in because he probably owns a fancy car," said Candy.

"Yes, I did. It's a really nice pick-up truck with tools in the back."

She said, "Then why let him in?"

Mitch said, "He helped build the place. So, if I don't let him in, I'd probably lose my job. What's your real name?"

"Candy."

"Candy?! Not Dolores?"

"It's a nickname."

"Well, Candy, do you prefer the hard stuff like Jolly Ranchers or the soft and chewy?"

"Both."

He gave her a poker face and said, "Well, I don't eat sweets, bad for your teeth." And held up his wedding ring finger.

Mitch opened the rope and let Candy and her friend enter. They strutted their miniskirts past Mitch, and he told them to have a good time.

"Sorry, folks. We are at capacity. It will be a few minutes longer." Lounging in the back of the group was Han.

Inside, the bandleader was playing on the keyboard. They had a drummer, bass player, and percussionist. Snifters of Hennessy were sitting on speakers and the side tables. The room had a good vibe with a throng of barflies. The dining room was packed as the staff moved methodically within a tight space. David saw OP watching the small television screen in the corner with a seat saved for him. The newscaster was reporting a search under way for the driver of a beached racing boat. They showed a blurry picture of a man walking across the sand, shooting a gun, and getting into a white SUV.

OP asked David, "Didn't that happen by you today?"

OP asked David, "Didn't that happen by you today?"

"Sure was."

"Did you see anything?"

David replied, "It's what the cops asked."

OP had a follow up question, "How are they going to find this guy?" The bartender, Lisa, came up and talked to them out of the corner of her mouth.

"You two again. Why don't you guys get married? Live a little."

David said, "You know that they're going to bring back smoking into these places? New law just got passed. I can't wait."

OP said, "Yah. I heard that, too, and it includes cigars."

She said, "You're such a liar."

"No, seriously," said David. "It will be less stressful for you, and everyone will be happier. You got nothing to worry about, except lung cancer, but you'll look cool. Cranberry soda, please?" OP motioned for another cocktail.

"Hey," OP said, and Lisa looked at him "Can you stop using your hands to scoop the ice into my drink? I don't want to get Ebola." She left them alone after mocking their laughter.

The music made David turn his head to watch.

"Don't get upset," OP said, "but we didn't install the floor today. The inspector came by and shut it down. Didn't want to call you with the bad news while you were enjoying yourself with tiddlywinks."

David said, "When do you think we can get the electrical in the floor?"

"As soon as you hire an electrician and get the right clips with tie downs. It all has to match up...are you okay?"

David was staring at him with a blank look on his face. He was motionless and said, "Remember in high school when the cops were chasing us, and I launched the Firebird into the gymnasium?"

"My favorite car. How can I forget it?"

David continued, "I might have done something similar tonight, so prepare yourself."

Lisa delivered the drinks and said, "I used my feet this time."

OP finished his drink and passed the glass. He said, "As long as it's the same price, it doesn't matter." She made a face and left.

OP turned to David and asked, "What happened?"

David searched for a starting point. "It's her fiancé, Thorpe. He had an event tonight."

"You told me. Only you would meet a woman as she's going down the aisle."

"She's not married, yet."

OP made a hissing sound and said, "Go ahead. Tell me what happened."

"I'm trying to, but you keep interrupting like you know what I'm going to say."

OP gave him the look and said, "I'll keep quiet."

"This is screwy because she was giving me clues, but it didn't add up to what was happening."

OP kept listening, and David paused as if to say something when OP said, "Is this going to be in English, or do you need a whiteboard?"

And then, David spilled the beans about Thorpe's party. A few drinks later, the front door opened innocuously as Han and two other security guards entered. They scanned the crowd and found David. Slowly, they moved in, undetected, from three different angles.

"Wait a second," OP said. "Did someone actually laugh at your jokes?"

"I don't know for sure, but I did get a smirk from her. Which is as good as a laugh, so it counts."

"Why didn't you win the pool game?"

David shook his head and said, "I should have."

OP took a sip of his drink and said, "It's because you were thinking about the blue dress."

"I wasn't the only one. The heads were turning, and she made me feel like I wasn't intruding."

"Sounds like you didn't need a pool stick for that game."

"Slow down, Nietzsche." David continued. "What the hell was I supposed to do?"

"She's a heater, Dave. Nothing to do, and after hearing your story, I'm going to ask Juanita to dress up in a tiger suit next Halloween."

David didn't laugh at OP's joke and said, "Hope the guy I hit in the head with the door is all right."

OP agreed and said, "You'll know when the police show up at your place. Unless the guy wants to walk around the rest of his life with a speech impediment. You should never mess with a franchised player. How rich is this guy?"

"He's nothing. The most he could buy is a couple NFL football teams and an island in Hawaii."

"No shit," OP said. "Not good news for you."

"What do you mean?"

OP paused and looked at his drink. It was hard for David to imagine the magnitude of such wealth. OP said, "This guy could bury you in more ways than you can imagine. Do you think he'll try to hurt you?"

"For feeding a tiger? Come on."

"You're an idiot. He doesn't care about the animal. He's jealous because you're hitting on his woman. You were checking her out while playing pool, weren't you? The guy probably recorded the whole thing. They're engaged. Men kill for less."

David thought for a second; it was something to consider as a possibility.

David said, "I was polite."

OP tossed a napkin in the garbage about ten feet away and said, "You made out with her, didn't you?"

"No."

"I don't care if you did. Can't stop Fate."

"What do you think he'll do?"

"Are you sure you never kissed her?" OP asked, then smiled.

"I'd remember if we did."

OP shrugged and said, *"Whatever."*

"Nothing happened," David mumbled. OP believed him but enjoyed busting his chops more than anything else. Someone tapped David on the shoulder. It was Han.

"Hello, David."

"Hey, Han. What are you doing here?"

"Sorry to bother you, but Thorpe wants the Yinwyan back." David said he didn't have it. The other two guards came in from opposite directions. OP stood up with his back to the bar, and he was the smallest of the group. David remained seated and swiveled his stool around. Han said, "And the flash drive."

Han introduced himself to OP, who replied, succinctly, "OP."

One of the guards started talking in Mandarin, and all OP heard was, "Opie Taylor. Xiang *Andy Griffith Show?*"

"No," OP said. "Not the TV show." He leaned into the guard and tilted his head to looked up at him.

The guard said, "Then, shut up and let them talk." His English accent was horrible. Han got in between them and told his man to relax. David knew that the wheels were ready to come off. OP had a fuse shorter than a chewed-up fingernail, and he was drinking the hard stuff tonight, so his tank was ready to blow. The only thing for David to do was gently get out of the way.

"Let me give you some advice," David said. The guard smiled and mumbled in Chinese.

He pointed his finger at him saying, "You're going about this all the wrong way."

Han put his hand on the guard's arm saying, "We're not here to make things worse."

"Han," David said, "I don't know anything about a flash drive or the Yinwyan."

Han said, "The statue is very important, and the flash drive looks like a skateboard. Mr. Thorpe doesn't care that you fed his cat."

OP and the two guards squared off. David whispered to Han, "As big as this guy thinks he is, it's best to leave my boy alone."

The guard said in Chinese, "No problems. He's my favorite monkey on *The Andy Griffith Show*," and then proceeded to pat OP on the top of his head. The invasion of his personal space sent electricity pulsing through OP's body. A waiter carrying a tray of dirty dishes lost his grip, and the plates crashed loudly on the Spanish tile. OP's right fist collapsed in perfect order. His engines were already revving at a high RPM. There was no struggle or camouflaging of his anger. Mechanically, his right foot took a slight step back until his hips were clear for a power rotation.

A split second later, his left foot went forward like it was one of the last steps of a long flight of stairs. His weight transferred from his toes, to his legs, and through his hips. His torso rotated with perfection through his limbs as the overhand, right knuckle sandwich connected to a closed jaw. Contact! Bing! The guard was struck like an axe splitting wood. The music stopped as the room gazed at them. Han looked at the man embedded into the dry wall. The guard didn't move an inch.

David watched Han look calmly unfazed by the violence. It seemed as if he could go brush his teeth afterwards and was taking his time to think about what to do next. Han put his head down and shook off the disappointment. The other guard stood back and waited for orders. It was hard for David to read what was going to happen next. The lead vocalist on stage said in an Essex accent, "Chill out, people. What are we fighting for?" No one answered his question.

Han said to OP, "That wasn't very nice."

David stepped in front of Han and said, "We don't call him OP because of *The Andy Griffith Show*. OP is an acronym for One Punch. Your boy was patting him on the head, and that was disrespectful. He should've kept his hands to himself."

Han looked over David's shoulder at OP and said, "A name well-deserved." Mitch came in and stood in the middle of the action as everyone appeared calm. He asked David to explain while Han and the other guard picked up the limp body of their comrade to drag him out of the restaurant. The music started up again.

"You guys better leave out the back," Mitch said.

They were given keys to both vehicles by the valet and took off. While driving, David picked up the skateboard. He pulled it apart with his fingers and found the flash drive. The slow version of *That's Life* played on the radio. He was driving with his hands on the wheel, lost in the lights of the night. Streetlamps passed, reflecting off the hood of his truck, and he let the song take over his thoughts. It felt as if the day was never going to end. He would drive back tomorrow to Thorpe's and return what was taken.

CHAPTER 15

DAVID PULLED UP to a warehouse in an industrial district. He liked the run-down look of the building, which was surrounded by a residential community near the freeway. Florida was too flat, and the place because it reminded him of certain parts of Cleveland where he grew up. The door opened to bells ringing in the distance. A train was coming, and the sound of 150-ton boxcars were pounding down the iron railways. It was the Union Pacific line, running late, and it let him know there was work to be done in the studio. No way was he getting any sleep tonight, not for the next couple hours, anyways. Too much had happened, and now, he had a skateboard that was doing its own set of mental tricks.

Tackle and Charlie gave him a full welcome at the door. He had just walked them before going to the party, but they made it seem it was if he'd been gone for weeks. He instantly forgot about everything that had happened. After the hugs and hellos, he took them both outside to take care of business.

Fifteen minutes later, he was in the kitchen grinding up some fresh coffee. He didn't mind the caffeine buzz this late and wanted the extra energy while the image of the Yinwyan was still fresh. He took out a blank sheet of paper and re-sketched his drawing from the notebook. As the pot was brewing, he immersed himself into adding sufficient shading and texture. By the time the brew stopped, he had what he wanted. Tackle smashed into his legs, causing some drops to hit the floor. Charlie investigated the cleanup. David looked around and knew that a dumpster being delivered couldn't happen fast enough. The place was a pigsty, and it was time to clean house. No more living with the clutter, and he made a promise to clean things up.

The disorder started after his mother's passing, or at least that was what Van der Slootzin pointed out. The grieving forced him to not let go, but after this morning, he was ready to move on and get organized. His father had been absent, a gambler, and a heavy drinker. It was his mom who listened, understood him, and worked two jobs to keep the family together. It didn't matter how they grew up; they always had something to eat.

David hit the power button on the sound system. The jukebox list punched up on the monitor, and he pressed the "random" selection. The mood was getting set as he looked at the blocks of wood in neatly stacked piles of plastic containers. The shape of the Yinwyan would have fit any number of the raw oak or black walnut pieces. He wanted something softer, so he picked out a piece of butternut. After some inspection, he determined that the darker tones and grains would pop after polishing. Charlie and Tackle sat in the corner watching with bored interest. He put on a pair of clear protection goggles and made a few cuts on the band saw.

Getting the shape was easy, and the work was fast. The caffeine kicked in, and David had what he wanted in no time. The hand chisels were next, then things slowed down dramatically. He preferred this part of the process. He wanted to get a sense of what the lost master was thinking, and he fell into a meditative state. The shapes were to his liking, as he whittled away with no care for perfection. This model was just the first one, and it could take five or six renditions to get the desired look. The chips piled up at his feet, and an hour vanished without him realizing it. He looked over at the dogs, and they had lifted their heads in caution. They started barking and running out of the room. David turned off the music.

The front door sounded like it was getting broken down, and outside, a police cruiser was parked with the engine running. David cracked open a window latch at eye level to see who was making all of the noise. The door was made of reinforced steel and metal strapping. It was one of the first things that he repaired after purchasing the building. He saw Baby Glenn and Marci, both in uniform.

David unlocked the door. He looked past them both and said, "Is the coast clear?"

"What? Why?" Baby Glenn paused and said, "Is everything all right?"

David didn't answer and stepped outside to look around. Tackle and Charlie attacked them for hugs and kisses. Marci picked up Charlie, and Tackle went to Baby Glenn. They took a moment, and David said, "What's going on?"

Baby Glenn said, "We just stopped by to show you some pictures. See if you recognized the face of the man who was driving the boat this morning." David waited for Baby Glenn to pull out some pictures from an envelope. He leafed through them and stopped at one in particular.

David said, "It's hard to say with the hat and sunglasses on, but it could be him."

Baby Glenn said, "Are you sure with all those bullets flying?"

"This one looks the closest, but I can't say for sure. I was in the water."

Marci said, "He's the only one we don't have a positive ID on, but we'll keep trying."

Baby Glenn asked, "Is this a bad time?"

David looked at them both and said "No, I'm just doing some work in the studio."

Baby Glenn turned to Marci and said, "Explains why we got the answering machine. We left you a few messages, and you had us worried for a bit."

"How come?" David asked.

"Things have escalated."

Baby Glenn continued, "They found the white SUV the guy took off in under the bridge. Had four dead bodies, all drug cartel henchmen. Thought we'd stop by and warn you to keep things locked up for the next couple days until we get a better handle on the situation. It's better to be safe than sorry."

David appreciated the heads-up and asked if they wanted some coffee. "Just made a fresh pot." He saw Marci and Baby Glenn look over his shoulder at the inside of the house.

She said, "I need some sleep. We're just checking in to let you know. Another time."

Baby Glenn said, "Roger that. I'll run some more searches for this character in the morning and keep you posted. Stay safe." They shook hands and left.

David didn't know what to think yet and watched them drive off. He whispered, "Thanks for stopping by. Now, I can sleep with my eyes open."

WHILE DRIVING AWAY, Marci and Baby Glenn didn't see Kayla sliding down in the car seat to avoid detection. She checked her gun to make sure it was loaded, then put it away in her purse. She didn't know what to make of David or why the police were at his door. It would be a fast conversation to get some answers for Christopher, and maybe save her parents' contractor along the way. Christopher never bugged out, but tonight, he did. He almost looked relieved when she said she'd go and talk to

David. He didn't get protective or all macho about the idea, even though she had expected some pushback. There was a lot she didn't understand about David, and he didn't seem like the type of person that Christopher would ever be connected to. The file on him stated that he was a contractor, had never served, and had gone to a small community college outside of Cleveland. He played football, was arrested for disturbing the peace, and had a 780-credit score. So, why did he live in a commercial building? The best part of working through all this information was that the headaches hadn't returned, and it was remarkable. She got out of the car and walked to the front door as it started to rain.

The knock didn't produce much of a sound. It was too sturdy. Kayla kicked it with her foot. David opened the latch and looked surprised to see her.

"You've had a busy night," she said.

David replied, "What are you doing here?"

Kayla pulled out a hundred-dollar bill and put it through the crevice. "Felt bad for taking your money."

David grabbed the C-note and said, "Who's with you?" Before she could answer, he opened the door as it started to downpour. He was glad that she was alone and instantly felt embarrassed because she'd see how he lived. He blocked her from entering.

Kayla said, "Aren't you going to let me in?"

David said, "Enter at your own risk, I'm in a transitional phase." He couldn't fight the shame of it anymore and was glad to get it out in the open.

He moved to the side. Kayla stopped in the hallway after seeing all the stuff piled up around the place. He closed the door. "Somehow, I get the feeling that you didn't come all the way here just for this." He walked past her while rubbing the Franklin between his fingers. "But I appreciate the gesture. It's good to see you again." She saw all of the stuff laying around and stood up straighter while following him into the kitchen.

"No, I didn't, but Christopher asked me to."

"Does he still think that I took his statue?"

"Ya, but I told him you're not the type. Oh, my gosh! Your dogs are so cute. What are their names?"

"He's Charlie, and the troublemaker is Tackle." Kayla smiled, and both canines wagged their tails.

"They look ferocious." Charlie had completely flipped over and closed his eyes. Tackle was asking for the same amount of pampering.

"Come on, you two, show some respect." Both went to a sitting position, and she petted them on the head. He asked if she wanted any coffee. She said yes, and they went into the kitchen.

The floor was done in black-and-white tile that needed to be cleaned. David took out some paper towels to wipe off a coffee mug. He said, "It's a bit rustic in here." She stayed in the center away from the table and benches. One chair had a stack of newspapers piled halfway up to the ceiling. Garbage bags full of clothes were in the corner, and a mattress was propped up against the wall. The room had a warm quality, reminiscent of the 1800s. David watched her touch the Rumford-designed pots and pans hanging from the ceiling on a metal bracket.

"Those were my mom's. She collected the stuff."

Kayla said, "I heard she passed."

"It's been over a year now."

"My condolences."

David expressed thanks as Kayla checked out the Elmira antique gas stove. Its legs made it look like it could walk, and it was positioned against a brick wall.

David said, "It's old, but it works." He gave Tackle some pats on the head and saw her approval of Charlie. He knew that if she didn't like these two, then there was no sense in making room for her, but she did. He started clearing out the junk around the table, and a chair soon became available. Then, he forced himself to stop. Kayla didn't seem to be too interested in sitting down at the moment. Instead, she was inspecting the glass door refrigerators. It surprised him when she asked, "Why do you have a futon in your kitchen?"

"Good question, and I have an answer. It was put there for one of my workers. They never came by to pick it up." He could see that she understood but was still inquisitive.

"The place doesn't look so bad."

"Now, you're being nice. Thanks. Do you take cream, sugar, or both?" She went with cream. He handed her the coffee.

"Where did you get the stove?"

"Ms. Krancinski. Swedish woman living out of Tamarac. No one would take it, and I thought it was too pretty for the garbage truck. Not too many green stoves in the world." They both took a sip of coffee as Kayla got up to look inside the oven. She closed it and scanned the rest of the kitchen. David watched her take it all in. He broke the silence by saying, "I'm not a thief, even if Christopher thinks I stole the Yinwyan."

"I know you're not. Wouldn't be here if I thought you were," she replied.

"Then, why did you show up?"

"To tell you how grateful I am to you for feeding Tatiana. I've already put a few calls in and will find her a sanctuary soon. You can bet your ass that'll get done. And on a lighter note, I had to help out Mom's GC before things got out of hand."

As slow as men were at figuring out women, reading the signs on Kayla seemed clear, but he'd been wrong before. Was she was interested? Engaged, yes, but maybe she was having second thoughts. He felt comfortable because she was the first one who had stuck around for longer than a minute after seeing the place. Not even the plumbing company lasted as long as she had.

"How's the guy with the bright-colored clothes that don't match?"

"Aaron? He'll be all right," she said.

"He got hit pretty hard on the head by the door. I stuffed the Yinwyan by his hands on the couch."

"How did you get it?"

"It was on the floor in two pieces when I entered. Didn't expect to ever see it again. Kind of like you right now."

She smiled and said, "Then, what happened?"

"After I smashed Aaron with the door?"

She smiled again and said, "Yes."

Her smile made him brighten up and act out while saying, "Well, I did your door handle-hockey trick."

"I'm sure it was amazing."

"You know how to make a person feel good." Then, he remembered the skateboard and wanted to give it back. "Let me get you what I think they really want. Follow me." She did and soon saw the living room.

Before handing the keychain over to Kayla, David saw her looking around. He said, "Try to think of it as a work in progress. A dumpster is showing up on Monday, and most of this mess will be gone in a few days." It was like a warehouse of openness with a large sectional couch near a baby grand piano. Magazines, *Star Wars* figurines, toys, board games, and books were in unmanageable piles.

She said, "Can I look through some of this stuff before you throw it out?" In her hand was a paperback by Ian Fleming. David looked at the exposed cement floors, trying to make space for her to walk through.

Kayla pushed a shopping cart with an engine in it out of the way to get closer to the light. She asked, "Have you lived here long?"

"Couple years," he answered as he pushed a rolled-up rug onto a bigger pile of plastic bags.

Kayla asked, "What's going on with all of the garbage?" There was a wall of them with wood and concrete chips punctured through the sides.

"It's from my last demolition job. It needs to be taken to the dump. Waiting for the right time."

Kayla said, "But why are they in the living room?"

David replied, "They're in the hallway, too. This is just the overflow." One of the walls was covered in skateboards all lined up in symmetrical order. All nine stacks of five were evenly matched to pegs. David took one of the boards off the wall and grabbed the mini skateboard tucked between the truck and the wheel. He handed it to Kayla.

"This is it?" She pulled it apart to reveal that it was a flash drive of some kind. She said, "Ooohh. So secretive. What do you think it is?"

"Paperwork?"

"Probably not, and since Christopher didn't mention anything about the flash drive, I don't want anything to do with it. You never gave it to me."

"You sure? Han was asking for it. I'd really like for you to give it to him."

Kayla took it and put it on the table near her purse. She asked, "You sure you haven't seen what's on it?"

"What for? Don't have a computer. Could use the one at the library tomorrow, but I'm kind of busy." He left and returned a few moments later with the partial replica of the Yinwyan.

She said, "You did this from just seeing it?"

He nodded.

"Good work. You should get into the art business full-time and retire from construction...after you finish my parent's place." And she gave it back to him. "Why did you take the drive?" David did a double-take from the wall of skateboards back to her.

"No reason." The sarcasm was thicker than roofing cement. She saw the lunacy of the question and continued to look around. He asked, "Can I ask you something?"

"Sure."

"Why do you want to marry him? Not putting him down. I think he's a good guy, but he doesn't seem your type. No offense."

"It's a long story."

But David kept pushing. "You're not going to offend me. All my trash is in plain sight."

She said, "I've known Christopher most of my life. He's always shown up for me as a true friend. Although we don't see eye to eye on everything, he's been extremely influential, has opened doors for me, and has never disrespected me. Do we know each other explicitly? I don't think two people ever really do. But he's an important person to me and very generous. But we don't need to get into any of this right now. You're a good artist. Didn't see that in you this morning." He wanted to ask another question, but she had diverted him too smoothly.

Instead, he said, "What did you see?"

Kayla answered unapologetically, "Someone who likes old stoves." She slid a bunch of notebooks away and sat on the corner of the couch. Then, she scanned the artwork. Getting more comfortable, she said, "This reminds me of a community tent we had in Afghanistan. We had some good times in that place."

"Really?"

"Free time in the military needs these kinds of hangouts. Ours was set up in a warehouse. Had so much junk in it that we nicknamed it 'the dump.'"

Abruptly, David asked, "Are you getting married soon?"

"Next week."

David let it go and changed the subject by saying, "I'm in the process of downsizing. Like I said, by Monday, most of it will be gone."

"You have a lot to do."

He bit his lip and liked her honesty. Then, he replied, "Couple of hours will do the job."

She said, "Maybe twenty minutes, tops."

A comfortable silence fell upon the room as Kayla asked, "How do you make sense of it all?"

"I didn't for a long time until recently. Now, it all organized," and he pointed to his head.

"How so?"

"There's nothing to figure out, really. Just do your natural. The outside world doesn't have to fix anything, nor should it. As soon as I saw that, things got easier."

"I'm not sure I understand?" Kayla asked.

"I'm still trying to figure it out. But Slootzin at the hospital seems to say it better."

"You still go to Van der Slootzin?"

"Not very often, but I've had enough sessions." He could tell that she loved animals by the way Tackle and Charlie were hanging onto her like a pair of handcuffs. He didn't want to like this woman any more than he did, so he made up some faults she might possess, like snoring really loudly or laughing like a hyena.

Kayla interrupted by asking, "Are you okay?"

"Sorry, am I staring?"

"Yes."

And he said, "It's been a long day. I'm zoning out." As interesting as she was to hang out with, he wasn't trying to stir up any trouble with her fiancé. It was his best attempt to see if she took the hint for bed time. She didn't pick it up and looked wide awake. He asked, "What are you going to do after you're done serving?"

"I might have a few more years before that happens. But when I get out, I want to work with horses. Let me show you something." She pulled out her wallet to show him a picture of Biscuit. It was beautiful, and David saw her eyes light up as she talked about how they connected with each other. She went on and on about the friendship and told him they'd go riding one day. After she finished talking, she sat back and put the picture away. Tackle came over to sit on his lap. Charlie wasn't moving from Kayla.

"What do you call this?" Kayla asked, pointing to the painting in blue. It had an orange color with two faces, and it made her stand up to get a closer look.

"I haven't named it. Any suggestions?"

"Same person, different days."

David said, "Seems to be two sides to everything. Just like people. You know everything about your future husband?"

Kayla sat down on the couch and said, "We're not down the aisle yet, and we'll get to know each other more, as time goes on."

"Having second thoughts?"

David could see that her mind was going a million miles per hour, and she was being genuine. "There must be a lot of pressure on you right now."

"Seems so, but I don't feel it," she said. He failed to mention that she could use string on her ring to make it fit the finger. Then, Thorpe popped into his mind; the guy probably had someone parked outside his place right now. He could be planning vengeance for all he knew, and she could be in on the act. David's mind was getting paranoid, so he put a stop to it. Why was she here, though? Why was she not with Christopher? While she wasn't looking, David stretched out his arms to no answers in exasperation, as the day was digging into tomorrow. Tackle looked up at him and found a better place to rest.

David said, "Besides him suing the shit out of me, is there anything else I should know about Christopher Thorpe?"

Kayla took a moment and said, "Number one, he doesn't sue unless there's a guaranteed payday in it for him. Secondly, he might be selling secrets to China and is one of the most dangerous people you could ever hope to know. Your best plan would be to move to a remote island, but it wouldn't help."

"How come?"

She replied, "Because he has unlimited resources and could easily find you, then kill you."

CHAPTER 16

A FRESH LAYER OF snow dumped on top of a bed of Minnesotan ice. The whole city was on lockdown thanks to the blanket of white. Salvatore Waste Management company in the outskirts of St. Paul was closed. They'd been taking out the garbage for businesses for the last twenty-five years. The owner, Joe, started out with one dump truck he purchased for twenty thousand dollars. He was looking out the back of the shop window, watching as the team assembled to plow out a few of their accounts. At sixty years of age, he felt as good as ever. At six feet four inches, he weighed 240 pounds, but he had a lean build. Most of the size was in his shoulders. As the crews left, he peeled the rind off an orange and went back into the office to crunch some numbers for the week. On his desk was a picture of his only granddaughter with him at the Big Mountain Cupcake Festival.

Joe was sitting on a small fortune. and the only thing that motivated him was his grandkid, Lexi. He wasn't into fishing, playing golf, or building model ships. It was watching her grow up and making himself available for any family activities that helped him forget the past. He kept it simple, worked hard, and stayed busy. Working nights gave him the time to avoid staff interruptions, phone calls, and the opportunity to see the crew. It also helped him avoid the nightmares which still came, but less often.

The phone rang, and he let his reading glasses fall to his chest as he answered.

Joe answered pleasantly, "Hello."

"Joe?" He tried to place the voice but couldn't.

"Who is this?" he replied. Christopher was on the other end.

"The father you never knew, that's who." He immediately recognized the voice, and it wasn't a call he was expecting.

"What do you want?"

"Come on, Joe," Christopher said. "How have you been?"

"Working. What can I do you for?"

Christopher gave the code by asking to order a box of "Oops-a-Daisies."

Silence ensued. Joe told him that he didn't fill those orders anymore and said, "We're out of stock."

"No way. Impossible. They're my favorite." The old Joe would have snapped at the chance because he always enjoyed a good payday.

Joe said, "I think you have the wrong number, mister. I'm hanging up now."

"You can't hang up, Joe. We need a favor."

The exhale that Joe let out said it all. "Oops-a-Daisies have expired."

"Of course they have, and we'll take a Pie-In-the-Sky to go along with the order and an Afternoon Delight. Are those available?"

Joe took out a pen to write down the order, knowing that Thorpe wouldn't stop. Joe's business was partially financed by Christopher. He also knew that Christopher would have his place burned down if he didn't comply. Instead, Joe did what he could by limiting his available resources. "No more Pie-In-the-

Skies, plus Ladders and Toasters are off the menu. I'm getting too old. All I have available are the Okey Dokies, a Mae West, or any of the Gee Whizzes."

The other end of the phone was silent as Christopher was undoubtedly reading the key codes for each available action. Ladders were breaking and entering. Toasters stood for arson, no suicide. Okey-Dokies was a hit and run, meaning an awful injury with no investigation. The Mae West gave Joe full control over the lives of those who must die. A Gee Whiz meant people were going to have to get hurt. It also stood for a money back guarantee on any failed mission.

Christopher said, "You are getting up there with the limited menu, my friend. The garbage business must be good. Oh, well, it's great to have you back on the team. I'll take a half dozen Dokies. Just find the answers, and the Mae West goes without saying."

Joe said, "Never thought I'd work for you again."

"Then, you should have changed your number." The connection ended.

Joe looked at the phone and put it back on the receiver. His watch gave him about an hour of clean up. He knew to go slow under these conditions. He needed time to think because he might have to kill a man, and the roads were icy.

A FLIP PHONE vibrated on a coffee table in the desert. The place was a cave carved out of the side of a mountain. Duke was asleep with a pizza box near him on the floor. All that was left were some uneaten crusts. Spread out before him were smutty magazines, porno tapes, and an arsenal of firearms. A manual for a timer switch was folded across his chest. The place was littered with cases of empty beer bottles, rolled up hundred-dollar bills, boxes of hypodermic needles, and several empty vials of Superdrol. The weed-smoking, hippie, gym rat was knocked out cold from blazing some Afghan-purple mist. He'd told his friend to lace it, as a joke, and the dealer obliged. The phone kept on ringing without going to voicemail. Tied to the couch a few feet away was a baby lamb. The buzzing sound finally woke the man out of a stupor.

Answering, he said, "Speak now, or lick my hairy armpits."

"That's pretty vile, and I can do without the visual," Christopher replied. Duke was already reaching for a cigarette.

"I was wondering when you were going to call about the square groupers." Duke had failed to deliver the cocaine in the torpedoes, as they had gone straight out to sea. It was a complete failure, and his plan was to blow something up to make him feel better. Instead, he decided to waste a few billion brain cells by going on a drug binge. It was the only way to celebrate still being alive after he'd had to smoke the buyers in the white SUV. He didn't like the idea of people laughing at him, talking behind his back, and looking into his life. Vegas was on hold as he looked down at the backpack of cocaine and some extra cash left over from his mule-running enterprise that was privately funded by the man he was now speaking to.

"No problem," Christopher said. "Not why I'm calling. That whole enterprise was a favor for a friend. We did verify with Tonka of the purchase, and you're welcome for us not giving your location to the buyers." Duke figured Captain Dolan sold him out.

Duke said, "Sorry, boss. I didn't believe them when they said the torpedoes didn't make it. Then, one of them pulled a gun and left me no choice."

"Relax. Forget about it. This is the deal. I'll sweep the entire thing under the rug, the buy money, and remote-controlled tampons, I mean torpedoes, if you can make it here to Miami in less than twelve hours."

"Can I go to Vegas first, roll the bones, and then go to Miami?" Duke could hear Christopher recoil at the thought and then cursed him out.

"How about doing the job first to make up for the losses?" Duke had visions of snapping Christopher's neck and knew that biting the golden goose would be a problem, but Duke still entertained the thought. He noticed that Christopher wasn't saying anything and remembered how quiet the man got when in the worst kind of trouble. Duke shut up and listened.

Christopher said, "You can go right after I get married."

Duke said, "Congratulations! Wow. What gem is marrying you? You should honeymoon at Circus Circus, they have the best suites. Unless you're still keeping the pinky finger in the air while sipping that rum." Christopher looked in the mirror. He was drinking brandy out of a snifter with his fourth finger vertical.

He placed the drink on the dresser and said, "See, this is why I need you. You're so intuitive. The job I have needs special attention. You available?"

"Always, boss."

"Then, be in Miami in twelve hours." The phone went silent. A smile appeared on Duke's face, then a frown. He knew that all was not forgiven and needed to be prepared to punch Christopher's ticket before the man killed him.

Duke picked up the Superdrol syringe and primed the metal stinger. He injected the concoction into his buttocks and then gave his nose a runner's blast. The lamb glanced at the fool and kept chewing on some nearby pizza crust. Duke was ready to go.

"Oh, Lucius," he said.

On the far side of the room, Duke led the lamb to a gate with metal bars. He untied the innocent animal and pulled the lever. After placing it inside the cell, he closed the gate. A clicking noise began that ended with an automatic lock. Immediately, he grabbed a large, black duffel bag to fill up his gear for the trip. He finished it off with some flares, a pair of pliers, and a box of Baby Ruth candy bars as he slipped on his work boots. Moments later, a large predator got a death grip on its lunch.

CHAPTER 17

DAVID LOOKED OVER at Kayla and said, "Tell me you're kidding?"

She got up and stared at a piece of art while saying, "Christopher is one of the richest men in the world. His family has connections dating back 160 years in Washington. They have blue-blood money, and it is rumored that one his great, great, great, great-grandfathers fought with Washington. The family business is logistically spider-webbed throughout the planet and can supply any country with unlimited resources. His ambition and will to win flies way under the radar for a silver spoon kid. The man can negotiate, hunt, and destroy a Fortune 500 company in a blink of an eye. You saw his walls. This is his life, and as long as our family has known him, he's been nothing but a complete gentleman. But it doesn't make me naïve to the fact that he'll do whatever it takes to extract vengeance when push comes to shove. He's Machiavellian."

David looked at the heavy bag in the corner of his gym area. He got down on himself for not doing his 200 leg kicks for the day. Kayla got up to look at the deer head. She asked, "Did you do this?"

"No, but you're looking at it from the wrong angle," he said and pulled her over to the other side. "It's an optical illusion." She was speechless. "I traded for it with a guy named Deininger."

"How does he do it?"

"He wouldn't tell me. I think it's about not paying attention to the noise and knowing what's valuable, or in this case, the focus point. Not totally sure. I can get lost in the objects, details, or layering. Flawless."

Kayla said, "It doesn't even seem possible." She changed perspectives, and with each angle, some new object was revealed in the piece.

She moved on, and he followed her to another painting and asked, "Should I be worried about Christopher?"

She smiled and said, "No. I'll straighten everything out with him the next time we talk."

She went back to the painting and asked, "This is original?"

"Yes."

"What is it?"

"The Sandwich."

"Like a cheeseburger?"

David looked over and said, "A cheeseburger isn't a sandwich. This is more like a pastrami on rye." David picked up a few bottle caps on the floor and tossed them into a barrel of aluminum cans.

"I don't see it. What happened to the frame?" she asked.

"Nothing. You see something wrong with it?" And he looked behind the canvas.

"Do you paint unrecognizable food because you're always hungry?"

"Never gave it much thought, really. Would you like something to eat?"

"What do you have?"

"I just went grocery shopping."

"As long as you let me cook. I haven't made anything in a while."

David winced and let out a sigh. He stopped in his tracks and said, "How about—no. You eat, I'll cook, and let you do the clean up."

She pushed him from behind and said, "Let's see what you have."

While walking into the kitchen, David said, "How about I let you chop some fruit, and we can both clean up together?" She stood in the doorway with her hand on her hip like at the pool table. He'd seen that same stance from her mother when she demanded that he take down a wall. It was in the family's DNA, and this one looked to have mastered the art of war. He didn't stand a chance, so he grabbed a box of blue tip matches.

"Okay. Have it your way. Let me get the pilot lit," he said.

"You don't see too many gas stoves in Florida."

"Luckily, we're zoned for it."

"Where did you find it again?"

"Old Lady Kracinski. I was driving down a tight street one day in Broward, going slow to read some directions. Cars were parked on both sides as I looked outside the passenger window to hear a hideous grinding noise. To my surprise, I saw this old grandma pushing a stove across the sidewalk all by herself. It made me stop."

He watched Kayla try to push the thing. She had no chance. "It's heavy."

He lifted up the metal burner plate and left it open. He continued, "So, I parked my truck and got out to help. When I got close, I saw that she had on was one of those nightgowns from the 1950s, with the tissue tucked under the sleeve, and was sporting a pair of worn-out slippers. I looked at the scratch marks on the concrete and figured that she had already pushed the thing about fifteen feet."

David lit the stove and closed the top. He said, "They were going to toss it away in the garbage. I offered to restore it. She agreed, and when I went back a few months later to tell her that the job was finished, she had passed. The family told me to keep it."

He finished with, "It's a sensitive piece of equipment, so be careful," then gave it a few pats on the side.

"I bet it is," Kayla replied. "She sounded like she was tough as nails."

"With a beautiful smile."

Kayla nudged the stove a bit, and David said, "I don't know how she did it!"

Kayla opened the oven door and said, "I bet it makes wonderful bread. Let me see what you have."

He stood in her way and said, "You sure about this? I can get it done faster." It was a weak attempt, and she didn't even bother to take a step back. She just pushed him out of the way. He pointed out the pantry and spice cupboard. "Are you sure you know how to cook? It doesn't look like it."

"Excuse me? I'll have you know that I was Cordon Bleu-certified and have been to a war zone twice. I think I can handle your kitchen." Then, she jabbed him in the ribs like a boxer. David quickly backed off while hitting the stove. The pilot light went out.

"Take it easy. What are you, Roy Jones Jr. going for a liver shot?" Kayla laughed and told him to get out so she could do her thing. She said it would take about twenty minutes and everything would be ready. David looked at the clock on the wall and highly doubted it. She pointed to the door.

"You're kicking me out of my own place?"

"I cook better alone," she replied. "Out. I can find whatever I need."

He didn't have a choice, and she watched him leave. Cooking always helped him work out his problems, and now, she had taken over the space. What was he supposed to do? She was too much of a distraction, so he looked outside the window to see if anything was suspicious. Nothing. Just an empty street. He said to himself, "This is never going to end," and rubbed his rib cage.

He called out down the hall, "Don't cut yourself." And cautioned, "Be careful."

"I will, leave me alone."

David peeked inside and saw her going through the inventory in the fridge. Kayla had a way about her that kicked up his energy—or was it the coffee? He was going to have to buy some more of those Costa Rican beans. He walked to the living room and decided to keep himself busy by doing a quick clean up job in the bathroom.

It took only a few minutes for Kayla to chop up some strawberries, mix the pancake batter, and wash the chicken thighs. She pulled out some cheese from the crisper and cut a chunk of Manchego for herself. The house was a mess, but David managed to keep the cooking area tidy.

Kayla grabbed a sauté pan hanging above the stove. It wasn't grimy, so she turned on the heat to the front burner. The flame didn't appear. She tried another burner, and nothing. Then, she grabbed the box of blue tip matches on the counter.

David had finished with the one bathroom and started picking up laundry. He wiped the mirror with an old shirt. While walking back to catch the replay of the Heat Bulls game, he heard the stove open up. Why was the grid being lifted?

As soon as he turned the corner, a large flame exploded through the doorway. It extinguished itself immediately, but the fireball froze him in his tracks. His heart started racing as he rushed into the kitchen. The place was smoldering with a small pile of papers burning on the ground. He covered his nose with his arm and stomped them out. He turned around and saw Kayla on the floor, pinned up against the futon. She must've hit the wall like a cannon ball.

The fire alarm started blaring. He bent down to see sparklers burning through her hair like a fuse. It smelled awful. He jumped up and grabbed the first bowl of liquid he could find and tossed it over her head. She got slimed with pancake mix and woke up coughing into the batter. David shut off the gas valve and then got up on the chair to take the battery out of the alarm. The smoke in the room lingered like one would find on a battlefield. He opened a window above the sink and the front door. Then, he soaked a dishtowel in water and checked in on how she was doing. He avoided looking at her, fearing the worst.

Kayla removed the batter from her eyes with her fingers. She took the dishtowel and slowly wiped the mush from her face. She felt like she had been hit by a truck. She asked, "What happened?" His heart raced in his chest, and he hoped that she was going to be all right. She looked okay, but he couldn't tell for sure.

"Are you hurt? Did you hit your head?" David thought she looked like a burnt marshmallow. He helped remove some debris from her clothes.

She said, "You threw pancake mix on me?"

"Your hair was sizzling like bacon. It was all I had to put out the flames." He helped her into the chair and got another dishtowel.

"Now, I know the real reason why you have the futon in your kitchen."

"Old Ms. Kracinski has never done that before. I don't think I tightened down the back gasket enough."

Kayla said, "I don't think you did, either. Better check it out after I leave." A wave of relief overcame David as he realized that she was going to be fine. His emotions turned on a dime, and it took some doing to hold back his laughter. It was so wrong and way too soon for any humor to be found in the situation.

David was amazed that Kayla was able to take a direct hit from the Howitzer stove and live. He wanted to give her some encouragement, but suddenly, he found another burst of laughter to suppress. He knew that if he started, he wouldn't be able to stop, and she might kill him after getting back on her feet.

As she cleaned up, she asked, "Why are you smiling?"

"I'm not smiling. This is serious." His cover-up wasn't working. "This is so serious. Can you move your arms and legs?" He started squeezing Kayla's bicep, and she offered no resistance.

She asked, "How bad do I look?"

"Hard to tell," he said. "Let me get a better look. Your eyebrows are..." He looked at her head sideways as a clump of hair fell into her hands.

"Where's your bathroom?"

"You shouldn't move right now. Just relax."

Kayla grabbed David's arm and almost pulled him to the floor as she got up. Her strength had returned in force. Then, she squeezed harder while repeating, "Where's the lady's room?"

He saw venom in her eyes and immediately said, "Follow me," and helped her walk with his guilt following right behind. He wanted to talk about the latest upgrade to his house, but he decided not to bring it up. Instead, he was going to leave it as a surprise for her to say something nice about it after she was finished.

Kayla entered and closed the door in his face. He'd just recently remodeled the master bath with a majestic blue trim and white marble tile. It had a double sink with a mounted mirror and recessed lighting. He was proud of the wow factor it produced at first glance. He'd copied it from one of the mansion hotels he saw in a magazine. His favorite part was the walk-in shower that was double the standard size. He thought that it would be cool if she noticed as he stared at the door, but under the given circumstances, he couldn't press for any acknowledgements. She probably had other things on her mind.

David left to investigate the mess. He saw that the cheese was still out to snack on. He double-checked the stove to make sure the gas valve was off. Tackle and Charlie started barking in the bedroom. He went back and stood near the door. He heard crying at first, and then, he didn't.

"Are you okay?" he yelled. Kayla didn't reply, and then, he heard the door lock. He went and sat on the bed to wait for it to open. That was when the shower started.

KAYLA STEPPED UNDER the overhead pour spout and saw a lot of hair falling to the floor. It clogged up the drain as she touched her eyebrows. The good news was that she wasn't dead. She replayed the scene in her head, and it was a good sign that she wasn't in shock. The overhead water spout felt good, relaxing, and she grabbed the stool to sit under it. All the hysteria bubbled up and washed away. She used her foot to push the clumps of hair that were blocking the drain. *It would grow back*, she thought, *and I've been through worse*. It was unbelievable that that she'd been saved from breaking her neck by a futon. How was she going to explain this incident to work? Or in the wedding photos? She'd become the monster bride of Halloween.

The water started turning cold, and it straightened her back. Her muscles contracted while she adjusted. She inspected a few scrapes, then smiled. They needed Kracinski's stove in Afghanistan. She turned off the water and closed her eyes to listen to it drain. Why hadn't Christopher told her about the drive? Something important must have been on it, but it would never go in her report if they asked her to write one up. She didn't want to know what was inside it. She stood up and dried off. The bathroom was impressive. After wiping the steam off the mirror, she noticed the colors of the room. It suited her eye. The light switch cover was in the shape of a guitar.

Kayla remembered how she used to dress up like Blondie and Patti Smith. No one could tell her a thing, and she had felt free, even though everyone thought that she was just a wannabe. She'd seen garage bands in high school with her best friend, Lisa, and they'd walked around like a couple of badasses. One night, the singer, Bobby Thompson, was jumping around, trying to look cool when he stepped on a rake. It popped up and knocked him into the drums. It was times like those which turned her onto punk bands like the Sex Pistols, Dead Kennedys, and Ramones. Those bands with attitudes stressed the hell out of her parents. It gave her dad the most fits, but she learned that no one could stop her from being free, except the military.

Kayla rubbed her fingers on the fluffy, clean towel. The bathroom wasn't a match for the rest of the place. It was clean, decorated, and didn't belong. Everything was new, and she saw it as David trying to make an improvement. She picked up the blow dryer when David knocked on the door again and asked, "Are you okay?" She asked for her purse while getting dressed. He went to the living room and brought back the satchel. She took the bag without him seeing inside and closed the door again in his face.

Kayla dumped the contents of the bag onto the counter. She shifted through her belongings and put the gun back. The pack of cigarettes got pushed aside as she took out a stick of bubble gum, then played with the lid on the S.T. Dupont. She opened and closed it few times and tucked it into her jeans. She picked up the eyeliner and recalled her favorite outfit just before going to college. She wished that she'd had this hairstyle back then, and she turned her head from side to side. Why not apply some faux eyebrows? She said to herself, "If you can't beat 'em, join 'em."

Getting lost in her makeover was beyond fulfilling. It felt primal with an uncontrollable urge to not give a shit. It was as if a street lamp shined on her, filling her with rebellious urges. She felt flawless as she finished the makeover. Taking a step back to evaluate her own artistry, she confirmed that it wouldn't pass any social standards.

It felt as if she was back in her own skin. The dirty, pink top looked fantastic with the burn holes. She tore off the sleeves and let her bra show through. It was a deep red hue that made listening to rock 'n' roll sexy. Her jeans fit, she knew it, and could still run a seven-minute mile in them. Then, she stopped. Something was missing. Was it a belt? Spikes? No, she needed something extra heavy.

Speaking with a bit of force, Kayla yelled out, "Do you have a leather jacket?" David made it sound like he didn't understand what she was saying, so she repeated it.

He went to the closet and got one out. It was worn-down and beat-up. He said, "It's been through some long winters and then got ran over by a bus. You probably don't want this one. What do you need a jacket for? This is Florida."

The door unlocked, and Kayla snatched it from David, saying, "It'll work." His schoolboy face said it all. She put it on and looked in the mirror one more time. It needed no one's final approval. She walked out of the chamber and said, "You got anything else around here that blows up I should know about?"

CHAPTER 18

THE YACHT NAMED "Nice Day" was docked near the intercoastal. Christopher was in his office on board and eating with Han. He looked at the monitor to see Aaron walking up the gangplank. He was rolling on a small dose of Special K, and the last thing he wanted to do was have a conversation with this kid before his bachelor party. The medical report folder on the desk said that Aaron had suffered a concussion. He was told to not go to sleep, and Christopher had the perfect solution. Miriam was waiting for Aaron on the upper deck.

Christopher said to Han, "Can we take him out to sea with us and dump his body overboard?" Han mentioned that the dock has cameras and that his car went through the front gate. Christopher said, "For a second there, I thought it was good idea." He had to come up with another solution. Crew members were directing Aaron at each turn to see the boss.

Finally, one held open the door, and Aaron entered. Han and Christopher had plastic bibs around their necks. TV surveillance monitors covered one of the walls with news networks, stock prices, and sporting events on multiple screens. The rest of the place looked like it was Captain Nemo's lair. Starfish-shaped bookends, framed maps, and exotic fish prints adorned the interior. Behind his desk was a painting of a single lion fish. Christopher pointed for Aaron to have a seat. He chewed his food and asked Han, "Pass the hollandaise over."

Christopher asked, "You hungry?" Aaron declined. Steel lobster crackers broke through the hard bone of chitin. Christopher used a small mini fork to procure the meat in the claw. "What did the doctor say about the concussion?"

Aaron replied, "Not to go to sleep for at least twenty-four hours."

He nodded and asked, "Do you think it's good advice?"

"Why wouldn't it be?"

Christopher sipped a 1990 Chevalier Montrachet. The aroma filled his nose with honey and made him want to drink more than he should. The grapes were a golden curtain of apricots and pears that cascaded past his tonsils. The finish was longer than normal. He squeezed off a long pause in between eating and taking sips of his drink to size up Aaron. He said, "You look like a fish that doesn't know it's out of water." Aaron couldn't figure out the riddle.

Christopher didn't give him time to respond and said, "Tokyo is calling. Five groups are waiting, and they all depend on me. Not a fan of excuses, Aaron."

Aaron nodded again and said, "I know."

"So, what is the problem?"

"I can't find the skateboard," Aaron said. "I looked all over for it. I think that guy took it."

"You mean the one who busted down the door, took the Yinwyan, and fed my tiger? What's his name?"

"David Wolfe," said Han.

"I was walking out to give you the flash drive," Aaron continued, "and then bam. He broke in."

"Then snatched the Yinwyan."

"For real," said Aaron.

"The Yinwyan? Wait a second...any more coleslaw left, Han?" A plastic container was passed to him. Christopher said, "They make great coleslaw. You sure you don't want a taste?" He loaded a few scoops onto his plate and told Aaron, "Don't worry, it's why I called for you, so we can figure something out."

"See those cameras?" Christopher asked, turning his gaze back to Aaron. "We have the same equipment in the house, driveway, entrance, hallway, and bar where we watched you take the statue."

Aaron said, "I was interested in researching it and didn't think you'd mind. I was going to put it back, but now, it's broken."

Christopher asked with his mouth full of food, "It's broken?" Han stopped eating.

"That's the confusing part. I don't know how it happened."

"It's confusing. How? Like a fuzzy dog can't find a bone? Or more a like crossword puzzle with too many missing clues? Better yet, how about something a truck ran over? That would cause confusion. No?"

"I was researching the origins of the sculpture on the laptop, and then, the knock came at the door. I must have had it in my hand when I got knocked out."

Christopher had already moved on and showed his phone to Aaron, then Han. He said, "Another Tokyo number. They've been calling me every twenty minutes. Go on, they're just board members."

Aaron said, "Can't we get another set of recovery keys? You said we had a backup?"

Christopher squeezed some fresh lemon over his hands and lifted the lid of a wooden box. Steam came out, and a hot towel was inside. He freshened up.

Christopher said, "Let's slow down a second, my friend. Be a turtle with me as we get this straight. You know what we do, right? Like for real, real? Not the pretend stuff with political campaigns, lobbying, and caviar?"

"Of course, you run the family business." Christopher watched the other man carefully and smiled with pity, because Aaron clearly didn't know.

Christopher said to Han, "He makes it sound so easy. Why don't I have this attitude?"

Han kept eating his food. Christopher said, "How far do you think someone will go to protect a multi-level conglomerate, with many of its businesses marked as unrelated and classified?"

"A long way."

Christopher got paranoid and told Han, "Make sure he isn't wearing a wire and give me his phone." Han got up and checked. Then, he turned the power button on Aaron's phone off.

Christopher said, "We like you, Aaron. We think highly of you, and you're doing a fine job. If you weren't unscrupulous, then you might not be good at your job. You like to write code, you could work for anyone, but you're in for some bad luck for you if you don't find the skateboard."

Christopher finished his statement as Han broke the claw of the crustacean with the lobster crackers.

Aaron jumped a bit by the sound and said, "Why don't you have the kitchen break it all up for you?"

Christopher snapped, "What the fuck, Aaron? What's wrong with you? Aaron, you're a deer in headlights." Christopher continued, "I'm trying to talk to you, in a serious conversation, while trying to teach you something. Then, you go yapping away off-topic. What the fuck? If you're talking about bullshit, then how can you be listening to me?" The silence hung in the air. Christopher took a sip of wine, then said, "Do you think it's your job to redirect the conversation?"

The only noise in the room was Han chewing food. Christopher continued, "And how will it work out if you're fighting to squeeze in some irrelevant words? Do you know how long I've been eating lobsters?"

Aaron said that he didn't.

"Of course, you don't. Before you were born would be the correct answer, but good for you in pointing out that you don't know. That is a good starting point. As a matter of fact, I can have a galley on board to break this shit up for me. Used to do it, too, all the time. Sauté them in butter, oil, and garlic. Only, I prefer to break them apart myself, pull the limbs off to get at the meat. Can I be allowed the luxury without your criticism?"

Aaron said that he could.

Christopher turned to Han and asked, "Where was I?"

Han said with a mouthful of food, "How you get paid."

"Thank you," Christopher said. "Thank you, Han. See, Aaron, he can eat, not talk, and pay attention. You have a lot to learn from Han. We need the skateboard. It's our coded asset that sets up a lot of funding for multiple entities. No one gets paid without the board members happy, and the disk contains my set of permission keys. So, my job is to get the keys, make the transfer, and have it done by yesterday. Which means that you're in the hot seat to find it and bring it to the safe house tonight. Capiche?"

"But what if I can't find it?"

"Wow, Aaron. Think positive. You're killing me here. How can you win with this attitude?" Christopher said to Han, "You're going to have to help the poor bastard."

"It's okay," Aaron replied. "I'll find it."

Christopher said, "Don't worry. Han won't get in your way, and if you run into any trouble, then he'll be a good person to have on your side." Aaron just looked at the carpet.

Christopher said, "I don't think you got it. You look lost. Give me a recap." Aaron wiped his palms on his pant legs. Christopher softly said, "Let me see if you have the proper retention skills before I send you on your way. What did I just tell you to do? Go. Greenlight...Go!"

"Get the flash drive and bring it back to you at the safe house by tonight."

"This is the Aaron I want to see more often," said Christopher. "Lucky for you, my fiancée is helping us out, and you also have Han, so count your blessings. I haven't heard from her yet, but she's talking to this David guy. If I hear anything, I'll let you know. Keep your phone on, and we'll talk. Don't get lost. Now go be all you can be."

Aaron thanked him and Christopher said, "Your job is on the line, son. Good luck." Han escorted Aaron out as Miriam entered.

"Am I almost done here?" asked Miriam as she slumped into the chair. She looked amazing for being so exhausted. Christopher wanted to rub her shoulders but thought it best to leave her be. She had been twenty-three when they first met at the casino and she was hosting a golf tournament. As much as he liked having her around to brag about her good looks, she was excellent at the job.

She said, "You ready for your stag party to begin?"

"Not yet. Get Farnsworth on the phone, please."

"But it's Saturday? Technically speaking, you told me to never call him on a Saturday."

He touched the top of her shoulder and said, "Well, then, we're just going to have to break the rules this time."

Miriam said, "I'll get him on the phone." He was used to her professionalism, and she played the game of dealing with his smart-ass locker room demeanor pretty well. He pushed her, but the pay was better than decent, and the perks were compelling. She held it all together better than most and had only confronted him once about working the entire weekend like she was now. He followed her into another room, knowing that she was tired.

Christopher said, "What are you going to do after law school?"

"Taking offers. You know of any opportunities?"

"We can find a place on our legal team. Pick the city you want to live in, and I'll make it happen."

Miriam's head picked up. "What's the salary?"

"This world is made for alphas. What are you bringing to the table besides brains, leadership, and good looks?"

"What else is there?"

"I only hire killers. If you aren't one, then we're going to have to find someone to teach you how to become one. You can grow into the job, and it's not very glamorous." She absorbed what he said instead of responding right away.

Christopher said, "You're not going to start getting weird on me now after all these years, are you?"

"Not a chance. I'm just ready to go home. It's been a long day."

Christopher smiled and said, "Forget the Farnshit guy. You've done enough. My stag party just started. Send the girls to the hot tub. See you tomorrow." Miriam left. He watched her go and never doubted her loyalty. He went back to get his wine and watched the monitors as two scantily dressed women walked up the plank.

———————————

DAVID AND KAYLA sat on the rooftop talking as the sun rose. She had gone to sleep on the couch around 3:30. He couldn't close his eyes and ended up doing some more work on the Yin-wyan. Now, it was a peaceful morning. She smelled the coffee as he brought the two mugs up to the roof, and her burnt eyebrows perked up ever so slightly. He continued, "It's the beans. I grind them fresh."

She said, "You do realize that I will have to get even with you and your stove one day."

"Can't let Ms. Kracinski win, can you?"

Kayla smiled. "No."

"I should probably get it fixed by someone who knows what they're doing. It's been like that for a while."

"How long?"

"Over a year."

"Never crossed your mind to tell me?"

"I tried to warn you. Correct me if I'm wrong, but I said more than once to let me handle it, but no. You're Julia Child-certified."

"Cordon Bleu."

"You ended up doing better than I thought."

"How so?"

"You cooked up a rebel without a cause." He sat back and soaked up the morning sun. David said, "I've decided to buy a new stove and keep Kracinski as a side piece."

Kayla asked, "You ever been married?"

"No. Came close a couple times but eventually stopped trying."

"Why did you stop?"

"I have an aversion to authority." She smiled and he continued, "Either I'm not the settling type, or my life is too complicated. Slootzin hasn't figured it out yet. My last girlfriend could get me to do anything, but she didn't like dogs, so it was a deal breaker."

"She didn't like Charlie and Tackle?"

"Can you imagine? She liked birds. Had an African Grey. Always fed it out of her mouth, and it would relieve itself on her flannel shirts. Beyond repelling."

"Shut up. You're kidding, right?"

"Of course, she just didn't like dogs."

"I can see why you get along with my dad."

"Hate to be a party pooper, but I can't duck Christopher any longer. I'm going to go over now and drop off the flash drive, then apologize for feeding his cat."

"I'll go with you."

"No, I don't think so. This is going to be humiliating for me. You've done enough by coming over last night." David saw the look again and didn't know how she was so skilled about getting her way, but he said without skipping a beat, "Unless you're up to it, I mean. Can't say I won't enjoy the company." She smiled and David said, "Besides, this new look you have is a knockout. I've never met a rock star before."

"You want my autograph?"

"Sure. But remember one thing."

"What?"

They started walking downstairs, and David said, "The jacket is a loan. You're going to have to return it eventually."

"It's fits so nicely, you might have to fight me for it."

"Aren't you getting married this week?"

She kept walking and said, "Damn. I knew that I was forgetting something." He had to hand it to her. She played to a different kind of music.

He said, "You know them New Yorkers would pay top dollar for a haircut like yours."

She turned around and said, "How much do you think it would cost?"

"At least $300 bucks for the blow torch method."

———

KAYLA AND DAVID walked out to his truck through the garage. He saw her reading a text, and she announced, "He's at the yacht."

"What's wrong?"

"Not sure. He's saying that they have to depart and we might not make it on time. Wouldn't tell me the reason." They walked past a covered-up vehicle, and she said, "What's this?"

"Beefcake, my fun car."

Kayla looked under the tarp at a BMW M20. David said, "It's had some engine work; this is the 77 model. Changed the body a bit to make it wider and couldn't resist putting on a hood scoop with the extra horsepower."

"You prefer German engineering over American muscle?"

David replied, "Not really, this was a gift from someone who owed me a lot of money." He took the tarp off and popped the hood. The engine was clean as a whistle.

She said, "Looks like a screamer."

"The throttle kit is custom. Put in a new gearbox. A bit uncomfortable if you don't like to go fast. The hydraulic hand-brake system wasn't installed by me. Local garage, Victor Russo's, did it instead."

"Is it street legal?"

He closed the hood and said, "I get away with it."

After opening the door, she asked, "No A/C?"

"It's a work in progress. I'll get to it eventually. Needs a paint job first."

She said, "Looks good enough to drive," then tried to open the driver's side door.

"What are you doing?"

"I want to drive." David failed to see the logic. She continued, "I figured we'd go together. I'm coming back this direction, anyway, and I know how to drive fast."

David used his best lecture voice when he said, "It'll take months for you to learn how to drive this car. Way too much power for you." It was as if she wasn't listening. "Come on, relax, remember the stove. There are too many moving parts. Let's get today off on the right foot. Watch me, take a few notes, and I promise that I'll bring you to the track another time for a joy ride."

She stood with her arms akimbo again. He climbed in through the driver's seat window without looking back. Her shadow hadn't moved. David cursed under his breath and moved over to the passenger side.

Kayla climbed through the window as well, making David's heartbeat increase. "If you crash this car, I want backstage passes to a Cypress Hill concert." His words landed like drops of water on a duck's back.

Kayla was stunned and said, "Cypress Hill? We should go regardless."

Once inside, he closely watched Kayla survey the interior. She glanced to the backseat and said, "What kind of blanket is that, Navaho?"

"Genuine Tijuana. I went there to get a root canal to save some money. Only problem was that the doctor showed up with blood all over his shirt. Sometimes, it pays to spend the extra thousand."

"I don't believe you."

"You're learning. Now, let's forget the color commenting for a second and focus. Adjust the seat. Your legs are too far back." She couldn't find the lever, and he reached across her body while saying, "May I?" Kayla gave permission. He pressed on her inner thigh and found the release button to scooched her up a bit.

She said, "Very nice," and liked the angle on her back as he helped her with the safety harness.

Kayla started playing around, and David thought she was enjoying things too much. He said, "Hey, focus," as she wiggled at the gearbox. She pushed his hand away and then tucked her hair behind her ear.

"Can you run it all by me again? I wasn't paying attention. What are you doing?"

"I just want to make sure that you have the right position."

"What if I'm a natural?"

"No problem. It can happen once every hundred years. Let me go over the ground rules. No risky moves with this side of the car, or my side, for that matter. Don't hit anyone, and no smoking while driving."

"Anything else?"

"Yes. Don't grind the gearbox like a spoon in the garbage disposal. Try to do be smooth and easy like a cheese farmer."

"What's a cheese farmer?"

"They're a bit smelly, but they make good cheese. This is a high-octane vehicle, so it smells a bit."

She took a sniff and said, "It's not too bad."

"We haven't started the engine yet." David put the key in the ignition, touched the buttons, flipped the switches, and said, "Push the green start button." Kayla did, and the engine roared to life. The chassis absorbed the purring as best it could. An AM/FM radio was ripped out of the dash. He talked a bit louder due to the engine rumbling.

"Are you sure you can drive stick?"

"I owned a 911. I got this." He had to trust her now. Kayla asked, "Why two shifters?"

"You'll never have to worry about this one. Just use this one."

"Can I hit this button?"

"Not now," David said. "It's a kill switch."

"Why does it sound so choppy?"

David pretended like he didn't hear her over the mechanical music. It was screaming for octane as it idled, but then, the engine died. He instructed her to start it again.

She pushed in the clutch and hit the button. He carefully watched her repeat the actions, and then, she engaged the shifter. The pedal was stiff and slipped off her foot. The car was in reverse and smashed into the workbench as the engine cut off.

David opened the passenger door and got out to investigate. Kayla got out of the driver's side door. "Why did we climb through the windows if the doors work?" Then, she saw the back bumper on the ground. Anger didn't hit David immediately. He put his hands in his pockets and blamed himself for letting her get behind the wheel. He looked at where the bumper had cracked off, then back to her. She asked again, "Why did we climb through the windows?"

David said, "You're supposed to climb through the window with these kinds of cars. Don't you ever go to the movies?"

David picked the bumper up and put it on the workbench. Kayla said, "What movies?"

"Can't think of any right now...Two Lane Blacktop with James Taylor."

"Never heard of it." She apologized and gave him a puppy-dog look. He walked past her and said, "Well, that makes us even. We'll take the pickup."

CHAPTER 19

HAN AND AARON were parked down the street as they watched David and Kayla leave. They slowly pulled up to the front door. Businesses were closed down for the weekend. Han released the trunk and pulled out a crowbar. He tried to wedge it between the lock and the door jam, but nothing budged. It was too secure. He put his ear to the door and heard dogs barking. Then, he went around back and broke in through the window to the laundry room. Both dogs started wagging their tails and laying down at his feet, wanting to be rubbed. Han stopped and absorbed the affection. Once in the living room, he waded through the mess. The place was in complete disorder. He looked at the wall of skateboards and figured that it was a good place to start searching for the flash drive. Then, on top of the dining room table, he noticed the replica Yinwyan. It looked almost as good as the original. He grabbed a brown paper bag from a stack on the table and stuffed the object inside. Then, he walked outside as Aaron came out from hiding behind the bushes. Han told him to get in the car.

THE YACHT WAS anchored out at sea as two women sunbathed on the upper deck. A yachtie was carrying a cell phone to the stern. Christopher and a diving buddy got out of the water in their scuba gear. They had lobsters in a netted bag. He took two of them out and yelled up to the girls, "What did you think was going to happen?!" They looked over the side to see him holding two crustaceans.

They couldn't understand what he was saying because of the sounds of the ocean and the sun in their eyes. They gave him a fake expression of astonishment and spectacular delight. One of the creatures kicked its tail ferociously.

A guard held the phone to Christopher's ear with an emergency call. Christopher was smiling, but soon, his expression changed to a frown. Han was not giving him the news he wanted. They couldn't find the flash drive. Christopher ended the call and looked up at the sunbathers.

One of the women watched Christopher place the ocean floor trophies in a cooler. She asked, "Is it possible to be a vegan and still eat lobster?"

The other was applying sunscreen and replied, "It's hard to say. I have a cousin who's a pescatarian, and she eats prime rib every year at Christmas."

Christopher's phone started ringing again. Kayla's name appeared on the screen as he looked down at where he had thrown it on the towels. He didn't feel like talking and avoided the call. He was having too good of a time. A text from her showed up next, and he didn't respond.

BACK AT THE marina, Kayla put the phone in her back pocket. "They're probably too far out. Can you believe it? The fiancée has been blown off." David could see that it didn't sit well with her. She said, "You up for a boat ride?"

"Sure. Are we going to commandeer a vessel?" She started walking to the west end of the marina.

"Follow me. Dad has a boat here."

They boarded a Mercury 42-foot Huntress. David asked, "You know how to drive one of these?"

"It's not my first rodeo."

David stayed silent and texted OP to let him know that he wasn't going to be stopping by the job site today. OP replied that he was taking the day off, too. David looked at the boat and said, "Should I batten down the hatches?"

Kayla replied, "Not yet. Let me get the key first." She started digging around and found the spare one to opened the lower cabin deck. A moment later, she came out and started the engine.

It was a process to cast away, and he followed her commands. The engine warmed up as they did a systems check. After about twenty minutes of work and changing into boating attire, she said, "Untie the lines."

"Aye, aye, Captain."

They made a pit stop at a refueling station before going out through the inlet. Almost eight hundred dollars later, they were good to go.

The seats on board made the ride ultra-smooth. Kayla told him that they were going to one of her favorite dive spots. He enjoyed just being able to sit back and relax. All this time that he had lived in Florida, and today was his first ride out to sea. Viewing the landscape from half a mile out was like looking at a foreign country. He watched her keep a consistent speed, check out the gauges, and plot a course. She pointed out the sand bars, fishing spots, and land markers, like an experienced captain. He got the feeling that she was slowly departing from the idea of being married, and he felt responsible. Their final destination was a snorkeling preserve near Ocean Reef, Key Largo.

Kayla told David the story of how her parents had been coming down here for years. She talked, and he listened. He couldn't believe that she had her first solo sailing adventure to the Bahamas at sixteen. She tacked and jibbed her way with the telling of this yarn like a proper sailor. There was a sense of pride behind her words, but it wasn't bragging. She gave most of the credit for her sailing adventure to her Uncle Tony, and yet, she still went alone.

A few hours later, they had arrived, and the cut the engine. She dropped anchor and gave him a pair of shorts. He stripped down as she went below deck. He loved the location and stretched out until she returned in a bikini, asking him to applying some suntan lotion.

"Can you put some on my back?" He got up and applied the Banana Boat for her.

"Is this where you kill people and dump them over the side?"

"Just the ones I don't like."

"Perfect," he said and added, "Good to know we're friends. Any sharks around?"

"This is Florida. Always sharks. No big deal. But we might see a few man-of-wars. Those are the ones we have to look out for." David took off his shirt, and Kayla suited him up with a weight belt, fins, mask, and snorkel. He watched her follow suit as she explained how the weighted vest would help him go down farther than normal. He had thought his swimming days were over for the next twenty years, but here he was. They descended into an underwater preserve. Exotic fish were huddled near the coral reef. Sunlight beamed from above as a sea turtle casually passed them by, then a sand shark drifted away. They went back up for air.

David said, "Those long-tentacled things are called man-of-war?"

"Yes, and stay away from them. The only antidote for their sting is human pee." She suggested making it a short swim, then submerged again. He followed her. It was a mystical world of underwater beauty. The visual colors and silent atmosphere were so vibrant. He understood why it was easy for people to fall in love with the ocean. On their next turn up for air, clouds billowed in the sky. The shadows under the surface moved as darkness appeared from above. The blocked sunlight muted the colors under the surface. Regardless, he felt good to be alive and exploring.

David tapped Kayla on the shoulder after spotting multiple long-tentacled creatures. They floated back to the surface, and she made the call that it had gotten too dangerous. They swam to the boat, and she went first up the ladder. David watched her as the boat swayed with the wake. A jellyfish lingered on the hull. David kicked off his fins and put them on the ledge. He took one more dip with his head under the water. The siphonophore floated out from under the hull and on top of his mask. As he climbed up the ladder, the silent stingers attacked a section of his forehead.

The tiny venom stingers were already in his blood stream before the pain blasted away. Kayla saw David pull the blue, gooey animal away from his ear. The pain was unbearable, and he threw the goggles off. The jellyfish landed on the deck like a raw egg. He sat down and wanted to rub away the excruciating pain and stinging sensation.

Kayla held his arms and yelled, "Don't touch it!" She inspected the tentacles and said, "They'll break off and rub into your skin. It'll only make it worse." He sat back and suffered. She returned with some vinegar and water.

David said, "You're not going to go number one on my forehead, are you?"

"Only land-lubbers pee on stingers anymore. It's a myth. The proper way is with vinegar and water. Now, lean back." Kayla covered his eyes with a towel and then poured the mixture over the inflamed area. "I told you to watch out for those things."

"I was distracted by watching someone climb up the ladder."

Kayla smiled. She replied, "You wanted to make sure I didn't slip and fall?" She kept pouring liquid over his forehead.

"Exactly." She removed the towel over his eyes, and he looked up at her and said, "Do you love him?"

"Of course I do. He's a good man."

"But not love, love."

"What the hell? We're not in high school. What are you referring to?"

He pushed on, "So, why marry him?" She left and came back with a pair of tweezers and a credit card. Then, she started pulling out some of the larger barbs which were sticking out and hard to see.

"Do you have to be in love to marry someone? Some people get married for other reasons."

"So, you're settling?"

"What's wrong with that Mr. Twenty-One Questions? Not everything is what it seems to be right now. But stop talking, or this stinger might get into your eye and turn you blind."

The sun streaked out in between the clouds. Kayla looked at him, and he couldn't tell what she was thinking. He tried to stand up and got woozy. He stumbled and grabbed her arm before falling.

"We better get you below deck, sailor."

He said, "Sounds like a fantastic idea." She slung his arm around her shoulder and supported his frame. Once he was in bed, she started to boil some water to help with the swelling.

"What are my chances, Doc?" David yelled.

She replied, "Looks like we're going to have to cut off one of your arms and donate your brain to science. *If* they'll take it."

"Focus, Doc. This is serious. I'm dying over here. Take care of Tackle and Charlie for me, will ya?"

She came back into the room with the hot water and a washcloth. "Yes, sir."

Then, he did the fake cough with a low, dying whisper, "Tell your mom and dad that I'm sorry that I didn't get to finish the kitchen." She gave him the look again as he continued like he was on his last breath, "What if the test results come back positive?" She put a hot towel on his face and positioned it so he could see her.

"Then you're as good as dead."

David then snuggled under the covers and held them close to his chin. She kept gently compressing the hot cloth on his forehead.

"Thanks for giving it to me straight, Doc. Normally, I don't trust the medical professionals, but you're different."

"You're welcome. Come up top after you're done." He did the fake cough again.

As she got up to leave, he said in a normal voice, "You might be too smart of a friend for me."

"Might?"

"I prefer a woman who can fail calculus or trigonometry."

"You find that attractive?" She asked while tossing him a protein bar.

"Not really, but it makes me feel better in the short-term." She started eating one herself.

"And what's your long-term plan?"

David settled into the pillows and closed his eyes. "My long-term plan? That's a great question."

"How so?"

David opened one eye to look at her and said, "Look where I'm laying down, Captain. Not a bad place to be, wouldn't yah say? Don't want to be in no place other than the spot where I'm at right now." Then, he started to drift away with the waves gently crashing against the boat.

By the time Kayla turned to leave, David was busy counting sheep, but the weekend wasn't over yet. The engine started up as he slumbered on a distant shore in another world.

CHAPTER 20

O P WAS ON the couch watching the news. The coffee table had a few bills spread out next to the calculator and a Mickey Mouse phone. The wire stretched across the floor. He got it from a previous customer as a gift and had it connected. He preferred a cash tip, but the lady was so nice, he couldn't refuse her generosity. He couldn't refuse her generosity. When he looked it up on eBay, the thing was worth three hundred dollars in great condition. His was mint, like his wife, Juanita. She was in the kitchen cooking empanadas. They were his favorite, and she made them from a family recipe.

They had first met at a bank and made each other smile from a simple hello while depositing funds. They became inseparable, yet from completely different parts of the world. OP loved how she spoke English with a Puerto Rican accent and enjoyed watching football. As sweet as Juanita was, she had a dark side as an immigration attorney. She was a natural introvert with a mean streak for people she didn't know or who thought her incompetent. She had a way of speaking down to others, even though she was only five foot two.

Juanita wanted a man who worked with his hands, and she got one with OP. Her entire family loved him not because he made her happy. She was hard to please, and often times, didn't know where he stood because she was unpredictable. Then, there was her proclivity for fancy clothes, nice cars, and expensive dinners. She had him figured out after he laid tile down in her condo and charmed her with a marble finish. The rest of her family put him to work on the weekends. He happily obliged. She grew to appreciate his old-fashioned values and unassuming ways with a Casanova love for romance.

Juanita walked into the room and OP saw her look at the papers and say, "Poppy, ya tienes hambre?"

He said, "Yes, please." He was too stubborn to ask her for help. He liked the fact that she took a backseat as he wrestled with balancing the checkbook. She learned early on to let him struggle with the easy problems, till he asked for help.

She picked up one of the statements and said, "You'd better slow down with the Amex, baby." He took the paper out of her hand and looked at it, then sat up on the edge of the sofa to use the calculator.

"I ordered a new couch," said Juanita.

"Why? I love this thing."

She didn't pay him any attention and said, "You'll see." He let it go and went back to the numbers.

These were sweet words to his ears. She didn't buy cheap. The last thing he ever wanted was for her to stop buying stuff because it was what she loved to do. As much as he didn't care, OP put up some resistance; otherwise, she'd think he'd gone soft. He knew that if she ever wanted to become an interior designer rather than a lawyer, she'd kill it. The phone started ringing, and she looked at the ID.

"No name."

OP asked, "Can you answer it for me, please? I'm buried right now." Then, he got up and walked into the kitchen to get another beer.

When Juanita answered the phone, Joe said, "Hello. Is OP available?"

Juanita replied, "He's not home yet. Whom may I ask is calling?" Joe introduced himself and said that he was a friend of David Wolfe's. Juanita relaxed into a friendly manner.

Joe asked, "Do you know when he'll be back?" She said that she didn't. Joe asked, "Do you know if David is still out with Kayla?"

Juanita said, "We haven't seen either of them today. Is everything okay?"

"Yes," he responded. "All is well. A mutual friend wants him to do some construction work on their roof, and they're having a hard time getting a hold of one another."

"He normally works from home," Juanita said. "Do you have his address? Oh, you do. Well, I know David was out on a boat today, so why don't you try his cell phone?"

OP came back in the room and motioned for her to give him the phone.

"Hold on a second, OP just walked in." Joe hung up.

"Hello?" The line was dead. OP looked at the screen, "Who was it?"

Juanita said, "Some older gringo named Joe. He sounded funny. Like some of your relatives."

"Russian?"

"No. Something else."

"Probably one of Thorpe's people."

"He has David's address. You might want to call him."

Instead, he sent a text. OP saw Juanita start to worry.

OP said, "David's been hanging out with Thorpe's fiancée all day. I think she's interested in his tool set." Juanita shook her head at the reference.

OP continued, "She's defecting. It happens."

"More like crossing the border." He filled her in on the gossip and explained the situation. It felt good to get the councilors free advice.

Juanita listened as OP put the phone down and pulled her close to let her know the accounting department was closed for the night.

HAN AND AARON entered a tiny, vintage elevator. They stood close to one another, and Aaron cracked a smile. Han was emotionless as he pressed the button for the penthouse. He said to Aaron, "Don't say anything stupid." Afterwards, they climbed a few stairs and accessed the roof via a spring-loaded door. Christopher was looking out into the distance at some police helicopters hovering in the sky. The news channels were farther away. He was wearing a Panama Jack hat and resting his hands on a duck cane. His ankle and ear didn't hurt so much from the fall the other day with Kayla. He'd taken enough drugs and sucked down enough booze to kill all of the pain.

Han glanced at Aaron, who looked deathly afraid. They stopped about twenty feet from the edge. Christopher said, "Come closer. I want you to see this."

"How are you?" asked Aaron.

"Incredible. Our hack team is in the building, slaving away because of you. I had to put two more people on to complete the job. We're paying them in pizza, cash, and cocaine." Aaron apologized again for not being able to find the flash drive and offered to help with the coding. "Don't worry about it, and let me come up with the ideas. You don't think I can fix this problem? It's my job."

Christopher saw Aaron look to Han for help. Christopher said, "Han can't help you." Han stepped up and handed over an almost completed statue of the Yinwyan. "Not bad." He gave it no more thought and tossed it to the ground. "Only it's not the original." Han went over and picked it up and put it back in the bag. Christopher said, "I'm glad you didn't kill him. He can be useful."

Aaron started rambling, and Christopher said, "Relax. It's a joke."

Aaron said, "I just wanted to get a closer look at the statue. The guy jumped me. When I woke up, I didn't know what to do."

Christopher said, "There are more of those than you think." He regretted making the admission but was feeling too good to critique himself. Han looked away as if uninterested. Christopher took a sip of tequila out of a flask and screwed the cap back into place. He remembered how the doctor told him not to mix anything with alcohol. His next words were on the tip of his tongue; only, he became captivated by the full moon and closed his eyes to take in a moment of peace. It'd been a day, and now, he had to muster up a way to deal with having to wait until the hackers broke the code for a new flash drive.

"You know, Aaron," Christopher began, "my father told me that there would be times like this." He pointed with his cane to the Yinwyan Han was holding. "My father gave it to me a few weeks before their plane crashed, said it would help me to become a better person. This is why I keep it near the booze to remind me to drink more. Dad had always found a way to push me." He saw the sorry look on Aaron's face, and the drugs that Christopher had ingested earlier made the other man's face look contorted.

Aaron said, "We're a lot alike in that regard."

Christopher said, "I think so. We're both selfish, and that's a good thing. It doesn't win us a lot of friends, but it does make us valuable." Aaron was getting scared because Christopher wasn't making any sense to him. The man looked wasted and sober at the same time.

Aaron noticed a few more bodyguards come out from the shadows, but they kept their distance. He blurted out, "The statue is in my office, bottom drawer."

Han stood there, motionless. Christopher looked at him and then faced Aaron. Duke stepped out of the shadows and said, "This is a funny place to meet." He slapped the neck of one of the guards and knocked the man out.

"What are you doing?" Christopher was seething and bent down to check on the unconscious man.

Duke said, "I don't know. You told me to come to the house, and here I am. I thought you wanted me to help you out?"

Christopher said, "Clearly, that was a mistake on my part. Han, don't do anything, please." Duke spun around and pointed a gun at Han. Christopher said, "What the fuck are you doing now? Calm down. This isn't why I've brought you in." Duke didn't holster the weapon, but he lowered his arm. Joe came out of the shadows but stayed in the darkness. Christopher said, "I need you for a different mission. We can all kill each other afterwards." Aaron's neck and shoulders started to tighten. Christopher said, "I need you to find the flash drive."

Aaron said, "I wasn't going to sell it to anyone. I was on my way..." Christopher cut him off and said, "Shut up, Aaron. I already knew you took the Yinwyan. Forget about it."

Christopher said to Duke, "Will you relax and give me a second to explain," then motioned for Han to relax. Joe pulled out a 357 and stepped back away from the conflict. Christopher said, "I've been told that we have a spy in our midst trying to access the database. They're already tracking us, and it's put me on edge. The only thing I need is the flash drive."

Duke said, "Sounds like you're making plans for an exit strategy."

Christopher agreed and said, "Duke, I need you to team up with Aaron. Retrace his steps to find the flash drive and see if you can beat the hacker's timeframe."

Han grabbed Christopher's arm. "You sure it's wise to keep him around?"

Christopher had no choice. There was no place to run or country to hide in. He said, "We'll have to make it work." Then, he turned to Duke and said, "Go to this David guy's house and see what you can find. In the meantime, keep me posted."

Duke pointed to Aaron. "Should we throw him out in the trash when done?"

Christopher said, "No. Don't be ridiculous. Don't do a fucking thing with him."

Duke said, "You guys are a bunch of Twinkies. What do you want me to do with the kid? I'm not some baggage handler."

Christopher said, "Find out anything you can, and meet us back at the house. Don't hurt the guy. We have enough problems." They all left Duke alone with Aaron.

It was everything that Duke didn't want to hear as he watched them leave. He didn't trust anyone and wanted to kill Christopher. Only, the guy in the back looked familiar. He saw him draw his weapon, and Duke didn't know if he'd live after getting off the first couple shots. So, he redirected his focus elsewhere. He asked the kid, "Where's the flash drive?"

Aaron said, "I don't know. We should go look for it."

Duke picked up Aaron and turned him upside down. "Empty your pockets." Then, Duke shook him.

Aaron yelled, "Let me go, you animal!" Change fell out, as did car keys and a rabbit's foot.

Duke said, "You got that right," then formed a plan of his own. The paranoia in his head said that Christopher was coming after him for messing up the drug run. It was why Christopher brought Duke back to Florida. He tightened his hands on Aaron's shirt. A second later, he launched Aaron over the edge of the building. The shock of not being able to find his feet didn't last long as the impending doom filled Aaron's brain. A split second later, he lost all consciousness as a Cadillac broke his fall. Han, Christopher, and the bodyguards were leaving as the crash occurred. They looked up at Duke, who gave them a salute.

Christopher looked away, feeling genuine hatred for the man. He had no choice now and watched Han start to go back up the stairs. Christopher grabbed his arm and said, "Another time. We have too much to do."

Duke looked off into the distance and admired the skyline.

A BUILDING HAD collapsed, and they were short-staffed at the hospital. Kayla's father called as they were docking the boat to ask for help. David drove her over, and they saw that the place was littered with emergency vehicles and news teams. They said their goodbyes at the front entrance. He broke the ice by saying, "It was good hanging out with you today, despite getting zapped in the face and almost dying."

She said, "You pulled through all right. I had a good time myself." It was obvious to both of them that it had to end. He was trying to think of something normal to say when he saw an elderly woman shuffling towards them. While they looked through the windshield, the elderly woman started struggling with a thick, aluminum walker. It had cut out tennis balls on the bottom of each peg.

David said, "I'll handle everything with Christopher in the morning...is she all right?" The elderly woman hit a lip on the sidewalk and fell to the curb.

They both jumped out of the car to help. Some orderlies were nearby and gave their support. David stepped back to let them do their thing. Kayla shrugged and waved goodbye. It was the first time that he'd seen a face plant by a little, old lady. *What are the odds?*

CHAPTER 21

CHARLIE AND TACKLE were eating away in separate bowls as David settled in for the night. He got into some comfortable clothes and started looking around for the replica Yinwyan, but it was gone. He searched the place and found the window broken in the back. He checked the gun stash, and it wasn't touched. He decided not call the police, given his earlier actions at Thorpe's. Instead, he cut a piece of plywood to board up the window, and then made a sandwich. What was done was done, and it wouldn't be a problem to make another replica later.

Standing at the kitchen sink, David washed dishes and saw the wall stained black from the flame bursts. He stacked the bowls and glasses in a neat pile. The window reflected his image as he contemplated the past forty-eight hours. With the water running he started to relax as a figure appeared from behind. A rubberized billy club glanced the backside of his head and struck his shoulder.

David buckled but didn't fall. He turned around to face the intruder with his arms protecting his head. He went to tackle him and got bitch-slapped into the cabinets by a hand that could palm a bowling ball. He hit the ground hard and was slow to move afterwards. The giant in front of him told him to relax. He thought about getting up but decided that he was satisfied with just sitting on the floor. The big man pulled out a gun. "Just stay on the floor for a minute until your blood starts circulating again." David didn't move an inch and waited for instructions. He got the answer pretty quick when Joe said, "Thorpe wants the flash drive. Told me to get it. I'm Joe." He extended his hand, and David shook it.

He simply said, "Nice to meet you, Joe. I'm David."

Joe said, "I know. Nothing is going to happen to you unless you do something stupid." Then, Joe ordered David to get up and follow him. They both walked into the living room, and Joe said, "You need a maid."

David watched the uninvited hammerhead walk around like he hated his job. He looked mad, and it was probably why he tried to split his head wide open. Then, Joe asked, "You okay?"

"I don't know. How do I look?"

Joe said, "Scared shitless," as he picked up a pile of wires, extension cords, and cables. He glanced at David like he was cuckoo and said, "What are you, one of those newborn recyclers?"

"It's for my artwork, and I collect the rest, just in case I need them."

"In case of what? Home Depot shuts down?" David asked for some water. Joe told David to sit down and got a bottle from the twenty-four-pack stacked near the wall. Charlie came crawling up to Joe and laid down at his shoes. He picked him up and his heart melted. Tackle went to David.

"This guy is a sweetheart," said Joe. Charlie instantly fell asleep in the arms of the lug. Joe pet Charlie and walked around like he was in a gallery. "Thorpe isn't too happy with you. But he's in a bad situation. Not sure what it is."

David said, "Neither do I."

"You got that right." The sculpture of the deer held his gaze, and he walked over to see scraps of garbage hanging from the board. As the image came to view of an actual deer head with antlers, he froze in his tracks. The optical illusion captured his imagination. Nothing was what it appeared to be; he took his time returning to David. He sat back down, and Charlie hadn't moved an inch the entire time.

Charlie's talent for making fast friends was applied, and it might have saved David's life. He smiled at Joe, and they sat in an uncomfortable silence. David touched the back of his head and it felt like it was split in two. He closed his eyes and gently rubbed his fingers on his shoulder, then sat back on the couch to relax. The big man could shoot at any moment, and he didn't want to look, so he closed his eyes. Slowly, he opened them back up and saw Charlie still sleeping in Joe's arms.

Joe looked up and said, "Where did you get this thing? It's adorable."

"The pound." Joe didn't believe him.

"This is a good dog. What's his name?"

"Charlie."

"Get out of town. That's my brother's name. Hey, Charlie. You like tuna fish?"

David looked around for clues as to what was going to happen next. He'd never had his house broken into before and then had a conversation with the assailant. He searched around in his mind for the root cause of his recent adventures which had been happening at an alarming pace. Joe said, "Thorpe isn't too bad a guy, but you crossed the man up with his money. Mess with the cash, and it'll make people do some strange things."

"What do you want from me?"

Joe said, "We'll get to it," and then asked, "Do you feed these dogs human food? It's probably why they're so nice."

"No. Dry kibble only."

"What's your problem?"

"It's not good for the dogs to eat human food."

"So, then why do they eat it?" Joe asked, frowning. David had taken this exact point of view with his vet on multiple occasions, and the answer was because certain dogs needed specific foods based on their stomachs. He'd tried to urge Charlie to eat whatever he put in front of him, but it never took. A few vet bills later, and David decided to switch things up. Dog kibble with the occasional mutt pretzel stick wrapped in peanut butter kept Charlie happy. Plus, David's money stayed in the bank. Tackle's specialty was anything. He'd eat canned sardines, sauerkraut, hot dog relish, anything but cherry tomatoes.

David said, "I'm sorry, but do you have a dog?"

"No."

"You'd have to have a dog in order to understand."

Joe raised his gun and said, "No. I don't think I do." David kept his mouth shut on the subject. The man with a crooked nose looked like he'd been hurting people for a while. Then, Joe said, "Thorpe knows you didn't take the Yinwyan and said that you made a nice replica." That information was good to know, so now, David didn't have to look for it. David relaxed a bit. Then, Joe said, "But it doesn't mean he won't pay someone to slit your throat. He's a good guy if you don't know him on the drugs."

"Sounds like a real winner. Does he do a lot of drugs?"

"Is that a problem? He's rich, he can do whatever he wants. That's the type of person you're dealing with." David pressed his fingers over his ears again to see if it would stop the ringing. Joe stood up and went back to the deer head with antlers.

He pointed to the mounted deer head and asked David, "What do you call this one?"

David forced himself to say, "The Challenge."

The thought of grabbing the lamp and smashing it over Joe's head emerged. But would it do the trick? What if the cord got stuck behind the couch? The thing didn't stretch far enough. Maybe David could make a run for it, but then, he thought, it's best not to get shot in the back. What was he going to do? If he couldn't get the guy in the kitchen, then what chance did he have now? Maybe the iron skillet on the stove would do the trick. David kept rubbing his neck to figure things out.

"Do you want a bag of ice?" Joe asked. "Sorry, it's been a while since I swung one of those things. I used to be pretty good at it."

"It's nice to know the skills have waned."

Joe chuckled and grabbed David by the collar as he followed him back to the kitchen. He got some ice, and they returned, stopping at the deer head. Joe said, "I don't get it. What's the challenge?"

David started out by saying, "It's a long story." Then, he shared about growing up in Cleveland and how he liked drawing as a kid. Joe looked at his watch. David got the hint.

"The reality is, it's not my work," David said, changing his tone. "I traded with another artist for a dresser. It's a made-up name based on the truth that people don't tell you. The crap we all carry inside us is the challenge. Which is basically a lie we tell ourselves, and everyone else. Seems like nothing can be taken at face-value, and on top of it all, we give ourselves the worst advice."

Joe said, "Go on."

David continued as if he wasn't interrupted. "We all do it blindly and suffer unconsciously as situations escalate. It hurts the most when we destroy ourselves and those around us thinking it's someone else's fault. Nothing in this room is out of place for me, even though it needs to be cleaned, and you think it to be messy. It's why you mentioned that I need a maid. Yet, you see something completely different. You think I'm a slob?"

Joe said, "More nuts then lazy." He pointed to the deer head with his thumb to eye level and said, "But this makes sense now."

David picked up a Bad Company album and put it back in its sleeve. He said, "Yah, this place is a shithole, and I'll soon untie the knot that it has on me."

"How did you come to that conclusion?"

David replied, "I have a good therapist. It's been a combination of things and something the artist told me.

"What was it?" David continued, "He said the idea came to him from an accident in the dead of winter. He was driving like a maniac, feeling his oats on a snow-covered road when an elk popped out. Boom! Splattered it under a Ford." David slapped his hands together, and Joe was motionless. "No big deal, right? A lot of people would say, 'Now you get out, chop it up, and have steaks for the winter.' Not this guy. He said he didn't kill it, but instead, followed it. Watched it stumble through the snow that took him deep into the woods. The farther he went, the more he wanted to leave, and after a couple hundred yards, he caught up to it. The thing was mangled, and at the end of its life. Said he looked into the night and saw a shooting star burn across the sky."

Joe said, "Bullshit."

David continued, "I'm just telling you what he told me... then, the wolves showed up. They howled, it bounced off the trees, and echoed through his soul. Then, something tugged at his leg as he looked down, and saw the elk chewing at his pants. He pulled away and started moving back to civilization. The way I see it, truth or fiction, make sure you drive safe at night on a snowy, country road."

When David finished talking, Joe was snuggling with Charlie. He said, "You're one strange individual."

David kept going and said, "What I got out of what he was saying is what you just said. Nothing makes any sense; this is life. Why bother trying to figure it out? Just watch what's going on, and right now, I'm into tape. Crazy about the sticky paper.

Different colors, whatever I can find, electrical, duct, scotch, masking, medical, doesn't matter."

Joe scratched his head and said, "What are you talking about?"

David pulled out a tape collage of Tackle and Charlie together. Joe held it up to Charlie and said, "Close resemblance. Were you trained professionally?"

David managed to crack a smile and asked Joe, "Were you?"

"How can you tell?"

"Not completely sure. But I'd have to say it's the turtleneck."

"It keeps me warm."

"In Florida?"

David checked out Joe's shoes. They had a thin tread and were low to the ground. They were the kind of footgear wrestlers or power lifters wore. David said, "Even look at your shoes. You can keep your balance in those things when times get quarrelsome." His knuckles looked like kneecaps, but David didn't push his luck. He asked, "You look like you tip the scale around 260?" All six foot four inches of Joe wasn't interested in answering questions. He had a thin circumference, was scrappy looking, and the salt-and-pepper mophead. David asked, "Do you want me to get you the flash drive?"

Joe paused and shook his head. "No. I'm going to tell him you didn't have it."

David couldn't believe what he'd just heard. "But I do. It's right here."

Joe started looking at another painting. "I know where it is. It was an obvious place to start behind the skateboards."

"I don't understand?"

"If I take it back to Thorpe, then my job is over. At my age, it could mean the end for me. I've been doing this for too long. Know too many things. I'm expendable. It's best to have no urgency when you think it might be your last mission. Have to trust yourself and let the events play to their own music. I'll still verify and see what the trees shake to the ground before pulling a trigger. Don't worry. Thorpe isn't going to kill his newlywed's parents' general contractor. Besides, there's always a backup. Sure, he wants you out of the picture for hanging with his fiancée, but that's no reason to kill a guy. Thorpe's too much of a playboy. One man is already dead, and he doesn't want anyone else to die." Joe kept on petting Charlie and said, "He's something else, isn't he? Do you know his background?"

David said that he didn't.

Joe asked, "How much is this?" Joe was looking at a different painting. "The one with the funny faces."

"It's hard to figure out a price under these conditions. What's it worth to you? The perceived value…" David bit his tongue as Joe took out his gun and put it back into a more comfortable place.

"Give me a good price."

"You're in luck. We just happen to be having a 'holiday special' going on right now."

Joe smiled and put the gun back in its holster. He kept looking around until he rested his eyes on a farm landscape with rabbits in the corner. David could tell that he was more of a color guy and asked, "You like rabbits?"

"Are you selling this one?"

David breathed a sigh of relief but didn't answer. He got up and went to the kitchen.

"Where are you going?" Joe asked.

"I'm going to go and get some wrapping paper. I'll be back."

"Don't go too far." David thought about running out the front door but decided against it because Joe had Charlie. Of all the luck, he liked the farm painting, and it was from another trade. He returned a few minutes later with some brown paper bags and masking tape. He took the painting off the wall and grabbed a pair of scissors.

"This isn't one of my paintings, either. I got it at a thrift store for twenty dollars. It's a famous Haitian artist and worth a lot of money. The store didn't have a clue as to who it was. You've got good taste."

Joe said, "See how the barn rests away from the chickens? I've always wanted to own a farm."

"You'd be doing me a favor by taking it."

"How come?"

"You look like you need some art in your life."

"Always been difficult for me to appreciate it. Never understood it, really. Maybe this place isn't a junk yard, after all." Joe sat back on the couch and watched David meticulously cut the brown bags up and seal the painting with the masking tape. Charlie jumped off the lap of his new friend to watch David work.

Joe said, "I'm going to put this up in my office. I'm kind of glad I didn't knock you out with the smack to the head." He mused, "Back in the day, you would have never made it past the kitchen."

"Good to see that you've turned a corner."

"Tell you a secret," said Joe. "It was always difficult for me to kill someone after meeting their dog." David looked over from making a face on the wrapping paper.

"Really?"

"No. I'm kidding," said Joe. "But Charlie is such a good boy. How did you come up with the name?"

"It's the one they gave me at the pound. I kept it." Joe looked at him like he didn't believe him. David asked, "What should I do now?"

"Get the hell out of town. There's a madman loose with a contract out on a lot of people. You might be on his list."

It felt like a bad dream to David, and his head started to hurt. He wanted to get some food, but it was too late. Maybe he could go to the corner store for some ice cream. It was the best stress reliever, a pint of vanilla with peanut butter swirl. He handed him the painting. Joe said, "Cute, but remember, you never saw me before."

They walked outside together.

"Don't look so down," Joe said. "You're still alive, and by all rights, you should be dead." He continued, "Thorpe knows more than a dozen guys who can perform a task as good as me. But don't worry, Thorpe has other personal problems right now, like some hotshot Washington elites gunning for his family business."

They reached Joe's van, and he opened the back. On the floor was a Joe Momma Cupcake Travel Bag. "You in the cupcake business?" David asked.

"Take it easy, Picasso. It's just a bag." Joe's phone started ringing. It was Christopher. "Don't say a word," he warned. "Hey...he hasn't shown up yet, and I couldn't find the flash drive. What do you want me to do?" He unlocked the side – door to the van and waved for David to put the painting in the back.

"Motherfucker. Are you losing your touch?" Christopher demanded.

"Could be, I am older now. Maybe I should try to find your fiancée first? She's probably hanging out with this David guy."

"Don't worry about it. I got it covered. Just sit tight until he shows up. We're running out of time."

"Don't worry," Joe said. "I'll get the bastard." Christopher hung up as Joe winked at David.

Joe said, "This is what you have to do. Get as many friends together as you can. Do you have any?"

"I know a Russian. Is that any good?"

"If you can find a Cossack, then you'll have a chance. This is what you do. First thing tomorrow morning, drive over to Thorpe's with all your friends in tow and hand over the flash drive on the best of terms. It'll cool him down a bit, and you can see if he'll forget the whole thing. He won't ask about the Yinwyan because he knows you didn't take it. But be careful of this longhaired freak mulling about. He's dangerous. They call him Duke. He's an evil dude, so be on high alert."

David thought that it was as good a plan as any. The flash drive had to be returned. Joe got in the front seat and rolled down the window.

"You got any money?"

David said, "I've got a couple hundred dollars on me."

Joe laughed. "No, you idiot, like a nest egg. Thirty Gs in a shoebox, Krugerrand's, silver coins?" It had been a while since he looked at any of his 401(k)s. Joe said, "Just disappear for a few months."

"Never going to happen. I have too much work to do."

Joe looked at David and said, "Then, you need lay low for a few days or take a short vacation to Alaska."

"Not going to happen. I'm in the middle of a job."

Joe put the vehicle in gear. "Your choice. You're playing with the big boys now."

David asked, "What else?"

"What do you mean, 'What else?'"

"Anything you forgot to tell me?" David asked.

Joe fixed the rearview mirror and said, "Yah. I'd leave the fiancée alone if I were you. Guys like Christopher are territorial and kill for pride." He drove off as David called his Russian Cossack.

CHAPTER 22

NEWS CREWS WERE hanging out at the hospital and inter-viewing staff as Kayla walked out of the automatic doors. Some were standing back and smoking cigarettes, while others stood by, ready to ask questions. She took a deep breath and felt good for being able to contribute. A reporter thought that she was from the building collapse and asked. She declined, smiled, and kept on moving. She remembered her dad's reaction after he saw the new hair do. She didn't have to tell him how much everyone loved it; he heard it for himself. The last patient she talked to was a seventy-five-year-old retired bank executive. She looked up at Kayla from her wheelchair and said, "Styles sure have changed."

Kayla loved her dad for understanding why she decided to go through with the wedding. He gave her his support and joked about how he sold out for love, but the situation has changed. A staff member approached her and asked to take a picture together. Then, she saw Christopher's limousine pull up. The window rolled down and she asked, "What are you doing here?"

Christopher stuck his head out of the window and said, "Need a ride?"

Kayla looked inside and got in while saying, "Of course."

He took one look and said, "You play drums in a band now? What the hell happened?" She looked into his eyes and saw that they were redder than usual.

She asked, "Have you had any sleep since the last time we talked?"

"No. But forget about it. I'll be sleeping soon enough. What happened to you?"

She went for the small talk option. "You like it?" "You got ripped off. No, seriously. It looks ridiculous. What about the wedding photos? Am I going to have to get a Mohawk?" She looked away to compose herself. He said, "I'm just kidding. Relax. It looks great on you." She got the sarcasm.

Kayla turned her head toward him and burned a stare into his eyes. She said, "Well, I like it. What happened to you this morning? Why did you blow me off?" She was ready for the excuses.

"Another wasted business deal," he said as he rubbed his knee and added, "And I got a surprise background check done on someone very close to me."

"We need to talk," she said.

"Yes, we do."

The silence inside the car made her look at him twice. She could see that he had something to say. "I've been told you work for a unique branch in government."

She said, "I thought you already knew."

"Have you given them anything?"

"Who?"

He sat back in his seat to relax and said, "Something doesn't add up. Is your new friend in on it, too?"

"You need to get some rest, and I need to get home. Can we drive?"

"The guy smells fishy to me. An ungrateful fellow."

"How so?"

"Is he part of your team?"

"This is getting stranger by the second. What the hell are you talking about?"

He said, "James Farnsworth is buying, excuse me, taking over the family business. I'm being forced out. They're sending it to China."

"They can't force you to sell."

"No. No, they can't, but they *can* make my life very difficult."

"What's on the skateboard? David wanted to go give it to you this morning, but you were already gone. You sent Han to get it from him, and all you had to do was answer the phone if you wanted it back so badly."

Christopher gritted his teeth and started shaking his head. Just then, his cell started ringing. It was Tokyo again. Christopher said, "I have to take this," and got out of the vehicle.

When Christopher came back, Kayla asked, "Who was it?"

He looked over to her and saw that she had opened up his Chinook Water Flask. He picked it up to see it was empty. He bowed his head and said, "Don't be mad at me, but I'm going to be in some serious trouble tomorrow."

"No shit. How about right now?"

"You don't understand. This has been a fucking crazy past few days. This morning was a lot of work. Your file on me should have told you at least that much."

"My file? We've known each other a long time. I don't need a file on you. You get choices, my position doesn't offer a lot of options...what was in the water?"

He wanted to know more, but she was already fading. He said, "The water was meant for me, so I could sleep tonight. We're going to have to talk in the morning."

"What was in it?"

"Horse tranquilizer." Kayla looked at how much she had put away. "Before you pass out, one question. Was this entire getting married proposal part of some elaborate plan?"

She said, "You asked me. How long does it take to kick in?"

He said he didn't know.

She said, "I told them I wouldn't do anything. Your proposal was my way out."

"What do they want?"

"From what I can gather, access. It's a frame job or a smear campaign. Since I've told them nothing, they're pissed and plan on shipping me out to Nova Scotia on Monday. I agreed to marry you because then they can't make me do my job, but if they want, they could then send me to prison."

"Thanks for telling me."

"It was an easy decision."

"Why?"

She gave him a confused look and said, "This isn't the game I signed up for, and it came back to bite me in the ass. I thought it would work out for both of us and I could come clean later, but we're just two friends who shouldn't get married."

"Wow. That rolled right off the tongue easy enough. It still might work."

Kayla finished with, "The chances are thin. It's better that they did force our hand because now we both know." She grabbed his arm and said, "You know, I'm going to kick your ass when I wake up." She closed her eyes and struggled to reach in her jean pocket, then pulled out the engagement ring. It fell to the floor.

Christopher picked it up and said, "It was fun while it lasted. I had such good plans for us."

"I don't think so. If you cared so much, then you would have been at the dock this morning."

"I shouldn't have done any meetings today."

She said, "Quit lying, and you need to start finding a way to protect yourself." He picked up his phone again and read the text message: *The team is having a hard time with the backup. It will take a few hours longer.* He didn't reply and put the device in his pocket.

Kayla turned to him and said, "I've been meaning to tell you something. You don't have to say anything if you don't want to."

"Go ahead."

"You didn't really answer the question about your mother's cat. I understand that you were young, but it doesn't justify what you did. I'm not going to let you do it to Tatiana." Christopher looked at her for the longest time in silence and said he was sorry, but she was already out.

DAVID RANG THE doorbell outside of OP's house with Tackle and Charlie in tow. They were patiently waiting for an answer. He started pounding on the front door. OP finally answered in a speedo and goggles, with a beer in his hand.

David said, "You ever wear this to work, you're fired."

"Come on in, man. What's bothering you?"

David walked in, and the dogs waited for OP to wave them along. They proceeded after he acknowledged that it was okay. They entered with tails wagging.

"I've been trying to reach you," David continued.

OP said, "It's jacuzzi night." Juanita came in from the back-yard in a bikini and T-shirt. David apologized for the intrusion. OP interjected, "You come to talk about my electrical abilities?"

"Hey, Charlie!" Juanita picked him up and snuggled him while walking out of the room.

"You'll never see that dog again," said OP. Then, he started petting Tackle while saying, "They always forget about you, don't they."

David said, "I don't care about the floor right now," and that got OP's attention. He said, "You don't look so good."

"How can you tell?"

"Because you haven't opened the refrigerator yet, and you have blood on the side of your neck." David got a paper towel and blotted a small cut on the side of his neck. He looked on the stove and opened the sauté pan to see a few leftover stuffed pork chops.

OP got out a plate and some silverware. David sat at the table, ready to eat, and asked, "You have any cafécito?"

They always did, and OP said, "Juanita made some earlier. I'll heat it up." David only knew it as jet fuel. He preferred small doses or else it would make the inside of his skin itch.

David said, "Need your help with something."

"You look like you've seen a ghost."

David started filling him in on what had transpired after they left the bar. Then, he said, "The guy, Joe, was paid to kill me but didn't. It cost me a painting to stay alive, but something else is going on with the guy."

"He told you his name?" OP asked, then handed over a plate of pork chops with applesauce and green beans.

"No potatoes?"

"This is leftovers."

David admitted, "We actually had a pretty good time together."

OP gave the "uh-oh" remark. David understood what he was saying and slowly chewed his food, noticing what a difference applesauce made.

Charlie came back into the kitchen and jumped up onto David's lap. Juanita entered a few minutes later. She took out a bowl of grapes and sat down to listen to David talk. Tackle was sprawled out on the floor as everyone watched David eat.

OP said, "How did you know which room to bust into to get to the tiger?"

David said, "Lucky guess."

OP continued and asked, "And then, you saw the skateboard and wanted it for the rest of your collection?"

David nodded in response. Juanita continued with the follow-up questions. He liked how she saw through things and kept drilling him with the facts of the story. OP needed someone like her. No pleading the fifth in this house. David said, "It all happened so fast, and I'd do it again if I had the chance. My only mistake was taking the skateboard. I'll straighten that out tomorrow."

"I broke my arm skateboarding," OP interjected. "Did I ever tell you the story, baby?"

Both David and Juanita said, "Yes, you did."

She clarified, "More than once." Then, she went back to David to say, "Bad luck for you." David understood.

OP asked, "What are you going to do?"

David said, "It's why I'm here." He stretched out his shoulder, which felt painful and good at the same time. He continued with, "All I can do is return the flash drive tomorrow and hope that Thorpe lets me make amends."

Juanita asked, "So, we go with you tomorrow?"

"Doesn't hurt to have a lawyer in tow. If you think it's safe? I don't want to put you into any kind of trouble."

OP replied, "Makes me think of the Cleveland Indians."

Juanita groaned, "No baseball, please."

OP continued, "It's just like playing a double header. We have to have a strategy for these back-to-back games. It's not as simple as a hit, run, and score."

"You know they're thinking about changing the name of the team," David said.

"Never going to happen. Even if it did, they could call themselves the Cleveland Cranberries, and it wouldn't matter. They'll always be the Cleveland Indians." David never understood how a kid who spent eight years in Russia could love baseball more than him.

David said, "So, this is going to be a Dostoevsky squeeze play?"

OP said, "The harder you try, the worse it gets. You made your move, and now, you must bear the responsibility. But forget the diamond in the rough theory. Let's switch tactics and talk hockey."

Juanita and David simultaneously said, "Hockey!?"

She said, "You don't watch hockey."

"Sure, I do. When the Stanley Cup is on." Juanita relinquished the questioning.

"Well, in Russia, baby, hockey is as important as cheese is to a Wisconsinite." He continued without interruption. "Let's look at the obvious and apply pressure on the net. Not the goalie, but in the scoring area. The protector doesn't exist, only the net. And in order to do that, we have to establish what the defense is giving us. That gets done by moving the puck across the blue line. Push hard and put bodies into the boards. But don't get chippy. Smash 'em."

He drove his fist into his palm. "Knock out a few teeth. Break a nose or two. We have to send a few of them to the chiropractor. Then, with the home crowd against us, we use our spacing. We need this for what?" OP waited for them to answer, but they had no idea. "A-SOG. A shot on goal, get it near the net, take a rebound. We don't have to score to win; it's all about having a swarming mentality and the score comes naturally. And in this game, high sticking is allowed. As long as the flash drive gets dropped off, we're all good. Then, you say goodbye to your girl. Game over."

OP looked for approval. They were both speechless.

Juanita turned to David and said, "If I were you, I'd call the cops."

David said, "You had me at crossing the blue line, and then, it all went south. Can you say that again, only in English this time? Hold on a second first." He looked at his phone and decided to call Kayla.

CHRISTOPHER TALKED TO and straightened out Kayla as she slept. "You have my full blessing to take care of Tatiana. We do it first thing in the morning. And as far as my mother's cat is concerned, I'd forgotten all about that very moment until you brought it up yesterday. I was a troubled kid back then and trying to get the attention of someone I loved dearly. When she acted as if I didn't exist, I made sure that she remembered me. It was a childish act. Nothing more." He sat back in the seat when finished.

At this point, Christopher started looking out the window at the white building. He said, "Mother had everything a woman could ask for: brains, beauty, friends. I was an only child. Dad was rarely home, and Mother didn't exist to me. But look what they gave me. I can't complain. You would think that we were a family, but we weren't. We were oceans apart from one another."

Christopher looked over at Kayla and continued the one-way conversation. "What else could I do? I would never want to share with you such a thing. This was my burden." Her phone started ringing. Christopher's returned from his thoughts, which were a million miles away, and got out her phone.

"Hello, David."

The voice sent a chill down David's back. "Can I speak with Kayla?"

"She's busy right now and told me to answer. I'll tell her you called?"

"No problem," David said. "I'm glad we connected."

"Me, too. When do you plan on returning my skateboard?"

"How about right now?"

"No, now's a bad time. Kayla and I are busy. Just bring it by tomorrow at noon." Christopher hung up the phone. He took out a cigar and torched the end. Then, he told the driver to take the long way home. He had to contemplate his mother again.

———

A HUMMER PULLED up outside of David's home. Duke got out with a hammer and banged on the door a few times. No one answered. He saw the face latch at eye-level and gave it a couple of whacks. A crack in the latch allowed him to look inside, but he couldn't see anything. He smacked on the lock, and it started to bend, but it wasn't going to help due to the deadbolt. In frustration, he kept smashing the handle until it fell off the frame. He put his shoulder into the panel of the door, but it didn't budge an inch. He went back out to the vehicle and got a sledge hammer. After three or four attempts with the new tool, nothing moved. Considering himself a natural-born genius, he felt a blob of multicellular groupings seize together within his brain and produce a thought. What if he took out the winch and hooked it to the crack in the viewing latch? Perfect.

After hooking it up, he got back into the truck and slammed it in reverse. The attachment wasn't done properly. As the tension increased on the thousand-pound cable, it finally gave way and created a whiplash with the hook as it snapped off the door. The end flew into the windshield, and the spiderweb pattern of cracked glass made Duke slam on the brakes. He thought about ramming the vehicle into the front door to knock it off the hinges. Intelligence prevailed, and he took out a K-12 fire rescue saw. In less than a minute, he walked through the front door and gave it an inspection.

Little did Duke know that the opening was reinforced from the inside with 2.7-gauge metal framing attached to concrete. The header was a steel wide flange beam for commercial construction. Duke wanted to burn the place to the ground with every fiber in his body, and the only reason he didn't was because he didn't have any gasoline. But he'd get some soon enough as his nostrils flared.

Not having the ability to start a fire drove Duke into a poisonous rage. He liked the look of the place and didn't know what to destroy. He walked into the living room, and after one beat, he saw the baby grand piano. A song popped into his head by the Rolling Stones: "You can't always get what you want…"

CHAPTER 23

SUNDAY
0000 HRS

DAVID LOOKED AT the phone as if he had swallowed a moldy ham sandwich. It felt humbling as he mumbled to himself, "It's better this way." Those two needed to get back together, and he got a slight reprieve for not being a homewrecker. It would be good to get the exchange over with; nothing good ever came from these types of whacky connections. It was difficult to get her off his mind, and the rollercoaster ride over the last forty-eight hours didn't help. Juanita plopped the cafécito down for him, and he drained it. OP watched him, and David said, "Can you roll with me back to my place?"

David didn't have to ask twice as OP put on his shit-kicking boots. The three of them drove over to his place and left the dogs behind. They saw the front door cut in half as they pulled up. Juanita let out a shocked, "Oh, my God." They pushed the door open to see the walls covered with spray paint as they moved slowly through the house. OP pulled Juanita inside the kitchen and told her to remain calm. She knew that David had become a hoarder but didn't know to what extent. She saw the toaster hanging from the light fixture and covered her mouth. OP whispered to her again to not say anything. All three kept walking into the living room, where they saw Joe sitting on the couch.

David was in shock and asked, "What brought you back?"

OP asked, "Did you do all of this?" David held him back.

Joe said, "No." OP grabbed a pipe wrench from the tool bucket, and David told him to relax.

"The guy's name is Duke," Joe said while throwing a Baby Ruth candy bar on the coffee table.

The Baldwin baby grand piano was in splinters. David took a seat near Joe. OP said, "Well, this ball player is a real son-of-a-bitch. Look at this mess."

Joe asked, "Which one?" Juanita clutched her purse and jacket. She decided to remain standing.

Joe continued, "Look on the bright side. The place needed a vacuum, regardless."

"Some dusting would help." David said.

"What are you doing here?" OP asked Joe.

David reached for the skateboard flash drive, but it was gone. "Someone took the skateboard."

Joe reached into his pocket and gave it to him.

"Why didn't this Duke guy take it?"

"The guy who did this isn't the sharpest tool in the shed. He's used more for his brawn than brains. An A-type scumbag, gone rogue."

David said, "I just talked to Thorpe. What's this mean?"

Joe replied, "Thorpe already has another backup, or at least that's what I've been told."

David didn't understand. "Then, why does he want me to return it by tomorrow at noon?"

Joe said, "Don't know. Maybe to save face with his fiancée?"

"So, why trash the place?" OP asked.

Joe continued, "Thorpe had nothing to do with this. Duke was acting on his own. He might be trying to set up Thorpe. At the meeting tomorrow, some accident could happen, or maybe Thorpe really does just want to talk it out. Duke likes to ruin everything he touches, as you can see." Joe seemed to be telling the truth to David, who sat back to weigh his options. OP picked up the candy bar and threw it in the garbage. David knew that he had to drop the flash drive off, regardless, and then face Kayla, even if she did change her mind. It was her right.

David got up and opened a storage locker at the foot of his bed. It was his home protection kit. He pulled out two large duffel bags and brought them back to the living room. Inside one of the cases was an AR15. It had attachment points, pistol grip, site, and a banana clip. The sixteen-inch muzzle had a suppressor, and the funny part was that he rarely ever went to the range. All this hardware was only for emergency purposes. If ever there was a time, it was now.

Joe said, "What's with all this fire power, kemosabe? You can't do this; it's an empty-handed job. These are trained professionals you're going against. They'll murder you!"

"What if they come back?" asked David.

Joe replied, "They're not. This is the work of one man, a true psychopath."

OP asked, "So, then, what do we do next?"

Joe pointed to OP's head, and said, "Use this."

Juanita asked David, "I thought you were a pacifist?"

David replied, "I am. But don't tell anyone that I'm not. My inalienable rights are a hobby I'd like to keep, despite the present surroundings."

OP said, "This stuff is all for show. He never even goes to the range. When's the last time you even fired a gun?" And, for emphasis, he held one up.

David thought for a second. "Three years ago, on my birthday."

Joe opened up the bag and inspected the 9mm. "It couldn't hurt to have one of these with you."

David said, "I did get a cleaning kit."

"Are those K-rations?" OP asked. David nodded.

Juanita asked how they tasted, and David said, "The beef stroganoff is my favorite. Don't bother with the chop suey."

"Can I have this one?" OP said as he took the Salisbury steak packet.

"Let me get this straight," Joe said. "You bought gun cleaner but never fired the actual weapons?"

"Don't listen to this guy. I've shot every one of these at least once. I was just more interested in seeing how they were put together." Joe smiled at the lunacy.

David asked, "Did you see Thorpe and Kayla together?"

Joe didn't answer the question and instead said, "Thorpe's not stupid. He'll check to see if you have any weapons. The problem is that you have to protect yourself. Going in as a group might not be enough with Duke hanging around."

OP said, "Maybe someone we know gets in another way and they give us the guns once were inside."

Joe replied, "Like in the movies. Might work, but Thorpe is watching Kayla very closely. Apparently, she drugged herself accidentally and is sleeping it off."

The room went silent. David didn't believe what he had just heard and said, "No way. He's known her family his whole life. Her dad is the family physician." He went to pick up his phone to call Sam, but Joe held his arm.

"You could be putting her parents in danger if you go this route. It's best to go in clean, make the transfer, and get everyone out safely." Joe continued telling them that Thorpe had hurt his ankle and gone off the deep-end with painkillers, drinking, and who knew what else. "He hasn't slept in over seventy-two hours and has snapped like a dried stick in the woods. The man is extremely irrational right now, and the woman he wanted to marry is a spy."

David asked, "What do you mean?"

Joe said, "I saw the file on her at Thorpe's. Don't know if the marriage is going to work out on this one, and this Duke fellow is a madman. It's the reason I came back, since we have a history. You might need my help tomorrow."

David said, "What do we need to do?"

"Know our purpose. Get in, and get out. Take direct action and wait until the dust settles. Most of all, avoid the madman. Blend in, and remain calm."

OP said, "It sounds just like hockey."

Joe ordered everyone to get some rest. Nothing was going to happen until tomorrow, anyway, and it was best to get some sleep. They determined that they'd discuss the game plan in the morning. OP and Juanita went back home, and David was out like a light switch. Joe slept on the couch with a 38 special in his hand.

BY NOON ON Sunday, Christopher still hadn't gone to sleep and was watching guests arrive from the window above the front door. He looked down at Miriam working. She seemed to be avoiding him, and he felt bad for yelling at her about the guest list. It was the type of relationship they had, but it was unprofessional on his part. He knew that he'd pushed it too far and would apologize tomorrow. The drugs were wearing on his sense of reality. How far could this darkness go? The world was caving in, and it felt like his enemies were attacking him from every direction. It made him want to have a drink. Kayla was not up yet, and it weighed on his heart. He walked away through the crowd of political supporters, shaking hands as he did so, but noticed the strange looks from acquaintances.

The band was playing and magicians performing as Christopher walked up to a crowded bar. He asked, "Does anyone want to do a shot of Jager?" Many of the political freeloaders chimed in. Han sent him a text about Kayla, saying that she was still sleeping. Christopher had ordered Han to send updates every ten minutes and to never leave her side. Christopher left the barflies and started making his way back to the office. He would stop along the way to do whatever was necessary to make it through the day as high as a kite.

Upon entering the office, Christopher looked at Han's emotionless stare. He stopped in front of Kayla on the couch as disappointment unraveled in his heart. He had to find a way to turn this around. He whispered to her, "Wake up, Kay." She looked so peaceful on the couch. Her unresponsiveness made him go over to check on the laptop to see if the signature release file from the backup skateboard had finished downloading. The screen icon was still spinning and showed as incomplete. Han stared out the window. Christopher said, "He could make it past our security team. Our safety is in your hands."

Han nodded and said, "We'll take care of it."

Christopher said, "Don't let her out of your sight." Then, he silently beat himself up for not stopping her from drinking the full bottle of water. Christopher asked, "How long has she been out?"

"Almost twelve hours."

Christopher had enough and said, "Give her the smelling salts. But be gentle." Han snapped the ends, and they watched her resurrect.

"Good morning, sleepy head," Christopher said. "How are you feeling?"

Kayla looked around and asked, "What happened?"

"You look fantastic," Christopher replied without answering the question. "Han, bring the food over." Han rolled over a cart of fresh OJ, frittatas, crepes, and sliced cantaloupe with raspberries.

He was pouring her a cup of coffee when she said, "I'm not hungry. How did I get here?" Her world swayed, and she was unsure of what was going on.

Christopher sat behind the desk and put on an Oakland Raider's football helmet. He then started tapping an egg in a vintage porcelain cup. It was topped with crackle-berry and finely minced onions. The facemask was custom made, so it could completely open up to eat, smoke, and drink. He opened the grill to commence eating. Then asked, "Are you sure don't want something light to eat?" He lifted up a jar of caviar and started digging in while watching her reaction.

She asked, "Why are you wearing that?"

"Well, it's almost football Sunday," he said, "and I'm famished." After cutting the top off of the egg, he continued, "I've had a long night worrying about you."

"What happened last night?"

"You drank my water and passed out. You must have been really tired."

Christopher knew that it was just a matter of time until Kayla figured it all out. He imagined telling her the truth as she struggled to process the information, but the situation was hopeless. His only concern right now was that she was all right. He could beg forgiveness for the next two or three months from around the world.

"You *drugged* me?"

"It was for me. I was drugging myself, but you drank it. Technically, it's my fault for not saying anything. I've been having a hard time sleeping lately. You took the wrong bottle. It's simple. Remember? I didn't hand you the water!"

Kayla took a deep breath. "You let me drink it."

Christopher brushed it off and said, "I was outside of the limo. By the time I realized it, you had the thing polished off."

While wiping his mouth with a napkin, he said, "It was a mishap. I take a lot of pills, darling. Fucking Universe. I apologize." He looked at her to see how all of this was landing. Then, he added, "You're fine, aren't you? I promise you that nothing happened. You're safe, Han never left your side, and I will take you wherever you want to go."

The statement had no question mark at the end. He hated himself for what had happened and hoped it wasn't something that would have to go to the lawyers. He saw her shooting daggers at his face. A second later, he watched her pick up a glass Davidoff ashtray that easily weighed five pounds and threw it at his head. It put a nick in the Raiders defense and ricocheted off the back wall.

Christopher could see that her brain was still foggy. She let out a grunt, and he marveled at her ability to find the strength to do such a thing. He knew that they prescribed him too much tranquilizer and would ask them to take down the dosage next time. She shook her arms free as the guards tried to helped her up, and no one knew what she was going to do next. He watched Han take a step back after she got his prized Louisville Slugger in her hands. With a firm, two-handed grip, she took a big swing. The second one was a base hit right up the middle and destroyed the laptop with the file downloading on it. The momentum sent her spinning and knocked her to the carpet. Christopher shook his head at what he had to endure. All of the air went out of his sails as he buried his head on the desk.

Kayla said, "I'm not blaming you, but you crossed the line." And he watched her stand up and move the hair from her face.

Christopher said, "Did you not hear anything I just told you?" She looked at Han and the other men in the room. "Han, talk to her."

Duke barged in with a gun in his hand and said, "What up, Count? You sick bastard. Everyone, take a step back." He surveyed the room and looked at the helmet on Christopher's head, then said, "And you thought I was weird."

Christopher took off the helmet and said, "We're having a bit of a tiff."

"Getting a divorce before the wedding? My kind of guy."

Han helped Kayla up off of the floor and pulled her off to the side.

Duke said to Han, "Get the bat out of her hands, and everyone needs to move over to the wall. Me and Christopher are going to have a pow-wow."

CHAPTER 24

David and OP stood outside of the garage bay door as it opened. OP was wearing a hockey jersey, and David had on a Nickelback shirt with the sleeves cut off. With his hat on backwards, he said, "We might as well give it a good spin before going in." Once inside, they took the bumper off the ground and duct taped it to the side panels. David popped the trunk to get to the fuel source cap. He walked over to the cabinet and pulled out two five-gallon drums of methanol to drain into the tank.

David and OP climbed through the windows and buckled up. Liftoff was about to commence. David pressed buttons, switches, and one lever to start the vehicle. Then, he punched the gas to ignite the engine guzzle. He slipped on some driving gloves as OP grabbed the "oh-shit" handle. First gear was engaged as David slowly pulled away. Once in the street, they stopped for David to click the bay door close via a remote control. He looked over to OP and got a thumbs up. Immediately, tires started spinning, but they weren't moving. Smoke exited the wheel wells, the rubber began to grip, and David warmed up the asphalt. He took off screaming down the street like Grant through Richmond. The suspension handled every curve and made him think of nothing but the next turn. He felt freedom with the pedal to the metal and all the horses guzzling as they were about to face the enemy.

Juanita was the first to pull up to the front circle drive. She was driving the getaway vehicle. They had used OP's work truck and put her friend's catering magnets on the side. She donned a waitress uniform with an old name-tag from her days of working through law school at Big Boy's restaurant. One of the guards at the front asked her what she was doing.

"We have a special delivery of steaks. Something about a hungry cat?" The guard motioned for the barricades to be removed and told her to go around back. She looked in the review mirror and saw Joe peeking out from underneath a tarp.

A black Cadillac Escalade rolled up to Thorpe's place with Mrs. Kelly in the passenger's seat. In the back were her two sons, Patrick and Danny. They played football for Stanford and University of Wisconsin. Both were on the o-line and could have gotten an academic scholarship to any school of their choice. It just so happened that God blessed them both with a six-foot-five-inch frame, 300 pounds of strength, and a good memory. The boys were graduating soon and were ready to have a good time.

They exited the vehicle, and Mrs. Kelly walked up to Miriam, who was texting on her phone.

"Hello, Miriam."

Miriam said, "Thanks for stopping by, Mrs. Kelly. I did not expect to see you. Would you like me to tell Christopher that you are here?"

"Please. He's the one who has to pass off on some documents for the Agricultural Act. I wonder what changed his mind?"

Miriam shrugged her shoulders.

"This is a very important piece of legislation and a very generous donation on his part." Mrs. Kelly turned to her boys and said, "This will only take a few minutes, boys." Miriam smiled brightly at them both, then got on the radio to let Christopher know that Mrs. Kelly had arrived.

Miriam said, "He'll be waiting for you in the library."

Danny took the lead and asked, "You work with my mom a lot?"

Patrick said, "Yeah, he doesn't get out much. I'm Patrick." They introduced themselves as Miriam smiled and shook their hands.

Danny said, "I'm more of the easy-going type. It's this guy you have to worry about. He's got the personality of a dead moth."

Patrick said, "Don't mind him. He lives in a tent under a bridge. Doesn't see people much." Miriam noticed his *Three Stooges* tie and complimented Patrick.

"See, Danny," Patrick said, "she recognizes a good Windsor knot." Miriam was a few years older than them, but the chemistry clicked.

They got her laughing, and she was excited to be talking to these two characters. She asked, "Would you two like a guided tour of the place?" They both thought that it was a fantastic suggestion. She gave her headset to another assistant and took a break with the giants. They started roughhousing amongst each other, and a shirt pocket was torn. Miriam turned around and said, "Now, both of you are going to have to behave yourselves, and don't break any of the furniture."

CHRISTOPHER WAS IN his office, having a conference call to explain the circumstances to Tokanowa Ichiowa and the other participants. Duke and Kayla were gone.

Tokanowa said, "A bird in the hand is better than two in the bush."

"No birds in this story, Tokanowa. No bush. No hands. Just tell me. Did the request go through? It's all I need to know."

The group of men and women on the other end of the call were silent. Christopher just stared at the laptop that Kayla took out with the Old Hickory.

"No. Never received."

"Give me a few more hours, and I'll resend."

Tokanowa said, "An emissary team is en route. They'll have the hard transfer ready." Christopher cut off the line as Joe walked into the room. Christopher asked, "Any news?"

"Nothing yet."

Christopher turned to the monitors in the room to see David and OP getting out of the car. Christopher said to Joe, "What are you doing here?"

"Came back to search the room. Start from scratch. This guy is getting too lucky."

"Lady Luck left me a couple days ago."

Joe looked at him and laughed, "You were born lucky enough. It'll turn around."

"I need to get lucky one more time. Will you help me save Kayla? That fucking monster took her." Christopher was being truthful, and Joe saw it. Christopher continued, "My back is up against a corner, Joe. Nothing can happen to her. I've called for every hitter I know, and in less than twenty minutes, this place will be a fortress. Nothing leaves this place." Christopher reached into his pocket and pulled out the ring he had given to Kayla. He shoved it into Joe's hand. "It's my talisman. Hold onto it, for good luck. We can't let anything happen to her." Christopher and Joe then looked at the camera feeds, and they all went blank.

Joe said, "He's in the control room. You better pull back all of your security."

Christopher said, "Don't let Duke touch a hair on her head." He looked down at the smashed computer bits and saw his life crumbling to the core. Failure hung in the air like a sword dangling above his head as he smashed his fist on the mahogany. In one swift motion, he cleared everything off of his desk. Christopher said, "I made a bargain with the devil, and I won't be able to live with myself if anything happens to her." Joe listened as Christopher opened a wooden cabinet behind his desk and pulled out a sawed-off shotgun.

Christopher said, "I know you two hate each other. He killed your friend. Some say on purpose. None of my business. But I beg you, finish him if I can't." He loaded the weapon and snapped it into position. He continued, "This is the worst losing streak ever, and it ends today."

Joe said, "Relax, Mr. Thorpe. We'll get this problem squared away."

Then, the door opened as David and OP were pushed into the room. Four guards followed behind them, and Duke was the last to enter. Joe stood down. Duke said, "Joe Mamma. Well, well, well. Here we are again."

Christopher put the sawed-off shotgun under the desk where Duke couldn't see it. He asked, "Where's Kayla?"

"She's in a safe place. I tied her up in the tigers crib, and strapped some C-4 onto the chair. A mouse fart will set it off." As he held up the trigger, and put it in his pocket. The room went silent.

Christopher sat down in the chair and put his hands on the weapon. He said, "That's not the answer I was looking for."

Duke pointed the gun at Christopher and tossed the skateboard drive onto the desk. He said, "Now, move the cash over to this account." And then, he slid over a folded-up piece of paper with routing numbers. "You do this one act, and everyone walks away pleasantly."

Christopher said, "Fucking moron. It's a multi-sig transfer. You need five other parties to agree."

"What can you do?"

Christopher looked at the device Duke gave him and said, "If you give me two hours, I can put thirty million in the account."

Duke agreed, and said, "You have thirty minutes."

Christopher said to David, "Sorry to drag you through all this."

David blamed himself.

OP asked, "Where's Kayla?" The guard told Duke that it was OP who knocked him out at the restaurant. Duke told him to handle it, and the guard picked up a vase and smashed it over OP's head. He buckled to the floor as three of the other guards held David back.

Duke said to Christopher, "By the way, these fellows are with me now."

Christopher said, "Can we maintain some composure, please?"

"I thought that's what we were doing? Was that from Ikea?"

"No, sixteenth century."

Duke laughed through his nose and said, "Damn. Do you have any crazy glue? Let's all sit down and relax, shall we?" David helped OP up as the guards grabbed David.

Duke asked, "Where you been, Joe? Heard you were looking for me?"

Joe said, "They weren't lying."

"Oh, yeah? That's hilarious, grandpa. Come on old, man. Draw on me, so I can put you out of your misery."

"Don't you want to beat it out of me? Or do you think you'd screw it up like you did with those remote-controlled tampons?"

"Torpedoes. They were torpedoes. Hand-to-hand? With you? It would be a dang good time. Let's get out of here, so we can have some room."

Duke turned to Christopher and said, "Finish what you have to do. Get it done in less than thirty minutes, and I'll let you have the trigger on your fiancé."

Duke turned to grab OP and dragged him away by the collar. Joe followed.

David tried to help, but the guards held him back. Joe put his hand on David's chest to push him back as well. With the flash drive in his hand, Christopher pulled out another laptop and said, "Please, be careful?"

Duke said, "Always." The four guards surrounding David and Christopher gave them common ground.

Christopher's stomach turned as he wondered where Han was. He thought about Kayla, and a bigger wave of concern came over him as the flash drive uploaded. He imagined the worst and covered his face.

David said, "Sorry about causing all these problems."

Christopher said, "It's not your fault. I have only myself to blame." He turned to the monitors on the wall and they were all blank. He had to get to Tatiana's pen and save Kayla. He started punching in numbers to login into his bank and after a few seconds, he had other ideas. Christopher reached for the sawed-off shotgun and stood up. "Put your guns down, or I'll split you in two." The guards didn't move an inch.

IN THE ADJOINING room, Duke put OP in a chair as Joe took off his jacket. Duke saw the gun and told Joe to toss it over. OP swayed in and out of consciousness as Duke stood nearby.

"You miss your partner?" Duke asked as he unloaded the ammo to the floor.

Blood trickled down OP's face. He heard them mumbling to one another as his knuckles curled into a fist. The blur in front of him had to be the enemy, so he unleashed a coil in his body to strike Duke with a sledgehammer-level of force. The bigfoot was tossed into a bookcase and out like a light. OP looked at Joe and saw him smile. A second later, Duke woke up and shrugged his shoulders at the blindsided attack.

The steroids absorbed most of the shock as Duke stood up and dusted off his shoulders. Joe was waiting patiently. Duke rubbed his jaw and smiled. That was all the aggravation he needed. He gave OP a front leg kick to the chest to send him crashing into the wall. His mind went foggy again, and he was out. Joe and Duke moved in on one another. The first shot was a haymaker by Joe, followed up by an elbow to the jaw, and an uppercut to the ribs. OP opened his eyes but remained on the floor. He was surprised by how light Joe was on his feet. He had a cadence with his fists like a gorilla swinging his arms from tree to tree. It verified something that they used to say back in Cleveland. A young person should leave those old timers alone when they had a face like a punching bag.

Joe grabbed a lock of Duke's hair and drove a knee into his forehead. Duke pulled a meat hook out from his back pocket and plunged it into Joe's shoulder. Duke got pushed in the back and dragged into a mirror. Joe tried to slam another knee into his opponent, but Duke blocked it. Joe took a better position with his arm and performed a hip toss to the floor.

Duke sprung up and used all his force to drive Joe through the double French doors. The momentum was so fierce that they couldn't stop, and both went over the balcony. OP watched them sail over. Christopher, David, and four guards entered the room. They looked at the broken room and slowly made their way to the balcony. Duke was impaled in the branches of the tree, and Joe lay still on the ground. Tatiana roared as Christopher saw Kayla not too far away, bound and gagged. A guard took advantage of Christopher being distracted and stole the moment by hitting him on the back of the head. He dropped to the ground and was out. It was David against four guards as a rugby scrum ensued. A lot of pushing and pulling happened until OP showed up and punched one of the guards in the temple. He was in a peaceful slumber before hitting the deck. David picked up a guard and tossed him over the side like a pile of lumber.

The remaining two pulled back. David never took his eyes off them and, with his peripheral vision, saw a perfect target. He didn't think twice and maneuvered his left leg behind the right as his body twisted in a split second. The twisting motion and snapping blow happened in a blink of an eye. The guards kneecap exploded as he dropped to the floor. He had no idea what had happened and instantly grabbed his knee in pain. The last one stopped to look. No one knew what to do next; they hadn't planned that far ahead. The remaining guard threw a roundhouse to David, and he blocked with an elbow. OP slowly moved in from the other side.

The guard climbed over the edge and dropped inside the den. He quickly made his way to the gate and hit the emergency exit button. The gated, steel door remained open with the hinges locked in place.

Tatiana watched as David and OP climbed down. Halfway to the ground, they heard a gunshot. The guard OP had knocked out had woken up and shot the chain off Tatiana. He stumbled back inside as the wild beast sniffed in their direction. She casually walked out of the cage while emitting a guttural growl and dragging the remaining linkage around her neck.

CHRISTOPHER HAD WOKEN up and watched David untie Kayla. He slowly walked away and out of sight. It was time to get his passport and a bag of cash. He looked at his watch. They'd be in the air in thirty minutes. As Christopher descended the stairs, he saw Han at the bottom with the extra guard detail. He asked, "Where have you been?"

"We got the control room back. It was boobytrapped. Where's Kayla?"

"She was in the tiger's cage. She's safe and amazingly alive. If you don't mind, I'd like you to follow me for a few minutes." Han was right behind him with several guards in tow.

———

OP HELPED JOE to his feet as he spit out a tooth. OP said, "That'll take some time to grow back. Put it under your pillow."

David finished untying Kayla. He asked, "You all right?"

She looked sluggish and rickety but strong enough to get to her feet. She said, "Tatiana was just staring at me. Her eyes were like florescent, green lightbulbs. It's as if she remembered me, and I never felt safer. We have to find her, but first, I have to put in a call to the bomb squad and get some tranquilizers." She looked under the chair and back at David, saying, "Ms. Kracinski would approve."

Joe walked up and said, "It ain't over till it's over. Juanita is waiting in the van. We should get going."

Kayla said, "I can't go till I see Christopher and make sure he's all right."

David agreed, and Joe said, "Can't hurt to check in on the man."

She said, "Don't worry, this is all getting squared away right now." She started walking inside without looking back.

———

INSIDE, THE GUESTS were milling about as usual. Danny, Patrick, and Miriam were relaxing together as they heard police sirens in the distance.

Mrs. Kelly got directed out of the library. Christopher told Han and the security detail to stand guard. After closing and locking the door, Christopher went over to the open window and slammed it shut. Then clicked a button to automatically shut the curtains. It got dark fast. He went to the fireplace mantel and pulled apart a panel in the frame to unveil a secret electronic keypad. After punching a few buttons, the fireplace was instantly drawn, and a safe behind the wall started to turn. It was connected to a heat sensor from the fireplace. It took a few seconds for the temperature to rise and release the bolts. He listened to the levers open behind the wall. A large shadow moved in the background of the room. He turned but saw nothing.

A hidden door slid open along the wall, revealing a treasure trove of Yinwyans, drawings, art, jewelry, and gold bars neatly stacked near vintage furnishings, firearms, and tiger pelts. Christopher turned his head towards a chilling noise. It wasn't the clock ticking above the mantel or the phone vibrating; it was the unthinkable. He unzipped the duffle bag and grabbed a gun. The safe door was wide open. He knew the room wasn't empty, and something didn't feel right.

Christopher could hear the sirens entering the long driveway. They'd be knocking down the door as soon as he touched his bags. It was too late for an exit, and it was time to lawyer up, unless he could escape through the kitchen.

From around the corner and out of the darkness, Tatiana emerged in a slow, low crawl. The heavy chain was soft as it bumped and dragged on the padded carpeting. She started to growl louder, breath heavier, and expose her teeth. The snarling came with the look of revenge shooting through her eyes. He turned to face her with defeated bravado. This was his fate, and he didn't hide from the fact as his life flashed before his eyes. Christopher said, "Hello, Mother."

Tatiana voiced her anger. "Couldn't get enough of me, could you?"

She was toying with him when he finally said, "Well, what are you waiting for?" He got the gun to parallel and fired off a shot. His pain was fast, and her kill was silent. Carnage ensued as she tore into his flesh and flung him around the room until his limbs detached. The finishing touch was to drag him about by the neck.

Outside, everyone was stepping away from the door except Han and Kayla. It was not what people were expecting to hear. Tatiana's roars had the guests running away. After things quieted down, Han slowly opened the door and peered inside. He located Tatiana laying over Christopher with her paws on his head to let everyone know that his body was her prize. The look on Han's face said it all and made Kayla turn cold. David wasn't too far away and watched her slowly walk away in disbelief. He wanted to go help her, but Joe put his hand on his shoulder and said, "Let her go."

Mrs. Kelly, Patrick, Danny, and Miriam were not too far away in the next room having a drink at the bar, and they were in total disbelief at the chaos. Miriam looked up at Danny's torn pocket and said, "I can sew it for you."

Less than a few minutes later, a CIA agent told Han to step aside. A sniper rifle slipped through the crack in the door as a tranquilizer dart put Tatiana gently to sleep.

Han slowly walked into the room with a few agents. The rest were given orders not to enter. They approached all the parts of Christopher that were still left to find his body bleeding out and his eyes wide open. One of the CIA agents lifted Tatiana's paw and measured the size of it next to his hand. He said, "Tony the tiger was on a mission."

The other agent replied, "You know, if you feed these things, they make great pets."

"Oh, sure. Get a load of the expert on wildlife over here."

Han didn't bother to look or listen. He had walked into the massive safe room and started taking pictures with his phone of the countless Yinwyan artifacts, sculptures, and relics. He picked up an original sketch of a ship called the Flor del la Mar. He put it down to view another of a cabin in the woods. An agent came up from behind him.

"It looks like your job's over. Congratulations."

Han said, "It's been a long time coming. Our country is in your debt."

The CIA agent replied, "Is that even possible?"

"No, but it feels good to work together again."

CHAPTER 25

SUNDAY
1400 HRS

1600 Pennsylvania Avenue NW,
Washington, DC 20500

THE PRESIDENT OF the United States, Michael Cooper, and the Chief of Staff, Hank Simmons, were in the Oval Office. James Farnsworth walked in like he owned the place and said, "Mr. President, we need to talk, in private."

The three of them went into the bathroom as James said, "Mr. President, Hank, it's been confirmed. Christopher Thorpe is dead." President Cooper put the lid down to sit on the toilet.

He asked, "How?"

"Eaten by a pet tiger," James replied. The president put his fingertips to his throat.

"What of the artifacts? The notebooks and his company?" Simmons asked.

"Didn't find the notebooks, but there were plenty of artifacts. The rest are being shipped back to Langley with some art work going to China. Seems they had a joint task force going on with the CIA. The family had ties to the region as far back as pre-World War II. Getting the company to move now is going to be a problem, but it's not our biggest issue, Mr. President,"

James continued. "His funding and sig-key signatures are needed as arbitrator. Which means they can't release any of the capital connected to our sub-campaign contracted bonds. We have to retrieve them before the end of the next election cycle or else."

Simmons said, "Or else what?"

"We lose them and default on the assets."

President Cooper said, "Can't we leverage anything? They're supposed to be in our hands."

James said, "They were, but now, there'll be an investigation."

The president didn't like what he was hearing. He'd known the Thorpe family for years. President Cooper said, "His father helped me get elected to Congress." He looked up from his spot on the porcelain throne to his Chief of Staff for guidance.

James stepped in and said, "Right now, we do nothing, absolutely nothing, except try to get the bounty in the house. They found a considerable amount of gold bars. I'll have someone on it, in it, and around it before sundown. Thorpe always followed the right channels and was a professional who was past his prime. I'll contact his team of hackers and squeeze them till they're all wearing orange jumpsuits and singing like canaries. We'll get our answers and have an untraceable funnel in less than twenty-four hours. Deny everything and claim grievance is my suggestion."

President Cooper said, "Sounds good to me."

Simmons asked, "Can they connect us?"

"Sure, they can, if they know where to look. I'll put together a statement; you can change it any way you like."

President Cooper wanted a more definitive answer. "Can they connect us?" "Deny, deny, deny," Simmons began. "Take it to the grave and deny. No one knows till they find out, and even then, we'll spin it."

After a moment, President Cooper said, "What a horrible way to go. Fangs ripping you apart."

James said, "I think I'd rather get shot."

President Cooper stood up immediately and walked to the door. "Don't ever say those words in my presence again."

James said, "My apologies, Mr. President. I really didn't want to say it with that tonality. My thoughts were to die peacefully in my sleep."

A FEW WEEKS later on a sunny beach in Florida, David and Kayla were relaxing under an umbrella. A discarded newspaper was off to the side with a headline reading, "Tiger Gets a New Home." Tatiana was going to a private sanctuary in Colorado. David whittled a piece of wood when he looked up and saw Marci walking toward them, with Baby Glenn was about fifty yards behind her. David waved, and she came over. He introduced her to Kayla. Baby Glenn showed up a few minutes later, completely out of breath. He waved to David and said, "We need to talk."

David got up and followed Baby Glenn a few feet away.

Baby Glenn asked, "You feeling good?"

"A lot better now. Thanks for asking. How you holding up?"

"Well, I'm going to be a dad in a few months, and it's going to be a pain in the ass. Hope I don't do anything stupid."

"You can't help it, so don't worry. One day at a time."

"You have kids?"

"No."

"Then, what the fuck do you know?"

David told him to take it easy. The guy was stressing out and taking it out on him, so he kept his mouth shut. Baby Glenn said, "CIA came in about our boat driver. He's gone. They closed the case, so you're in the clear."

"I didn't know that I was a suspect."

Baby Glenn felt his shoulders and said, "This is good news for you. We should workout sometime."

David sucked in his belly a bit saying, "I'm pretty busy these days."

"Who's the girl?"

"A new friend."

"Shut up," Baby Glenn responded. "She's too fine to be with you, and you're too ugly."

David looked at him and said, "I figured if you could get away with it, anybody can." He started to walk away, but Baby Glenn grabbed his shoulder.

"I'm looking to add a room to the house. When can you come by?"

"Oh. Now, I get it. Insult me to get in my good graces. Wait a second, are you asking, or is this coming from Marci?" They both turned to hear Marci and Kayla laughing out loud. The men wondered what about.

Baby Glenn said, while looking at Marci, "She's got me doing more repairs to the house then I can live with. If she ever talks to you about new rooms, windows, or impact doors, you tell her that they're horrible. And that you're too busy till I find out how much." The vein in his forehead started to activate. "I don't need you adding anything extra to my expenses. I'm on a strict budget, and if she presses you, then tell her you have an STD from a parakeet. I don't give a shit. You feel me?"

David said, "That's gross."

Baby Glenn grabbed his shoulder again and said, "As long as we understand each other." While they came to an agreement, two young men tried to start up a conversation with Marci and Kayla. Baby Glenn walked over as the kids made a fast exit. He told Marci to keep going with the workout, and they left. Marci smiled and waved back as David found his place back on the blanket next to Kayla.

"What was he saying?" Kayla asked.

"He wants me to add a room to their house with the baby on the way."

"Ya, I gave her my number. We're going to meet up at the gym after the baby and do a spin class together."

David fell back and covered his head. "Argh. I hate bikes."

"You used to be neighbors?"

"Yep." Kayla reminded him about dinner later on at her parent's house. He hoped that they didn't know about the failed permit inspection. She turned to him with a radiant smile, and he'd been wanting to kiss her for a while now. This was as good a chance as any. He asked, "What did your boss say?"

"They kicked me out with an honorable discharge. Seems they don't need my services any longer. They had a vote on it, and we parted ways." David waited for more info.

Kayla asked, "What's up? Why are you smiling all of a sudden?"

"Nothing," David said. "I was thinking about the heated floors in your mother's kitchen." Kayla knew that he was lying and watched him reach over to hook her arm with his as he pulled her closer. She'd been waiting for him to kiss her and didn't resist.

They locked up into each other before another word could be said as she coiled around him like a snake resting on a tree limb. He felt the grit of sand against his back as her thighs wrapped around his legs. The noise of the crowd intertwined with the break of the waves and the circling birds. The passage of time collided with a newfound touch. The connection was made long ago and caught up to them both with each breathe. It was two people sharing an unknown magic with sensations spinning in every direction. Their embrace held with growing intensity and intrigue, giving way to thoughts which drifted farther and farther within each other.

THE END

ACKNOWLEDGMENTS

THANK YOU TO all of the amazing people who helped me complete the process of writing a book. It can be difficult to navigate through the abyss of talented editors and reviewers available. They showed up with impeccable timing, like my neighbor, Laura Benmoussa, and brother, Vince O'Connor. Their viewpoints made a notable impact with helping me see some of the missing details. From the list of professionals in the trade of editing, I'd like to personally thank Suzanne Uchytil, Sarah Wu, Allison Heddon, Dolly Farha, and Lacy Challe. It wasn't easy, and they all gave me insightful feedback, guidance, and, above all, honesty with the project. Everyone's effort and dedication are very much appreciated. Till next time.

www.ingramcontent.com/pod-product-compliance
Lightning Source LLC
Chambersburg PA
CBHW020135310726
48970CB00006B/1887